First Day of Class...

"Amazing," Michael said. He turned to his friends and smirked. "The chick does philosophy. But she doesn't know the rules. Should we tell her?"

"Dr. Hastings doesn't like us to drink in class," Che said.

"Well, so? Who would be stupid enough to drink in class?" I said, not thinking.

Michael laughed loudly. "She thinks you mean drink as in imbibe, tipple, partake of alcoholic beverages."

I blushed. Now they would all think I was a lush...awesome.

Che said, "All in good time!" rather knowingly. "For now though—if he sees you drinking soda or whatever in class, he'll make you pour it out. Later on you can start bringing in coffee. By the end of the semester you can crack a keg in the middle of the room, and he won't care. But first you have to prove yourself."

I wondered how many times I was going to have to prove myself before this class even started. "Okay," I said, and tipped up my iced latte and downed its contents. I strode over to a waste basket to dispose of the empty cup—and as I turned to go back to my seat, I bumped into someone entering the classroom. Another student. Another man.

It was him. The Perfect Guy.

Catholic

Philosopher Chick

Makes Her Début

Also from Chesterton Press
for young people:

The Fairy Tale Novels
Fairy tales retold by Regina Doman
www.fairytalenovels.com

The Shadow of the Bear
Black as Night
Waking Rose
The Midnight Dancers
Alex O'Donnell & the 40 CyberThieves

The John Paul 2 High Series
by Christian M. Frank
www.johnpaul2high.com

Book One: Catholic, Reluctantly
Book Two: Trespasses Against Us
Book Three: Summer of My Dissent
Book Four: Undercover Papist

Look for more upcoming titles at
ChestertonPress.com

Catholic Philosopher Chick

Makes Her Début

By Rebecca Bratten Weiss

and Regina Doman

Chesterton Press
Front Royal, Virginia

Chesterton Press
P.O. Box 949
Front Royal, VA 22630
www.chestertonpress.com

Summary: In a massive change of lifestyle, former
NYC fashion writer Catelyn Frank travels to Texas to
start a doctorate in Catholic Thomistic philosophy and
search for Truth, Beauty, and the Perfect Guy.

ISBN: 978-0-9827677-6-4

Printed in the United States of America

www.chestertonpress.com

~

To my long-suffering husband, and my patient children, who tolerated my neglect of them while I was working on this. – RBW

Ditto. -- RD

1 ∼

Incipit Vita Nova

Finally! I had escaped. I had fled the frenetic rat-race of the Eastern seaboard and come, like a modern-day hermitess, to the Texan desert, in search of the Good, the True, and the Beautiful…

OKAY! I admit it! And the Perfect Guy!

At 24, I was already starting to feel like an old maid. With no dates in two years I was beginning to wonder anxiously if perhaps God had other plans for me. Yikes! Still, I continued to hope brazenly that God had that Special Someone in store. Preferably before I turned 30.

Perhaps it was pretentious of me to expect I would find the Perfect Guy while studying philosophy at the Dominican University of Houston. One does not usually associate the words "Philosophy" and "Perfect Guy." But then again, one would not normally associate "Young Jewish Catholic Woman" and "Lover of Saint Thomas Aquinas" either. Yet here I was.

I had left my fashion magazine job—given up the world of Dior dresses and Louboutin shoes—to devote myself to the writings of a thirteenth-century monk. But I liked to think of myself as a post-modern penitent, snatched from the fires of Cosmopolitan and caught up to something higher and purer.

So I took a deep breath and crossed myself as the airplane touched down. Saying a final prayer of thanks to my newfound mentor and all-around-go-to saint, Thomas Aquinas (a.k.a. the Angelic Doctor), I rose to my petite height of five-three (augmented by sky-high black heels) and tugged my bag out of the overhead compartment.

As I stepped out of the airplane tunnel, I smoothed the inevitable frizzies out of the sides of my dark-brown-with-honey-highlights curly hair, shouldered my bag, and set my face toward the desert. Well, the Houston International Airport. Definitely not the desert. Nor was it deserted. In my estimation, half the population was at the airport that day. Apparently it was "wear a ten-gallon hat!" day too. It looked like a (crowded) stage set of a Hollywood urban cowboy movie.

I tried not to gape as I headed for the baggage claim to seek out my gray-leopard-print luggage. I also tried not to jostle the cowboys, who, when jostled, were surprisingly polite. "Not a problem, ma'am," one of them said when I excused myself.

Ma'am!

I quickly halted and gave myself a lookover. I was, it must be confessed, on the heavier side of my ideal happy weight, but surely I didn't look matronly enough to deserve a 'Ma'am'? Did I?

I quickly tried to recollect myself. Body image is no longer primary, I told myself sternly. I was in pursuit of a more spiritual form of perfection. Not that I wanted to succumb to any banal idiocy about "finding myself" — but I wanted to find out more about this God who'd done such a turnaround in my comfortably angst-ridden career-driven lifestyle. I had always had an interest in Ultimate Questions. But it had taken a serious re-assessment of life goals in order for me to realize that what I really wanted was to be a philosopher.

Alas, I discovered now as I assessed myself, my image of myself as the Next Great Catholic Philosopher also included being a dress size 4.

I was feeling mild self-loathing, and self-loathing makes me hungry. So I halted at the nearest food stand and ordered a cinnabon. Because when you're having body-image issues, the very best thing to do is drown them in a sea of goopy fat-and-corn-syrup-laden carbs. So much for my diet.

The cinnabon was rather nasty, but strangely comforting. I realized it was oozing sticky stuff all over my chin. There I sat, matronly and sticky, in Texas of all places, surrounded by cowboys — and all because of St. Thomas Aquinas. I think that qualifies as irony.

A woman trotted past me wearing fire-engine red heels and addressed me. "Honey, did you lose an earring?"

Honey???!!!!???

Was this sarcasm? But the lady seemed devoid of mockery, even if she was a towering brown female like a geriatric Barbie doll, in shiny red from head to toe, with a magnificently inert helmet of silver-blond hair.

I glanced at the silver hoop she held and checked my lobes. "No, I don't think so." Why was she calling me honey? My native Philadelphian Jewish self wanted to tell her I wasn't her honey and never would be, but I recalled my new rule: What Would Aquinas Do? And so I tried to smile benignly as I scraped the last of the shredded napkin off my face. "Sorry."

"I see now, you got an earring in both ears," the geriatric Barbie drawled. "This one sure is pretty though." She dangled it before me on the tip of a long red lacquered unreal nail. "Too bad I didn't find botha them, coulda worn 'em myself. Haha, now don't tell 'em I said that, 'kay, honey?"

"Speaking of the deed is not equivalent with doing the deed," I said. I tried to sound oracular but instead I think I just came off as weird. Giving me an odd look, she trotted on, like an aged Miss-American contestant, earring still dangling from her finger.

I had to get the sticky stuff off my face before I caught a cab to Dominican U. The first impression I made at the university must be pristine, elegant, philosophical, maybe a teensy bit romantic? Mysterious? The Dark Lady Philosopher from the North. One who would never, ever eat a cinnabon.

I angled my way through the crowd towards the restroom, found a mirror, and checked my appearance. I was dressed for success, at least: wearing my favorite slimming trousers over stilettos, several silver necklaces layered with obsidian beads, and my silk shirt with the high ruffly collar a la Charles II, with a clever little one-button blazer: scholarly but not stuffy. Okay, well, maybe stuffy in the sense of being hot. I felt a slight unpleasant trickle under my armpits.

It also occurred to me that my attempt at philosophical finesse had probably come off as just plain rude to the woman in red: after all, she had been friendly and I had been stiff and weird. Pristine? Elegant? More like snobbish and uptight—and in no way saintly. I sighed again. The process of remodeling Cate into a kind, decent, charitable, disciplined, healthy, and *thin* human creature was clearly still in its infancy.

De-stickified, I emerged from the restroom attempting to get a new view of my surroundings, to look upon my fellow humans as creatures to love and opportunities for sanctity. It was then that I realized that

1) the aged Barbie Doll was not the only representative of her gender species at the airport and

2) I was wearing far more clothes than most other women in the room.

As I approached the luggage carrel, three unclad pairs of Barbie-like shining legs, topped by microscopic Daisy Dukes, blocked my view of the conveyer belt. Two of the legs' owners were blond, one brunette, they all had skin brown as well-oiled leather and chest sizes to be envied. As a well-trained feminist, I had rejected Barbies at a young age. But had I done it out of a rejection of a gender stereotype or just plain old jealousy, since my body type even then had been a polar opposite?

As I tried to sidle around the three pairs of legs, I remembered reading that according to basic principles of physics and anatomy, a real live woman with the Barbie figure would be incapable of standing up. She would just topple over. But here in front of me now were three girls living in blatant defiance of the fundamental laws of physics. They should not have been able to walk, especially in their high-heeled clogs, but they did. They seized their hot pink bags and strutted away through the parting crowd.

I supposed that I was witnessing a miracle. I ought to have been thanking God. I suspect the surrounding cowboys were.

Correctly proportioned and therefore non-miraculous, armored in dank silks, I seized my bags and hurried through the gap left by the retreating Barbies to the glass exit doors when I spotted a different sort of miracle.

This one was tall, dark, and handsome. And coming right towards me.

Even though I was obviously not his object, I swallowed and tried not to meet his eyes. He passed by but not before I had taken a complete body-picture of him. Six two, lean, broad-shouldered, black hair, a decent tan, and distinctly good taste in clothes. The black luggage and gray-and-black suit and strident walk proclaimed him as Not From Here. I hadn't gotten a good look at his eyes before I'd had to avert mine, but I could feel my subconscious rapidly recalculating the parameters of a Perfect Guy to accommodate this new specimen. *Those pecs alone...*

Again I chastised myself. The old Catelyn had hardly been a paragon of sexual virtue, and I was determined to Mend My Ways. This is where my newfound faith had answers and consolation for the sexual misery I'd endured through my undergraduate years. Now I was sworn to be chaste, trying hard to guard my Thought Life, and seeking my Vocation. Consecrated celibacy, becoming a nun, now intrigued me, and it wasn't too difficult for me to believe that my sojourn in Houston could be a stepping-stone on the road to some Religious Vocation. But whenever I saw a well-fitted member of the Male Gender, all such aspirations turned to dust in the furious fires of a healthy parental urge. Groaning, I tried to refocus myself. I was seeking the Good, the True, and the Beautiful. Where the Perfect Man fit in, I didn't know.

But presumably God did.

2 ⌇

The City of Man

I wheeled my luggage through the doors into what was apparently a landscape-size outdoor oven. The sun was blazing, and the taxis speeding past me seemed to be wavering mirages. In Philadelphia we complain about the heat all summer, but between public transportation and air conditioning, even someone slightly above her happy weight doesn't really suffer. But this was a new kind of heat completely. I found myself gasping and mopping my brow after three minutes, just before a non-mirage cab pulled to a stop in front of me.

I jumped inside with my bags, grateful for shade if not exactly comfort. "Dominican University of Houston," I managed to say.

As a city girl, I consider myself a connoisseur of cab-drivers, having grown familiar with the basic categories: the Rasta types with their beads and Rasta wisdom and ganja smell, the old hippies with their conspiracy theories, and the silent Arabs. If the Angelic Doctor had been a Philadelphian, he might have further extrapolated these. I quickly discovered that this cab driver was the old hippie conspiracy-theory type. His theory had something to do with the Lost Tribes of Israel, the Beatle's White Album and predictably, JFK.

"I always keep my clock set five minutes fast," he explained, "so don't be worrying that you might be late to wherever you're going."

"Oh, that's no problem," I said, determined to be charitable despite having narrowly escaped from a slow cooker, "I do the same thing myself. It's supposed to motivate me to get to places on time but of course I always do the subtraction in my head so I always end up late, anyway."

"Now, that's not why I do it," he said "I do it because of government monitoring, see? The CIA. This clock's on a computer, see? All the computers are tied together to one central computer..."

His explanation was like an inane but familiar lullaby of modern-thought-mishmash so I gazed out the windows at my first glimpse of my desert of refuge, Texas. I had anticipated stockyards, dusty taverns, Mexican workers on the corner, maybe even a few cowboys on horseback, dodging the tumbleweed. But the modern wasteland seemed composed of...

Strip malls. Nothing but strip malls. We zipped down the highway and all along the access roads were strip malls, with drug stores, shoe stores, cheap boutiques, dollar stores, payday lenders, pawnshops, hairdressers, tanning salons (LOTS of tanning salons), Mexican restaurants, Chinese restaurants, BBQ joints...over and over again, in a vicious cycle of repetition.

I am a big city girl; I grew up in Philadelphia, am comfortable in New York and Boston, in restaurants and boutiques and clubs and concert halls; I have been to London, Paris, Prague and Rome, know how to navigate trams and change money, am comfortable with wine menus in three languages, and having worked as a fashion writer for a year, am not (very) intimidated by the Beautiful People. But never in my life had I seen such a city as this, a city of strip malls. If I got lost here, I would be stranded forever in a labyrinth of strip malls: the Post-Modern Urban Wandering Jew.

I devoutly hoped that in choosing Houston for my quest of the true, the good and the beautiful, I wouldn't have to cross "beauty" off the list.

"First time in Texas?" asked the cab driver.

"Yes, actually. I guess there's a rodeo in town this weekend?"

"Rodeo? Naw, naw, I don't think so. The Livestock Show and Rodeo's the big one, but that's not 'til March."

"Oh." Then it occurred to me that perhaps Texans really do dress like that all the time, and that my big-city eastern-seaboard perspective might really be just another form of provincialism. I felt a little lost and confused.

"So, you a new student at Dominican?" the cabbie asked.

"Yes, I'm going there for grad school."

"Grad school. Good for you, get ahead in life, you won't have to end up driving a taxicab like yours truly. Whatcha gonna study?"

"Philosophy."

"Philosophy. How many angels dance on the head of a pin and all that? You Catholic?"

I straightened myself. *Be not ashamed of your faith.* "As of two years ago, yes."

"So you do whatever the Pope says, eh?"

"Well, actually, papal authority…"

"I dated a Catholic girl once. Man, she was a wild one!" To my discomfiture the hippie cabman proceeded to explain just how wild she had been, adding at the end, "she made me go to her church with her one Sunday, though…all that sitting and kneeling and standing…"

"We call it Catholic Calisthenics," I said politely. "Spiritual exercises. Required by papal authority."

His eyes widened slightly and then he snapped the new information into his reality. "Yeah, makes sense. Kind of like the Mormons, right? A health regimen?"

"You've got it." Sad to say, I didn't regret my misinformation. My other vice is sarcasm.

There it was: a big brick sign with white block letter, DOMINICAN UNIVERSITY OF HOUSTON, and there against the humid sky was the big Florentine bell-tower I had seen on all the brochures and web-sites. Here at last!

We rolled in between big hedges of privet. I wondered whether I would feel something different in the air, maybe the aroma of venerable old tomes laden with age-old wisdom, a whiff of frankincense, the golden dust of ages? I paid my fare, thanked the cabbie, and stepped out, breathing deeply and gazing round me, wanting to experience everything to the fullest.

What I smelled was: air pollution and a slight hint of rotten eggs. And nicotine smoke. Well, no big deal, I'm used to that. It almost seems pointless to quit smoking when you live in a megalopolis because at least when you're inhaling cigarette smoke you know what's getting into your lungs. When you're not smoking you're breathing in exhaust, sewage, factory smoke, and heaven only knows what else. What made this city air smell like rotten eggs? I'd rather not know.

What I saw was: a row of large block-like 1950s era buildings with flat roofs and depressing blank windows. This I had not expected: glossy pictures of the bell-tower, the neo-Romanesque chapel interior, the big classical fountain outside the graduate building, had prepared me for something more in the tradition of Dreaming Spires, not glum modernism. Whoever does the marketing for Dominican is brilliant, I thought. Brilliant, and not entirely trustworthy.

I tried to stay hopeful, reminding myself that these were the dorms I was looking at and okay, maybe I was going to have to live in one, but there were still the chapel, the bell-tower and the fountain to look forward to. Stone walls do not a prison make, nor modernistic buildings a cage. There was a paradise of intellectual beauty to anticipate...even if the buildings left a little—or a lot—to be desired. Hoping no one would notice the spreading damp patches under my armpits—I hoisted my bags and approached my new abode, Albert Hall.

I was met by a short, bouncy girl in running shorts and a blue Dominican University t-shirt perched behind a card table wearing a name tag. "Hi! Welcome to Albert Hall! I'm Jenny, your R.A. What's your name?"

Maybe it's because I'm from the urban northeast, but I'm not used to bubbly people. I am always wondering whether they are a) on some kind of happy pill or b) secretly making fun of me. But I smiled and responded politely. Jenny just went on bubbling:

"So this is your first year? Well, this is an AWESOME dorm to be in. I've lived here for three years! You should join our dorm volleyball team, it's AWESOME! Hey, I LOVE your shoes! Wow, how do you walk in those?"

"Practice, I guess," I said. "They're probably terrible for my feet—I'll be lame by the time I'm forty, most likely. But I need all the extra height I can get!"

"Here, let me help you with your bags. I don't want you to get some kind of fracture going up the stairs!"

Jenny seemed to be honestly and sincerely bubbly, in a friendly and unmedicated sort of way. She helped me haul my bags, gave me my registration and orientation packets and then showed me to a closet on the third floor, which, upon second glance, I realized was my room. I had lived in a dorm during my undergraduate years, but didn't remember it being this small. Maybe it would have been bigger if there hadn't been two of everything—two bookshelves, two desks, two beds...

"Am I having a roommate?" I asked, as the terrible truth suddenly dawned.

Jenny checked her list. "Sure, yeah, you are! I think she's a transfer from Sienna dorm. Hey, did I tell you there's a Dorm Social this evening so you can get to meet everyone? Are you going to the Orientation Sock Hop?"

I fumbled with my bags. "Uh, actually I wanted to see first about classes..."

"So you're a transfer, right?"

"Actually I'm a grad student."

"Oh, wow, no wonder you look older. We don't get many grad students who live in the dorms. I'm sorry, I didn't mean you look old. Just older. Actually, you look really young—I mean for grad school. You must be really smart!"

I could feel a generational gap (okay, it was only a few years, but it felt like half a century) yawning between us. "Where do most of the grad students live?"

"Oh, off campus. Why'd you decide to live in the dorms?"

Looking at the narrow shaft of a room, I was asking myself the same question. I was also wondering where the bathrooms were, since my suite of rooms obviously didn't include one. "I applied kind of at the last minute and only just got my acceptance letter—so it was just easier to sign up for campus housing. I figured I'd see how it is and maybe move off campus after a semester or so, after I've gotten a feel for the area."

"Oh that totally makes sense! Like I said, you must be smart! Wow, is this all your luggage? Most of the girls have tons and tons of stuff."

"Actually, these are just my travel bags. The rest of my stuff is being shipped here." I was wondering where I was going to put it all. My shoe collection alone would be bursting out of the tiny closet. I felt suddenly like a crass materialist. "I hope it will all fit... I probably brought along too much. But I just couldn't decide what to leave behind... I'm so not good at the whole detached-from-worldly-possessions thing."

"Neither am I," said Jenny sympathetically, "I would die without my music collection. It's awful."

"I think just about everything I own is a 'collection'" I said, a little ruefully. "Ah well."

"Hey, we can't all be saints right away, right?"

I thanked Jenny for her help, stowed my bags, and sat down at the dorm desk on the standard-issue dorm chair to look through the registration packet to prepare for my reason for being in school again: Philosophy Classes! I just hoped I could get into the classes I wanted: *if* I could decide which ones...

3 ～

The Frizzy-Haired
Dark Lady of Philosophy

I had been poring over the course catalog downloaded from the university website and had marked off my favorite gems on the plane ride. Now it only remained to discover what was being offered this semester at what times.

According to the orientation schedule, registration was going on now. There was to be a grad school orientation talk the next evening; the graduate dean, Dr. Lucia Moerio, would introduce the new students. I hoped they wouldn't all be more brilliant than me.

And the faculty—this was why I had picked Dominican University. According to Pearse and Melannie Glaston, my friends and fellow Aquinas-lovers who had made significant contributions to my conversion, Dominican had the best lineup of Thomistic studies on this side of the Atlantic. There was Dr. Lucia Moerio, who had taught St. Thomas to seminarians at the Papal College; Fr. Dominique-Marie Souer, who had pioneered a new translation of the *Summa Contra Gentiles*; Dr. Paul Hastings, editor of a prestigious series of commentaries on the Angelic Doctor; not to mention Professor Steven Carson whose dramatic conversion story from atheist to liberation theologian to Thomist had first sparked my interest in the Saint, back when I was barely more than an atheist myself. And there were lesser lights, of course, but as Pearse had told me, even the professors who were unknown outside of Dominican had incredible credentials.

Solidly orthodox, profoundly Catholic, rigorously academic... I was chanting Dominican's PR lines to myself as I smoothed down the registration schedule. How was I ever going to *choose?*

Then, as I wiped my brow yet again (the air conditioning hadn't quite taken effect), I realized I was confronted with an even more burning choice: what was I going to wear to registration? Those damp underarm patches had to go.

I zipped open my bags and gnawed my nails. Maybe just keep the present outfit, sans coat and blouse? If I started on a maniacal program of re-outfitting myself, I would end up disgruntled, knee-deep in a pool of self-loathing and discarded clothes, and probably wearing the same thing I'd started in. But my silver necklaces still felt hot and heavy and my obsidian earrings felt like weights. Clearly some re-accessorizing was in order...

An hour later, dressed at last in a chic new sleeveless blouse in sandstone linen with a light string of jade Chinese beads and matching earrings and one thick gold bangle, I was standing outside the Registrar's office clutching the course schedule. I had underlined the classes I wanted to sign up for this semester and was struggling with my inability to bilocate: Aesthetics, The Body-Mind Problem, Epistemology, Feminism and Personalism, Logic and Language, Metaphysics, Philosophy of the Human Person, Selected Problems in Ethics, Texts of Heidegger, and to crown it all off, a two-semester seminar class on the *Summa Theologica*, with Dr. Paul Hastings.

Oh, I wanted them all, but particularly the last one. The only trouble was that it was listed as Restricted to Second Year Graduate Students. But would the professor make any exceptions? Particularly for a pilgrim convert anxious to make up for years frittered away studying marketing and business? My parents had indulged my intellect in my grade and high school education, but when it came to college, which they paid for, they had insisted I do something practical. Hence the degree in Journalism and the job in the fashion industry. But now, in a fit of intergenerational rebellion, I had left behind a career to pursue the most arcane of arcane studies. And I was loving it.

I began to look around at the other students who had just picked up their packets from grad registration: a couple of guys behind me, one tall and one short, were perusing their rosters so intently I could not see their faces. In front of me several girls in loose drab clothes were talking to some equally-sloppily dressed crop-headed boys.

"…Omigosh I can't wait! I'm signing up for Steven Carson! I can't believe it! I'm really going to be a student of Steven Carson!"

"I wish I wish I WISH I could take Theology 301 with him, but my schedule won't give. I'm going to be stuck with Dr. Hans Ecking instead…"

"Did you see Carson on EWTN this past summer? When I heard him talking about the Blessed Mother my eyes were, like, opened…"

"I actually met him at chapel the other day! He is sooooo cooool."

"Well, I finally am going to get a chance to take his Spirituality of Francis and Dominic."

"I heard that one was full."

"Noooooo! Don't say that, Matt!"

"Don't have a cow. You can still take Christianity and Modernity—or that one on Catholic social teaching: I've heard that's good."

"Oh, I don't care, as long as I get into one of his classes. He's like, the whole reason I'm here at Dominican. He's the most awesome professor ever!"

At this point one of the girls turned and smiled at me. She was pale, thin, and wore silver-rimmed glasses that were sliding a bit down her small nose.

"Are you taking Steven Carson?" she asked, in lieu of a hello.

Now, I, too, owed something of my interest in Aquinas to Steven Carson. But I have another fault of which I must accuse myself: that of instantly failing to be interested in anything which seems to be popular at the moment. In other words, I tend to be a snob. Mea culpa, mea culpa, but it's true. Discovering that to these students, Steven Carson was the Catholic equivalent of Brad Pitt made me feel that studying under him would mean being one of a zillion nameless fans sitting rapt and dewy-eyed in a cavernous classroom.

"I'm a Philosophy major, so probably not," I said, "though I hope I can make it to one of his talks while I'm here. I'm actually a bigger fan of Dr. Paul Hastings…"

The crowd of ill-dressed students stared at me as though I had the Number of the Beast tattooed on my forehead.

"You're a fan of Dr. Hastings?" one of them asked.

"Who's that?" another asked.

"He's in the philosophy department," I said, "and he's as important as Carson, really, even if he's more academic than popular…he's probably better known outside specifically religious circles, actually. I'm really interested in his seminar on the Summa…"

"You think you're getting into the Suminar?"

The voice, from above me, spoke in tones heavily laced with condescension. I turned to face the tall boy who had been standing behind me. He smirked a bit, in a friendly sort of way; he was burly and ruggedly handsome: curly-haired with long-lashed brown eyes—and normally I'd say he was hot. Well, the old Catelyn would have let him buy her a drink. No, the old Catelyn would have bought *him* a drink.

That is, if he hadn't just spoken to me like a junior-high kid speaks to a kindergartener. He continued, "You can't take the Suminar."

"Suminar?"

"Hastings' class on the *Summa*. You know it's only for students who have passed their quals? And we had to pass a test, too, to get in. Bunch of people got rejected. And you're in your first year of the grad program. Am I right?"

I wasn't exactly eager to tell this overgrown boy that he was right, even if he did have incredibly long-lashed brown eyes and incredibly chiseled cheeks with a light dusting of golden hairs on them. "I thought I'd speak to him about it."

The tall boy laughed. "About making an exception? I'd love to see that. I'm telling you, you can't *just* have studied Aquinas. You can't just know the parameters of his thought. You've got to be in deep with him. You've got to be practically obsessed."

"An apt description," I said.

"Listen, take it from me: just sign up for the basics — ethics, metaphysics, history of phil classes. Got to get them under your belt before you play with the big boys, no offense." He grinned at me.

"None taken," I said. I lied. Mea culpa. I guess it was just another indication of my lack of humility. "But I've already had Ethics — I'm hoping I can get into the Selected Problems class. And I've read most of the major texts, Plato's dialogues, and —"

"That's great, good for you," he said, "but this is Dominican...there's a specific prejudice here that you haven't really studied an idea until you've studied it with one of our profs. That's why you have to take so many classes. It's part of the whole Spartan plan to torture us and work us to death and weed out the unfit until we're either dead or don't care anymore. Then we'll be the few, the proud...the PhDs."

"And teaching at the Community College of Soggy Bottom, Arkansas," said the shorter boy in a faux hick accent, with an imaginary chaw in one cheek. I almost giggled, but I was too annoyed.

"Maybe you will be," said the tall guy with a shrug of his very masculine shoulders, "I'll be a department head at some cushy little liberal arts school, smoking cigars and explaining to cute undergrad girls the difference between Eros and Agape."

I snorted and so did the shorter guy, who had a freckled baby face and wore a "Guinness is Good for You" t-shirt. "Keep dreaming," he said.

The big guy laughed. "Hey, good luck with asking Hastings!" he said to me, and winked. As though somehow the cheesy little 1950s gesture could make up for how totally insulting he had just been. Did I detect a whiff of chauvinism in the air, along with exhaust and rotten eggs?

Well, well, well... new Catelyn or not, I instinctively squared my shoulders and stuck my chin in the air. I might be a Catholic now, but I certainly wasn't going to be an intellectual doormat.

"Thanks," I said. "I'll see you in the Suminar."

I heard joint male laughter behind me as I marched away.

4 ～

Contra Sassy Goddess

I have to get into that class, I just have to! If only for the forsaken feminist cause...

I was still fuming as I walked. But then I remembered: anger, according to the Angelic Doctor, has no purpose but the rectification of injustice. So I stopped fuming and tried to plan.

How could I convince Dr. Hastings to let me into the...what had they called it? The Suminar. I prayed that a man of his intellect wouldn't be prey to the same misogyny as his students. What made it even more maddening was that the hulking student had been not only chauvinistic but also, woefully, attractive. Chalk it up to the fallenness of this world...

Half way back to the dorm I remembered I had forgotten to have my student ID made, so back I marched across the Quad in the scorching heat. Landscapers had attempted to beautify the campus with green and growing things. I don't know the names of flowers unless there's a shade of couture fabric named after them, so I don't know what these were, but they looked gorgeous and tropical: huge purple blossoms on twining vines, large lush bicolor cactus-looking things with streaks of bright yellow, others with long elegant white flowers, and even palm trees. The palm trees cheered me immensely, but also more strongly enforced my new-found conviction that a black trouser suit was about as comfy as a straitjacket in this climate.

I saw, down at the other end of the quad, the bland facade of the graduate school building—and of course the iconic fountain: even at a distance the murmur of the water sounded cool and soothing. People sat around it on benches, under the trees— girls in flimsy bright spaghetti-strap dresses, boys in shorts, some shirtless. Most of them were sitting glued to their phones, texting—but a few were reading. I would have to stake out a place to study near there, in the cool of the evening…and fish out some cotton dresses when my boxes arrived, too.

I slipped quickly into the bathroom to make sure my hair and makeup looked acceptable. In my experience, bureaucratic photographers are spiteful amateurs who are determined to make everyone look like a criminal, a granny, or a meth addict. They just lounge around looking bored until you happen to sneeze or squint and then—snap! I was not going to be a casualty of their malicious pastime, especially my first year at graduate school.

Looking in the bathroom mirror, I discovered to my horror that my new waterproof mascara was not waterproof in Houston humidity. Apparently also at some point I had vigorously rubbed one eye: a swoop of black descended across my left cheekbone, rather like the single tear in one of those "tragedy" masks. Murphy's Law said that it had been there for some time—most likely while I was talking to the winking male chauvinist. Fabulous. He probably thought I had been crying. Besides which, my hair had recently decided to abandon its customary character as a mop of winsome curls, and resolve itself into a frizzy brillo-pad instead.

There was no way I was having my photo taken now. I looked like a deranged minstrel, and besides that I was starving, not having eaten anything since my licentious cinnabon. I would just have to take care of my ID later. I tried to wipe the black teardrop off my face with a paper towel and hand soap but the mascara had decided (of course!) to be waterproof again.

Luckily I had my Dolce and Gabbana movie-star glasses with me: they hid most of my face. At this point, I wished they could hide my entire body. Back to the dorm I trudged again, sweating visibly, though with a supreme and heroic effort I maintained my confident poise, pretending I was six feet tall with a Grecian nose and glossy golden hair, lithe and slender in a breezy muslin dress...I marched down the hall to my room, resplendent in imagined elegance—

"Shut the damned door!"
I had opened the door with a flourish, and there before me stood, apparently, an underwear model. At any rate, she was in her underwear. She was also tall, lean, tanned, and scowling at me.

I slammed the door. Then I realized that was my room and that was my roommate and it was my fault for opening the door (though you'd think she would have heard the key turning and shouted out earlier?) and also that I was going to have to go back in again. I tapped tentatively.

"I'm so sorry," I called through the door, "I'm your roommate. Cate. Is it okay for me to come in now?"

"Um, it's a little late for asking, don't you think?"

I opened the door slowly; she was clad now in short short shorts and a crop-top with a big sparkly pink heart on it and the words "sassy goddess" in sloppy purple script. She was still scowling. She was not, however, as intimidating as she had been before, now that I saw that her honey-colored hair was brightly streaked with cheap, obvious highlights: *so* ten years ago. She had a long upper lip and a wide turned-up nose—not a model, just a very young, very fit, very badly brought-up girl.

"Jeez. You knock first. Think you can remember that? Unless you were like, born in a barn or something."

"I'm not in the habit of knocking on my own door," I said coldly, but then remembered, again, that it had been my fault, and tried to sound more conciliatory: "Sorry, I've just never shared a room before." This was true: the dorm suites in my old college were single units. And of course, as an only child, I had always had my own domain. I forced myself to smile: after all, there was no point in setting up everlasting enmity if I was going to have to be sharing space with this person. "I guess I'll have to get used to it. I'm sorry; I didn't get your name."

"No, that's because I didn't tell you. Duhhhh." She rolled her big blue eyes. I noticed that the floor was liberally strewn with various other pink sparkly miniscule items of what could generously be called clothing. My bed was a little oasis of tidy cotton earth-tones in a surging sea of pink Lycra. I sat down on it, and kicked off my heels. My feet were smarting. Probably smelly by now, too, but I was nearly past caring.

"That's right," I said. "I am aware of that. But in polite society one doesn't just say 'who are you?'" Hungry and crabby and sweaty as I was, my good intentions — both virtuous and pragmatic — were already worn thin. "So…" I went on, smiling fixedly, trying not to succumb to the vice of sarcasm.

"Huh?"

"Oh, never mind. Hi. I'm Cate. I'm from Philadelphia. I'm here for grad school. You're my roommate. You're here to be a sassy goddess, I see. Nice to meet you."

"Okay, you don't have to be so, like, random and weird. Seriously. You know you have make-up like, all over your face?"

I tossed my frizzy hair. "Oh, that's the way they're wearing it now in New York. They call it raccoon chic." She was staring at me, so I rambled on, "You know, part of the whole going-green animal rights movement. Some people are wearing bunny tails too. I myself prefer a fox-tail. Solidarity, baby."

The Sassy Goddess looked as though I were a raving lunatic. "Uh, okay. So, that's just lame," she said.

"Haha, just kidding. Yes, I know my make-up smeared. Thanks."

I realized that this conversation was doomed, and that she was not going to tell me her name, and that from the perspective of both Christian charity and basic humanistic sensibility I was just digging myself into a hole. I gathered together my toiletries and headed down to the bathroom for a long, long shower.

It didn't look as though I were destined to get along with any students at Dominican. I was either too old, the wrong gender, too fervent, or too much of an individualist. Now I was forced to come to grips with another reality: since my conversion, I had depended on my handful of Catholic friends for support while living in The World. I had never gotten the opportunities to spend as much time with them as I would have liked—but I had always looked forward to their company, and appreciated their warm acceptance of me. I hadn't really imagined what my new life would be like without those occasional get-togethers, because I assumed that a university like Dominican would be full of potential friends. But what if this wasn't true? What if I had merely exchanged one level of isolation for another?

What did Thomas have to say on the subject? I recalled a popular quote of his *"Friendship is the source of the greatest pleasures, and without friends, even the most agreeable pursuits become tedious."* If this were the case, what sort of life was in store for me? A life of solitary ascetic intellectualism? Would studying philosophy in a world without friendship end up being a cold and soul-destroying business? Apparently even a great intellectual and monastic giant like Thomas thought it might. The idea was truly depressing. I tried not to let it bother me as I glumly waited for the water in the shower to get warm.

5 ～

On the Matter of Inordinate Desire

Kimmy wasn't there when I got back. I discovered her name later when a friend of hers (a short bosomy girl with "you can look but you can't touch" printed in sparkly letters on the back of her hot pants) stopped by two minutes after I'd closed to the door, to ask whether Kimmy had already left for some party.

Evidently Kimmy had—and it had been a wild one, I discerned when I awoke the next morning to find her passed out under the covers, her discarded pink clothing on the floor, reeking of stale cigarette smoke and an odor in the air suggested gut-wrenching quantities of Boone's sickly-sweet something-or-other. I was surprised: I had expected students at Dominican, even undergrads rejoicing in their freedom, to be a bit more...what? Practicing their Catholic faith?

But could I really judge her? Remembering my sophomore year, when I had decided to cut loose a bit, I felt a little sorry for Kimmy, imagining the misery that lay before her, as she journeyed back from Party Place down Hangover Alley. I confess I also felt a little smug in my recently-acquired virtue. And, finally, I felt a little relieved: at least if I fell off the non-smokers' wagon and took a drag here and there, no one would eviscerate me. Maybe there was some leeway even in Catholic circles. Then I felt guilty for not cherishing more loving concern towards Kimmy in her physical and moral prostration, and said a prayer for her as I left the room for the communal bathroom down the hall.

As I engaged in my morning preening before the narrow-shelved mirror flanked by a dozen similar ones over generic white sinks, I observed the other girls coming and going in the bathroom. They were indeed a mix, somewhat like the crowd I remembered from my own college days, but there were more scapulars, miraculous medals, and other Catholic paraphernalia in evidence. Some of the students seemed lost, lonely and nearly in tears; some looked dour, Goth and sulky; others burst with noisy energy. Some were awkward in baggy plaid pajamas and others at ease in skimpy night-dresses.

As I turned down the corridor to the showers, I nearly collided with another girl who was coming out: we did a brief slapstick courteous back-and-forth in the doorway; finally I laughed and flattened myself against the wall. "Go ahead," I said, "or we'll be here all day." She smiled shyly and hurried past me; I noticed that she wore braids and a bulky yellow flannel night-gown covered with huge, horribly cute, smirking purple teddy-bears. It was a shame these Catholic girls had no fashion sense.

After my shower, I had to wait for a sink (I had forgotten to put on my moisturizer). Several undergrads were chattering about a boy band or teen dream or some such phenomenon as they brushed their teeth:

"He is so adorable I just want to take him home and cuddle him and squeeze him!"

"Oh, that's *all* you want to do?"

"Annie! Don't be bad!" She splashed her friend with water. Annie splashed her back, and got water on a third girl who shrieked, "Stop it guys!" Then they were all splashing each other and giggling and screaming; I threw my towel over my make-up case so it wouldn't get wet and stood silent, like disapproval on a monument, feeling a million years older than them.

Eventually with many hen-like noises they all chased one another from the bathroom leaving me in blissful peace to complete my transmogrification into the Amazing New Student who was going to track down Dr. Hastings, captivate him with her perspicacity, and get into that Summa class.

I had gone through agonies to plan and prepare my outfit the previous evening, but, as usually happens, when I was back in my room trying on the actual clothes, my projected vision fell flat. The jade-green cotton dress I had planned to wear had suddenly and mysteriously become too tight—I could *not* have suddenly gained weight! With all my sweating, I had probably lost at least five pounds in fluids yesterday. I willed myself to believe that the fabric had somehow shrunk in the heat. Apparently unbeknownst to me, my clothing had decided to diet along with me, in a spirit of community. How kind and supportive of it!

Kimmy groaned in her bed of pain as I silently, swiftly and with increasing despair tried and discarded every outfit in my present truncated wardrobe, to wit:

1) Teal pin-striped maxi-dress (no way! comfy but too girly, makes me look pregnant)

2) White linen capris with grey cashmere sleeveless turtleneck (are my hips that huge???)

3) Black pin-striped skirt with cotton blouse and matching vest (How did that skirt get so tight? I look like a stripper pretending to be a lawyer, ick)

4) Little Black Silk Dress (too evening-y)

5) Slick dark denim trousers with black frilly belted blouse (This cinched waist makes me look like one of the Toadstool People! Who are the Toadstool People? I don't know. But I am one of them.)

6) Dark red capris...(never mind, can't even get into them. I want to find out what diet my clothes are on because it sure seems to be working for them...)

7) Cashmere turtleneck (above) with denim trousers (above) and dark brown Italian leather strappy slingbacks with silver buckles, chunky Peruvian beaten-silver earrings (I hate the way I look and probably I will sweat a lot again but Kimmy is groaning and tossing and will wake up soon and how much time have I wasted already???)

8) Nix the turtleneck: my neck is itchy. Stretchy midnight-blue silk blouse with detail in red embroidery, denim trousers, etc. etc. etc. …Kimmy is waking up…

It was nine o'clock. Maybe I should just skip breakfast, I thought, given the fact that my bodily circumference had recently expanded to titanic proportions? But every single diet guide I had ever read was adamant about the necessity of breakfast. Good dieters eat a big nutritious breakfast filled with fresh fruit, low-fat proteins, whole grains—and then spend the rest of the day in stern, Spartan deprivation. If deprivation is necessary, I prefer to starve myself all day long and then feast on huge chunks of cheese and magnanimous goblets of wine come evening.

I wondered what Thomas Aquinas would say on the subject of dieting. Considering the fact that he had been hugely overweight—they'd had to cut a piece out of the table so he could squeeze himself in to dine with his brothers in the friary—maybe he would say it wasn't an important issue?

"Uhhhhhmmgggghhhhhmmhhutttuggkk,"
Kimmy said.

"Have a nice day," I whispered. That was the extent of our discourse. I grabbed my hefty old Summa from my desk, and tiptoed out the door. A quick breakfast and then I was to go off on my quest to convince Dr. Hastings of my brilliance.

In the cafeteria I discovered a quiet sunny corner, out of the way of undergrad traffic and set down my tray and my Summa. I flipped past the Virtues

for my soul. I hope so. I'd like to be a politician with a soul. If such a thing is possible."

"You want to go into politics?" I asked. "I'm Catelyn, by the way."

"I do! I'm Danielle," she shook my hand via coffee mugs. "I'm in my junior year here. I used to think that if I mastered logic and rhetoric I could go out into politics and convince everyone of what's good and right. But unfortunately it doesn't work that way...people don't work that way. Nothing against philosophy though," she quickly added, "I mean, it just has a different end, right?"

"Or it's a different pathway to the same end," I said, sipping my coffee and nibbling bacon, "truth, beauty, goodness..."

"I need all of those I can get," she said with a sigh, picking at her fruit. "I spent the summer being an intern in Washington D.C. for a pro-life senator. A real dose of reality. I guess I'm jaded now. I feel like I can never respect a politician again."

I tried cutting my waffle, but it seemed to be made of cardboard, so I gave up. "Oh, but some good people with sound principals have to go into politics or the whole system will become rotten," I said. "And there were some noble politicians. St. Thomas More, for instance...Okay, I know, that was five hundred years ago and he got his head chopped off but..."

Danielle made a wry face. "I'll take whatever comfort I can get. Well, politics is my life plan, if I don't get married and have a ton of kids instead. So hey, do you ever do pro-life work?"

"Actually, yes, I used to be part of the chapter of Feministas Pro Vita for a short time. Have you heard of them? Kind of like a pro-life Amnesty International?"

Her eyes widened. "Seriously? I'm president of the chapter here! Omigosh, okay, I totally want to be a politician and get your vote—um, sign you up right away!"

"You need some philosophers in your group?" I joked.

"We need incredibly smart people like you, regardless of their major! Not that I'm trying to use you for your brain—you seem really cool, too."

"Thanks. I'm trying for the cool-hip-jet-setting philosopher image...if that's not an oxymoron. I guess Derrida worked it?"

"Derrida?"

I flushed. I didn't want to look like a snob. "Post-modern philosopher. All you have to know about him is that he revolutionized post-modern thought, and could look really really cool and French, slouching in dark glasses and oozing continental suavity."

Danielle grinned. "Gotcha. Well, I think you could ooze American suavity well enough if you put your mind to it. Join our group on Facebook and you'll get my weekly updates, meeting times, events, etc. And we should hang out, too."

I suddenly realized that it was nearly ten and got up, clearing my tray. "Hey, I have to run—got to go beg a prof to let me in his class—but I really am interested in joining your group. Even if you do want to use me for my brain...it was really nice meeting you, Danielle!"

"Same here, Cate. Good luck pleading with the prof!"

"Thanks. Say a prayer for me!" I called over my shoulder as I headed off with my embarrassing tray of half-eaten food. Danielle was smart and cool, even if she was so willowy that I felt like a Jewish dumpling next to her. However, it was amazing to discover an undergraduate who could possibly be a friend: intelligent, socially aware, and, while not a sassy goddess, not dull either.

6 ⤳

Batman in Biblioteca

The morning was hazy and humid: I was sure I would be sweating again later, but now I was refreshed, happy I had not eaten all that overly-processed food on my plate, invigorated by a friendly intellectual conversation, ready for anything. I had briefly explored the campus the night before and located the important places: the chapel, the library, the graduate building and even a secret little shady nook, potentially a clandestine smoker's hideaway, should I fail in yet another of my resolutions.

I found the offices of the philosophy department and spent more time than was necessary perusing their bulletin boards, peering through the small windows at their offices—some tidy, some not, some dull, some delightfully full of books and paintings and leather chairs. I saw the back of several philosophical (and balding) heads, but Dr. Hastings was not in. I noted that his office was clean, his bookshelves orderly, but also that he had a large framed print of the *School of Athens* on his wall—and fountain pens in pen holders on his immaculate shining desk! And a coat-rack in the corner, with... a fedora on it? Fascinating. But, in the end, not sufficient to make up for the absence of the man himself.

I found the office of the department secretary: a middle-aged, plump and cheerful woman, who beamed at me and welcomed me to the University and told me that Dr. Hastings never seemed to be in his office when he was supposed to be, and probably was out for coffee, or else in the Rare Books room in the library, could she take a message?

No, I did not want to leave a message. I had to take on this problem in person, with all the forces of charm and rhetoric and intelligence I could muster. Reminding myself that the race is to the swift, I headed over to the library; perhaps I could find a comfortable and conspicuous perch outside the Rare Books room and settle in there with some obviously philosophical reading material that would be guaranteed to catch his attention and earn his respect. Luckily, I still had my big, moldy, impressive, leather-bound Summa with me.

The Rare Books room was right by the philosophy section, and right next to it were two tables, either of which would have been a perfect place for me to sit and wait. Except that one table was taken by a boy and a girl, who sat side-by-side, heads bent affectionately together over a notebook. They were whispering and cooing sweet nothings in each other's ears and stroking each other's wrists; protected by the impermeable aura that surrounds young couples in love—that whole attitude of "don't come near us, we love each other, that makes us so special—too bad you're lonely and single and don't have a place to sit but that's not OUR problem, we have to deal with the terrible task of being in luuuuuvvvvvv."

Gag. Did I ever act like that back a million years ago when I was dating someone? I hope to God I didn't. And if ever I stop being lonely and single, I hope I will retain a few shreds of my social sensibilities, and not practically make out in the library, of all places.

And the other table was dominated (of course!) by the handsomely rude winking guy who had so annoyed me the day before. When I say "dominated" I mean he was sprawled on one chair with his feet (in work boots!) on another chair, his book-bag on a third chair, and several books and notebooks strewn carelessly across the table. He was still more handsome than he had a right to be, but I was not in the mood to tangle with him again. I had business to accomplish.

So, one table was usurped by Cupid, the other by Patriarchy. What was a single young intellectual woman to do? Find something to read, I suppose, and watch for Dr. Hastings' emergence. I began to scan the shelves closely on the pretext of finding something important: Santayana, Sartre, Saussure, Schlick, Scheler... Sartre was right in front of me. Does anyone, outside emo types in coffee-shops, take Sartre seriously? Nevertheless, I snatched up one of his books, *Existentialism is a Humanism*. But when I tried to open it, my leather bag began to slide down my shoulder, and I had to grab at it: the weight of the Summa was against me, not a good omen. I dropped Sartre and the pages all fluttered like existentialist butterflies; out dropped a glossy folded magazine pull-out that magically unfolded as it fell to the floor: a giant Batman poster.

What was *that* doing in Sartre? I could not imagine. Some comic-book geek exacerbating his geekiness by studying up on French philosophy? No matter: the Dark Knight leered up at me shinily from the library floor, and in my haste to seize him before anyone noticed and blamed him on me, I dropped my leather bag with a boom.

The couple, startled out of the rosy realms of Amor, glared at me for disturbing their spun-sugar existence. I dared not look at the patriarch, but knelt and began hastily folding Batman. As I was stuffing him back into *Existentialism is a Humanism*, though, I saw the patriarch rise and approach me—no doubt to offer me his manly assistance in poster-folding. I felt my face go red.

"You don't need to be so embarrassed. It's not like it's Superman" he said.

"It's not mine," I said helplessly. "It fell out of this book I was trying to look at." I held up Sartre.

"Now *that*," he said, "is something to be embarrassed about."

For a moment I could think of nary a thing to say. I could hardly protest that I had just pulled

Existentialism is a Humanism off the shelf because I was hanging around in hopes that Dr. Hastings would show up, and because I wanted to look occupied, and because I was hoping that any tall terribly handsome chauvinistic types loafing in the library would leave me ALONE.

"You're not seriously thinking of commencing your philosophical erudition with old J.P Sartre, are you?" he folded his arms and shook his head. "I told you to get some real philosophy under your belt before…"

Wrath! "I commenced my philosophical erudition years ago," I snarled, "if you want to know, I came to collect this book because I'm a member of a clandestine drug cartel, and my confederates just sent me an encrypted message telling me to use this book for our next high-secret coded correspondence."

He stared at me. "Okay…what?"

"*That* is called being facetious," I said. "As in, duhh, what do you THINK I'm doing?"

"Well, what ARE you doing?"

"Wasting my time, apparently!"

"Does this have anything to do with the fact that Hastings is in there"—he jerked his thumb at the door of the Rare Books room—"and you are still hoping to get into his class?"

"Why do you care?"

"By which you mean, you ARE waiting for Hastings, aren't you? Come on, don't be shy. Tell me, why are you so desperate to get into that class? I could probably give you a few pointers."

"I don't—"

"—For one thing, don't go on about wanting to use philosophy to defend the faith, Hastings has a thing about that: he likes his students to be studying philosophy for its own sake."

I noticed that not only the lovey-dovey couple, but also a few students who had been quietly tucked away reading in carrels, were now glaring at us.

"And if you are going to gush about Truth, Beauty and Goodness, don't leave out Unity, like most people do. And don't mention Being. He has this theory about the Transcendental Properties: saying Being is a property of all beings is redundant. Seems kinda obvious to me, but that's his thing. And of course he hates the popular touch. Dry and witty is the way to go. Let's see, what else? Oh yes, don't refer to Aristotle as 'the Philosopher.' Hastings thinks Aristotle's influence on Aquinas is overrated."

My head was spinning. I think I HAD been planning on talking about Truth, Beauty and Goodness. And probably Aristotle, too. I think my mouth gaped a bit.

"Don't feel bad," he went on, chivalrous but still condescendingly, "he's a top-notch scholar, even if he is a pompous ass, and it is an upper-level class, and you're new. You'll learn the ropes soon enough. Don't despair: despair is the root of all sin, after all," he grinned and wagged a roguish, paternal finger at me.

Suddenly my brain snapped on again. "That's debatable," I said. "After all, consider what Thomas says." With a flourish, I quoted from memory: "'Now every sin consists in the desire for some mutable good, for which man has an inordinate desire, and the possession of which gives him inordinate pleasure.' Question 72, Article 1. Now whether or not you agree with Thomas on this is up for grabs, sure, but you can't just blithely state that despair is the root of all sin and expect me to bow to your superior judgment, can you?"

"She's got you there, Sean," said a voice behind us. Sean (so that was his name!) suddenly turned red all over and whirled around; I whirled too. A lean ironic-looking man with a supercilious nose had silently approached us and was regarding us with sardonic green eyes.

Sean sputtered. "Oh, hi, hi! How's it going Dr. Hastings?"

Hastings. With horror I realized I was still holding the Batman poster, which had unfolded itself again as if charmed: it seemed to be almost life-size, half-crumpled around my legs, obscuring my tailored trousers and strappy shoes. I was also holding Sartre. Then it occurred to me with pleasure that Sean was looking even more abashed than I felt: clearly he was wondering how long the professor had been listening to us, whether Dr. Hastings had heard himself called a pompous ass. Things were looking up.

"Will you all please SHUT UP!" Suddenly a voice rose querulously from over the rim of a carrel.

"No, I don't think so," said Dr. Hastings pleasantly. His voice was clipped just enough to suggest but not emulate a British accent. "Is that you, Michael? Well, maybe you should learn how to study even when there is a little racket going on. My logic professor in graduate school wrote his master-work while manning the big guns on a tank in Vietnam. *That* is true scholarship."

Sean chuckled a little but then caught himself, perhaps remembering that Vietnam was no laughing matter and he himself was possibly in disgrace at the moment. "See you round," he muttered, and made as if to slouch off.

"In class, tomorrow," said Hastings. "Or wait — did I give you permission to take that class? I don't quite remember —"

"Yeah, yeah, you did, I'm on the list, okay, bye, see you then, have a good one..." he ducked away, sputtering a bit, I thought. Leaving me with the professor. And the poster.

"I prefer Batman myself," said Hastings, smiling at the scowling image. "Although there is a whiff of Pelagianism in that whole do-it-yourself super-hero touch, don't you think?"

"Well, Pelagians deny original sin, don't they?" I responded, folding up the poster, marveling to find that both my mind and my mouth functioned again, just fine. "And the dark side of Batman's personality, as well as the Gotham touch — doesn't that rule out his being a Pelagian?"

"Good point."

"Actually, this isn't my poster," I added, still doggedly determined not to claim credit for it. "It fell out of Sartre. And the only reason I was looking at Sartre is that I was hanging out here hoping you would show up..."

"Really? You're not paparazzi I hope."

"No." I smiled, I hoped winningly, and introduced myself. "Catelyn Frank—I'm new in the grad philosophy program, and I observed your seminar on the Summa on the course list, and, I have to admit, I was seized by a desperate desire to take it—even though I know it's only for students who have completed their first year and all that—"

"What made you think I would be here?"

"*A priori* intuition?" I said on a whim, not wanting to give away the nice secretary, in case Hastings had been hoping to keep private his library hideout.

"*A priori* intuition of an empirical fact? Hardly likely. Never mind, though. So, you're a first-year student, and you want to take the Summa class. You might not believe this, Catelyn, but I have never had a student make that request of me before. Perhaps they know enough to be intimidated?"

I couldn't help squaring my shoulders. "Oh, don't worry, several students tried to make sure I was intimidated. But I decided it couldn't hurt to ask. I heard there was a test—"

"Yes, a test I try to keep extremely difficult. For one thing, I am rather a stickler on grammar—and you'd be amazed how few of these kids know how to write. I don't want to spend two semesters holding the hands of a bunch of grammatical infants, so to speak. Now, you may be thinking 'I was in AP English in High School' or even 'I have a B.A. in English,' but, young lady, I am afraid in most cases that means absolutely nothing."

My heart was singing (silently) within me: if there

is one area in which I have absolute confidence, it is the area of writing. I may not burst with poetic eloquence, but when it comes to clarity of expression and perfection of syntax, I have got it down. Naturally I did not say this to Hastings.

"Would you be willing to let me take the test, though?" I asked.

"Well, that would be setting an unusual precedent. However, I am not averse to setting unusual precedents; necessarily...you don't by chance have a Master's degree in philosophy already?"

"I'm afraid not," I said, and added, in a fit of stupidity, "I have a B.A. in Journalism and a B.S in Business—University of Pennsylvania, Summa cum Laude."

"Oh!" he looked surprised, but not impressed. "Not philosophy? I thought you already had a degree—"

"They were really good about making sure we got our liberal arts," I said. This seemed to evoke a pitying stare. Hastily, I added, "and I've been doing a lot of studying on my own. I used your commentary on the Summa."

Bingo: scholars are human too, and I think most of them cherish a secret belief that they ought to be more famous, more beloved, more revered than they ever really are. It is amazing how easily one may ingratiate oneself by a careful modicum of fawning.

"Yes, I could see you know your Aquinas," he said. "And you put Sean in his place rather nicely. He and his little friends have been getting too big for their collective britches of late, one might say. You know, that is something…yes, indeed. Catelyn?"

"Yes?"

"I think I will let you take that test. Do not count on passing it. But if you do pass — well, good for you! That should be sufficient to allow you into the class, I think. It occurred to me that thus far the class is entirely composed of male students, and one wouldn't want to have hordes of angry affirmative-action maniacs breathing down one's neck now, would one?"

"That does sound unpleasant," I said, trying not to sound jubilant. It was done! I had done it…or, well, no, actually it was not done. "Thank you so much!"

But the first hurdle was over. Now, as I walked away from Hastings in my strappy sandals, still holding the erstwhile Batman poster, I realized that all I had to do was prepare for an insanely difficult graduate-level test on a subject I had never majored in, a test that plenty of more prepared students had failed. A test I had just been told I would probably fail…

7 〜

Contra Gentile

Examination: Tomorrow morning.

Preparation: Spent the entire rest of the day in the library poring over Hasting's commentary on Aquinas.

Food: Sandwich and macchiato at the little student café while studying notes on Aquinas.

Personal grooming: Makeup off, check. Shower, check. (No bathtub and did not want to encourage mildew on copy of Summa by exposing it to further moisture.)

Prayer: Thomas Aquinas on the Eucharist. Turned into studying session, had to break it off. Wished I was into the rosary or some other non-intellectual Catholic devotion.

Finally I put on some Chopin, thinking I might indulge in a little relaxation and light reading for a sense of harmony and a brief escape.

As I lay in the half-light on the still-not-familiar dorm mattress, though, I felt a deep discontent. I was physically comfortable and rapidly recovering from philosophy-fever, but the old familiar loathing of being in my own skin was still haunting me.

For a time, in the past, I had thought that this feeling was simply the result of a poor body-image. Then I had realized that it went deeper than that—somehow I felt a vague guilt at the heart of my very being. I had, for a while tried to quench this guilt in a deluge of work, accomplishment, achievement, over-achievement…then, when that wore me out, I had turned briefly to hedonism. That had only augmented the guilt, as well as, ironically, setting into motion the whole chain of events that had led me to eventually quit my job and come to Dominican.

I turned off the music, put on some sandals. Time to find a different remedy. Going to church was still not easy for me; even after two years of being Catholic, I always had to force myself—but I was invariably happy I had made the effort and got there. I wanted to see inside the university chapel anyway, take a look at the architecture, check out Mass and reconciliation schedules—and considering what I had in store for me the next morning, I would need all the divine assistance I could get.

Now in the silver-violet cool of the evening it was pleasant to be out in the humid air—though I wanted a cigarette!—and, clad in a plain sand-colored cotton sundress and flat sandals, no longer a purveyor of image and status, I was happy to walk past the fountain and listen to its murmuring song. The chapel was down a set of steps, surrounded by a small jungle of vegetation—in the evening shadows I could see the faint rainbow of color filtered through rough post-modern chunks of stained glass, from the lighted interior.

It was cool and quiet there, and nearly empty, though there were a few people crouched in prayer in the small Eucharistic chapel off to the side of the narthex. I was uncomfortable praying in a crowd so I silently skirted the nave, observing the low, blockish arches, the flagged floor: the chapel was constructed in a kind of neo-Romanesque style. Gazing at the Real Presence, I felt that being here at Dominican University was a Life Changing Event. Incredibly important things were about to happen to me.

Hoping and praying that, if indeed something Life Changing was imminent, I wouldn't miss it because I was distracted by something frivolous like my mascara or failure to obtain my happy weight, I trudged down a side aisle. And there, standing in a lonely corner, to my delight, I found a statue of St Thomas Aquinas! He was, alas, represented as rather more slender than I had imagined him, but there was a solitary kneeler in front of him, and no one else around, so I could kneel down and spend a few moments catching up and commiserating with him. I had a lot to thank him for as well.

My conversation led me back to the nave, where I found myself joining in a rosary led by a few kneeling Dominican nuns in white habits. But my meditations on the Joyful Mysteries were distracted by my wondering if any of them taught at Dominican or if they were somehow connected to the University? The university was founded by friars, and the school website hadn't mentioned any nuns.

Part of me wanted to introduce myself to one of the nuns after the rosary, but I was anxious not to look too bubbly, eager, or pious. After a long deliberation with myself, I figured that I would wait until I felt more "called," and rested secure in that decision until the nuns filed out and left the chapel. Then I felt the guilt of a coward, and began to berate myself. So I finished prayer in roughly the same agitated and flagellating state of mind in which I had entered it. Hopefully it wasn't a waste of an hour...

By now the church was empty, but its vast space seemed to have something of the fullness of a tranquil sea. Trying to recapture the sense of quietude and magnanimity I had briefly found there, I took another deep breath as I stood in the vestibule. A faint smell trickled towards me on the humid air. Incense? The breath of angels? No: cigarette smoke!

My tranquility rolled away and gave in to a fierce conviction that the best possible way to celebrate life, hope and divine mercy would be to light one up. My second conviction was outrage: who in the world would be smoking practically inside a church building? No one is less tolerant of cigarette smoke than an ex-smoker under tension.

I glared out the open doors and saw the culprit immediately: a shaven head gleaming in the half-light above the spark of a cigarette. As I walked outside, half-ready to lecture him, he turned his dark eyes on me.

"You're very interesting," he said in a surprisingly

deep voice. He was a slight young man in torn blue-jeans that appeared to be spattered with white paint or chalk dust. I saw he was of medium height, olive-skinned, with strong eyebrows and a wispy goatee on his thin face. I did not find his appearance attractive, plus he had to be either gauche or ignorant to smoke so close to the church, but, (maybe because that hour of prayer had done me some good anyhow) I decided to give him the benefit of the doubt.

"Excuse me?" I said, smiling.

"I'm doing a study," he blew a puff of smoke straight at me. "How many people go in there to pray, and which statues they pray to. Yes, I know, I know, you venerate the saints, you don't worship the actual statues. I've heard the whole spiel before. But it is interesting."

"What's interesting? That I'm Catholic?"

"No, that you're a rudimentary pagan, along with the rest of the lumps in there. Listen: in the past half-hour — three cigarettes, I think — I've counted nine people going into the church. Three guys went in to pray to St Joseph. Everyone else went, including the nuns, and groveled before Mary, except for one guy who actually worshiped the Jesus statue, and you. Now, you — you seem to have a thing for fat old Aquinas."

"That's not a particularly respectful way to speak of a saint and a great philosopher," I said, charity giving way to irritation. Also I resented the term "lump." What was he suggesting?

"Just another dead white male. As far as him

being a saint—I think it's really funny how Jesus is supposed to be such a big deal in your religion, but he doesn't get as much face time as Mary does. I'm thinking that there's really something to that thesis about Mary being a front for the primeval Mother Goddess."

"Well, it's true that Mary is a mother figure and many people find her more accessible. But we go to Jesus through her—and we don't wor—"

"Yeah, yeah, yeah, I know, I've heard the whole explanation," he gestured impatiently with his cigarette. "But what you say and what you do is different. I've figured it all out. What you really want is to go back to the good old days: Greek polytheism. A god for everything, and none of them too perfect. Your devotion to Aquinas, a fat, bald man in a dress? I figured that out, too: he's just Silenus Christianized. You're subconsciously still a devotee of the Bacchic rites, I bet, and that's why—"

"That is such a total load of crap," I said, now angry (and really, really wanting a smoke). "It's not that we want to be pagans. It's not that the Greeks were right. They had…they had…a hint of the truth, you know?" My vocabulary was suffering because I was trying hard not to breathe the haunting smoke, which would only make my craving worse.

"No, I don't know. But I bet you want to tell me." He grinned. "I love it how people here are all so eager to set me straight."

I ignored this and went on: "Their gods and goddesses were like—well, in the imagination, representing something that they sort of hoped for.

Archetypes, you know. Like, the whole thing with Dionysus, the dying god: that's a prefigurement of Christ. So is Apollo. Anyway, all that stuff is great in poetry and mythology, but Plato himself saw that having a bunch of gods acting like people just didn't make sense. Zeus raping all those women, Artemis wreaking vengeance on people. Why would we want that? When we have a God who gives us perfect love?"

"Maybe because the idea of perfection is irritating to us."

"Maybe to YOU," I exclaimed, "But to me—perfection is inspiring!"

He gave me a long, pitying look. "Just keep telling yourself that," he said. "You'll really fit in around this place, then." He flicked his cigarette onto the cobblestones, ground it out with his heel, and, without another word, walked off into the shadows.

Well, so much for spiritual solace! I fumed a bit on the spot there, inhaling deep, long draughts of precious second-hand smoke, asking myself: was that what Aquinas would have done?

Probably he would not have called his opponent's opinion a load of crap, I decided, ruefully.

It struck me that my encounter at the church door had been a sort of test. I tried to pick apart what it could have meant. Why was I here? To study philosophy for its own sake? To launch a career in academia, become some famous jet-setting philosophic author? Or to serve God in humble obscurity? And how did He want me to serve Him? Suppose I didn't make it into the Suminar—suppose I failed in my studies — could I live with that? Could my ego?

The mysterious and unpleasant pagan smoker had not been impressed with me, clearly. But perhaps after all I was not here to impress? Perhaps — uncomfortable thought! — I was here to be humbled?

I pondered this and inwardly groaned. If so, a perfect opportunity for humiliation awaited me in the early hours of the coming dawn: Hasting's test.

8

In Turris Eburnea

I sat outside Dr. Hastings' office pretending not to be quaking inwardly with the terror of insufficiency. I had been given two hours to answer four essay prompts—no choices!—and had finished my final essay fifteen minutes before the time ran out. I wondered whether I should have taken the full two hours, whether I had said enough or whether I had missed or, ultimate horror, misspelled anything. Later in life I would discover that not all scholars are necessarily stellar in the spelling department, but in those salad days of youthful idealism, I expected my profs to be paragons of every intellectual perfection.

I watched them flitting about: mostly older men, a little paunchy, a little grey. I was right between the philosophy offices and the English offices, and noticed that the English profs in general looked more intriguing, at least on a base human level: one of them wore tie-dye under a ratty sports coat, and sat in the midst of poetic disorder with his door open and his feet up on the desk. A woman with wild hair and huge earrings stopped by his office and said in a deep grating voice: "Truth is not beauty, beauty is not truth."

"It is when I see you," he said. I could pick up a note of light jest in both voices. I found myself fascinated by this academic flirting.   Ah, if I found that my Vocation was to the married state, wouldn't it be lovely to trade banter with my Beloved, like a couple from an updated Austen novel?

A few students drifted down the hallway — mostly men in the philosophy section, mostly women in the English section. This segregation, I thought, might be sexist but it could also be conducive to my getting a date. Provided there was anyone worth dating in the philosophy section...

I noticed a tall girl lingering outside the office of the wild-haired woman. She merited a second look, and then a third, because of both her striking appearance and her style, which was distinct. She was thin and angular, not beautiful — her nose was long and sharp, her ears too prominent, her lips thin and her eyes too wide-set. But with her dead-white skin and waist-length red hair, she looked like someone you might see in a painting, or in a play. She wore beat-up boots of pale leather, a short lime-green skirt that appeared to have once been the bottom part of a flamenco dress, and a loose black jersey top with the sleeves cut off. Silver bangles jingled all up and down her arm. She bounced on her toes and fidgeted as she stood outside the door, apparently reading the material on the bulletin board — one paper seemed to be a call for auditions, but I couldn't tell what the play was. Watching her fidget, I felt mingled jealousy of her for being so tall and thin while I was built like a toadstool, exasperation for her inability to stand still, and a strong sense that I would like to get to know her.

"What's the play?" I asked.

The girl glanced sideways at me, and then back at the poster. She didn't seem to like what she saw. I wasn't sure why: was my Oscar de la Renta charcoal pantsuit too conservative for her?

"It should have been Macbeth," she said. "But they've substituted a tragicomedy instead, at the last minute. *The Tempest*. A bad omen."

"Oh," I said, not understanding how not doing a tragedy could be a bad omen. Was I being too analytical? "Are you a drama major?"

"Aye," the girl said, a deep monosyllable.

"I'm studying philosophy," I said, when she didn't say anything.

She glanced at me sideways. "I suspected as much," she said.

Just then, the wild-haired woman came out of the office, and the tall girl turned to her, exclaiming, "Oh, Ms. McCaffery! Is it true what I heard? That you're not directing the play after all?"

"Come into my office," said the other grimly, "and I will tell you all. My matter hath no voice, but to your most pregnant and vouchsafed ear."

I watched them go into the office a bit jealously. All this intellectual repartee! I wished I had been a part of it, but alas, I was not cool enough for the drama major, apparently, and probably looked about forty years old to her. I was reminded again of my suspended doom as a door opened behind me, and I turned to see Dr. Hastings.

I tried to look casual. He looked expressionless. I tried not to deduce the worst from this.

"Did you ever study G.E. Moore?" he asked.

"No," I said, unhappily. I wished that I had, but it was too late now—and lying about one's reading experience is a good way to look really, really foolish.

"I was wondering where you got the idea for your explanation of Natural Law. It's not exactly typical."

I felt sick. "Isn't it?" I asked.

"No. The average graduate student explains Natural Law theory in such a way as to fall prey to the naturalistic fallacy: now, this may not be an issue in conservative circles, but it's problematic if you wish to dialogue outside the box, so to speak. I imagined you had been influenced by the *Principia Ethica*."

Not being familiar with this work, I imagined that he was accusing me of something undesirable, something to be expected from a batman-loving, Sartre-reading neophyte—but I couldn't say much in my own defense; I think I gurgled a bit.

"Well, it's a little sloppy." He paused and I was waiting for the death-blow. "But it's an impressive discovery for even a graduate student to make without outside influence. You can congratulate yourself on having a rare analytic ability." He smiled now. "And so in consideration of this fact, I would be doing both you and the class a grave injustice, were I to prohibit you from joining us. I've made corrections on your essays," he handed them to me: they were now festooned with large, swooping notations in red, "please read them and try to avoid further errors in vocabulary."

I could scarcely believe my ears. "You mean—"

"Yes, you can take the class. You look a little stunned," he added, and grinned in a slightly sinister manner. "Perhaps you should look frightened as well. You're in for a lot of work."

My head still felt cloudy and my knees weak, as I headed back down the stairs. I was moving as though through deep water or sand. A clattering of feet behind me caused me to step briefly to the side: it was the red-haired drama major again, practically careening down the stairs with a thumping of boots and a jangle of bangles. She nearly bumped into me as she passed.

"Excuse me!" I exclaimed.

"Sorry!" she shouted, but did not stop in her headlong dash. Naturally, I thought. Why stop for an old philosophical fogey like me? After all, I didn't really want to be friends with someone so haphazard and rude. And why would I need to, now that I had gotten into the Suminar? I was certain that all sorts of splendors awaited me there. So long as I had the intellectual prowess to be equal to them...

You never get a second chance to make a first impression, I told myself grimly the following day, checking my outfit in the plate-glass windows of the academic building. Trite, but oh so true. Hopefully no one would guess how long it had taken me to put together this outfit. After four hours of analysis, re-evaluation, and ruthless editing, I was wearing my most ultra-slimming black suit with a single strand of thick silver links, tiny silver hoop earrings, and the highest black pumps I owned. I knew I was risking the Texas heat but I was gambling that the building's air conditioning would compensate. My hair was severely straightened, gelled, and in a low chignon. Professional, authoritative, alluring? I hoped. I approached the classroom with trepidation and paused near the door to look in. Dr. Hastings stood near the desk, writing something on a leather schedule, so I knew this was the right class.

The Summa class was in a large, circular room on the top floor with a large, circular table and no windows: it seemed like a secret and enclosed space, where great mysteries might be uttered — compared at least to the average rectangular room with rectangular windows and rectangular fluorescent lights. This room was lighted by a kind of golden strip around the periphery of the ceiling, so the glow was soft and less glaring.

I already had the single textbook: my distinguished old tome, which Hastings had looked at and approved. I'd hoped he'd be impressed by its venerable shabbiness, but he merely sniffed a bit, glanced over it, and said it would do.

So, shouldering my distressed leather J. Peterman bag, I stepped across the threshold and — was hit with It.

The Tingling.

I had experienced it once or twice before, very faintly, but never this intensely. The feeling was difficult to explain even to myself. My grandmother, who was probably the quintessential Jewish grandmother, used to call it "the Tingling."

According to her, whenever she was approaching some life-changing moment, she would get the Tingling. And I was having it now. Not that I was planning on telling anyone—I had my reputation as a cutting-edge intellectual to maintain (or at least develop), after all—but as I stepped into the classroom (trying to look as though I was a normal person NOT having a semi-mystical experience) I couldn't avoid the burning sense that: **Someone in this room is the one meant for you.**

Not exactly what you want to be thinking when you're trying to make a Great First Impression.

So there I was, standing in the door, large iced latte in hand, trying not to totter over in my shoes, having a Preternatural Experience, while the various male students lounged and cast odd glances in my direction.

Swiftly I jerked myself back into normal reality and made my tingling hands pull out the nearest chair and sit down. I set down my bag next to my tingling feet, and wished, not for the first time, that I was a normal Gentile person with a grandmother who wore velour sweatpants and watched Oprah and played bingo, instead of experiencing miniature theophanies in public. Then maybe Rumblings of

Destiny would have been excluded from my genetic makeup.

I spread out my book, my notebook, my pens, and then devoted all my energy towards the Feng Shui of locating the correct position for my latte—directly to my left would get in the way of the Summa. Directly to the right might put it at risk for being spilled if I grabbed a pen. Gradually I realized that I had to look around at the occupants of the room, or else appear scared or arrogant. I decided to seize the advantage and look around first. If one of these men was going to be my Eternal Destiny, I might as well see what he looked like.

There were six men in the room with me, excluding Dr. Hastings, who was leaving the room anyhow, carrying a folder of papers. I glanced at each of the students in turn.

To my left sat a small, dapper, dark young man in cowboy boots, skinny jeans and a baggy embroidered shirt. He was leaning back in a suave sort of way, lazily discoursing with the baby-faced boy that I had seen earlier. Him? My destiny? I immediately thought: no way. Not that I mind Latinos, but I couldn't see myself falling for someone who wore those clothes.

And Baby-Face? Freckled and dressed in a sloppy sort of manner, with beat-up converse sneakers and ripped jeans: polar opposite to the first guy, but again my innate fashion sense discounted him as my Perfect Match, not unless he took an intensive year-long course in learning how to dress. His American Eagle t-shirt was too baggy and half untucked, and his shoelaces were untied.

On the other side of these two sat a tall, broad-shouldered man, somewhat crouched over his book. I noticed that he had reddish hair and reddish skin and rather remarkable biceps, but his face was hidden by one large hand. He struck me as seeming a little older than the other two. Husband possibility? Hard to say, from this angle.

The next man in the room was regarding me with an unpleasant insolence, and unfortunately he was familiar. The bald pagan who had been practically smoking inside the church last night. Hardly likely. My imaginary Beloved would have to be Catholic, at the very least, and even if I were silly enough to go thinking I could change a man, this one seemed like an extremely improbable candidate for the RCIA and thus it was highly unlikely that I'd marry him over and above the current selection.

In the corner sat a blond long-haired boy with a pretty face wearing a too-tight Lacoste shirt, a too-tight denim suit jacket, and too-tight seersucker trousers. He looked like he would have been more comfortable headlining for an indie band than studying Aquinas. I could not for the life of me imagine him being my Destiny. In fact, the very sight of him brought to mind a series of cheesy pop song lyrics—which my Personal Revelation was starting to sound like, ugh.

The last student in the room was sitting directly across from me, intent on texting something on his phone. Just as I looked at him, he looked up at me. It was my nemesis. Sean.

My Eternal Destiny? I groaned. The entire situation was getting ridiculous. I realized at this point that evaluating this Personal Revelation was going to derail any attempt at normal thought and stuffed it into the deepest reaches of my subconscious, for now.

Sean stared at me in a pantomime of wild head-scratching eye-bugging disbelief, then got to his feet, exclaiming, "Well, congratulations! You did it! Or, did you? Don't tell me you're doing a philosophy class sit-in!"

"No, I took the test. Dr. Hastings said I could take the class." I said this with certain smugness. Sean did not seem perturbed; he came over and shook my hand—I noticed that his hands were dry and pleasantly callused—and said, "Well, well, well, whatdya know?"

"What?" the dark one asked.

"She's a first-year," Sean said.

"No way!"

"Yup. Hey, how'd you get in?"

"I talked to Hastings, he gave me the test."

"Amazing," Baby-face said. He turned to his friends and smirked. "The chick does philosophy. But she doesn't know the rules. Should we tell her?"

"Dr. Hastings doesn't like us to drink in class," the dark one said.

"Well, so? Who would be stupid enough to drink in class?" I said, not thinking.

Baby-face laughed loudly. "She thinks you mean drink as in imbibe, tipple, partake of alcoholic beverages."

I blushed. Now they would all think I was a lush…awesome.

The dark one said, "All in good time!" rather knowingly. He seemed to have the faintest suggestion of a Mexican accent. I confess I like Mexican accents. "For now though—if he sees you drinking soda or whatever in class, he'll make you pour it out. Later on you can start bringing in coffee. By the end of the semester you can crack a keg in the middle of the room, and he won't care. But first you have to prove yourself."

I wondered how many times I was going to have to prove myself before this class even started. "Okay," I said, and tipped up my iced latte and downed its contents. I strode over to a waste basket to dispose of the empty cup—and as I turned to go back to my seat, I bumped into someone entering the classroom. Another student. Another man.

It was him. The Perfect Guy.

9 ⤳

Homo Perfectus

Tall, dark, handsome, carrying a black leather messenger bag, wearing an outfit that was flawless: just the right balance of casual studiousness with formality: grey suit trousers and blazer, darker gray button shirt, no tie. Black hair, blue eyes, an intently piercing expression, now aimed in my direction. It was the Perfect Man, from the airport. And he was Catholic. And in my class in the Summa.

No wonder my Sense of Destiny was in overdrive. But wait—he hadn't been in the room during the actual moment of the Tingling. Did that mean—he couldn't be—?

"You have whipped cream on your nose," said Baby-face. Hurriedly, I wiped it off with my wrist and sat down. The Perfect Man didn't seem to mind. He smiled and said, "It's off now," and took a seat to my right, next to Dr. Hasting's paraphernalia.

"Hey Justin," Sean said.

"Hey Fowler," the Perfect Man said. He glanced in my direction. "Hello."

"I'm Catelyn Frank," I blurted out.

He smiled, but then a Bach concerto erupted from his pocket, and he pulled a cell phone out and got up, excusing himself into the hall.

"Well, well, well," said Baby-face, apparently continuing the conversation with a languid glance in my direction. "I have to say I'm thrilled we finally have a woman in the class."

I don't take kindly to being referred to in the third person, particularly as a representative of my gender, so I said nothing. Unfortunately, Baby-face went on.

"Yessir, a woman in a philosophy class. When's the last time that happened?"

Sean said, "Last year. We had Marcy, in Heidegger."

"I mean a *young* woman."

The dark young man shrugged. "There was Laura in Plato."

"Very funny, Che. Remember her little mustache?" Baby-face let out a long, melodramatic sigh.

Sean gave a half-smile. "Mmhmm," he agreed.

"Oh, the misery of reading the Symposium and realizing that we were doomed, doomed! Remember? 'Only by loving as many beautiful bodies as possible can one ascend to the philosophic heights!' But not only is it contrary to our ethics, it's also impossible when I look around and just see these ugly manly faces...sorry, but I'm not turning gay just to please Socrates!"

"I completely agree," said Che. "We need a woman to look at."

"That's right," I said. "The University gave me a special scholarship so all of you could have a woman to look at. I can't actually read or anything, you know."

I noticed that the older man with the biceps seemed to be amused by this conversation, but the skinny bald pagan was lounging in his chair staring at a wall.

"Oh, hey, I didn't mean it like that," said the dark guy the others were calling Che. He looked genuinely contrite. "I know you've got to be smart if you passed that test. It almost killed me. Took years off my life. Turned my hair gray, no kidding, you look at my head, you see this shiny black hair, but guess what? It's dyed. Rogaine, baby."

Having succumbed (justifiably?) to my vice of sarcasm, I was glad that Dr. Hastings stepped into the room at this point and class began.

Divested of caffeine, heated by the chauvinism around me, I tried not to pay attention to the roll call. But of course, I really *was* interested.

Sean Fowler: my patriarchal acquaintance. He seemed remarkably relaxed around Hastings, considering his humiliation in the library. He sat hunched forward a little, looking cheerful and interested. I was annoyed with myself for noticing that he had little curls of brown hair on the back of his neck, and that it was rather a nice neck, too.

Justin Hale: So that was the full name of the Perfect Man. I took the opportunity of glancing at him again when his name was called and noticed his skin was olive, his profile aquiline, and (Oh! Did he just glance my way on purpose?) startlingly pale blue eyes under slanted eyebrows. I found myself wiping my nose again just to make sure I was presentable.

Bartholomew Ingram: that was the older man with reddish hair and the biceps. He was not handsome but seemed to ooze virility: the strong, silent type, I guessed.

Hector Mendoza: that was Che's real name, apparently. The dapper Mexican seemed to be a good sort in spite of his sexist remarks and his overdone suavity; somehow it was difficult to be really irritated at him. Even now he was glancing at me with a slightly anxious expression to see if I was still mad. I pretended I was.

Garrett Oakleigh: this was the Indie rockstar. He didn't look particularly smart, and I wondered how in the world he had passed the test. I guessed from the way that he was fiddling with a pen that he was a smoker. A smoker currently craving a cigarette. I sympathized with him.

Nathaniel Santorini, who informed the professor that he only answered to the name Nat: So this was the bald pagan, who couldn't help reminding me of a Nazi skinhead. After all, the Nazis were pagans too, even if they pretended to be Christians. He continued to lounge indolently and insolently even as his name was called, just giving a small nod to Hastings, who seemed a little annoyed, a little amused.

Baby-face turned out to be Michael Schaeffer. He raised his hand when his name was called, and asked, pointing to me, "And what about her?"

"Oh yes, and Catelyn," Dr. Hastings added, "your name will be added to the roster after the paperwork has gone through...but let me get your name down now...what was your last name again? Oh yes, Catelyn Frank, good. And so—"

And so class began.

Hastings started out by giving us some background which, he added, he didn't think we ought to need, but which perhaps we did and maybe we were ashamed to ask certain questions, and perhaps we should be ashamed, but that was no reason to remain in ignorance...I hoped he was not thinking of me, specifically. I tried hard to focus on Aquinas, my beloved Philosopher, and keep all thoughts of Earthly Things, such as Weddings, far from my mind.

"The important thing for you all to remember is that Aquinas would not have considered himself a philosopher in the sense we use today. We think of philosophy as a specific discipline, with a set of principles which more or less have to be observed.

"In the thirteenth century this would not have been the case. If you were studying philosophy, you would have been expected to know a good deal more than what any of you here know today—but, on the other hand," and here he smirked his slightly malicious smirk again, "you would not be tested on it.

"Aquinas considered that he was doing not so much philosophy as natural theology. What this means, from our perspective, is that we have to enter in, to some extent, to the spirit of thirteenth century monastic spirituality.

"Have you ever looked closely at an illuminated manuscript from that period? If you have not, I advise that you remedy this. Look closely at the art, at the calligraphy, the marginalia. The grotesque images may at times confuse you, but they are not there simply to provoke laughter. Nor are they there simply to make a dry text seem more interesting. Seeking into the allegorical significance of such illuminated works is part of the process of understanding them. The men who made them prayed while they worked. And perhaps expected us to pray while we study.

"So the process of what we would today call 'philosophizing,' for Thomas and his contemporaries was not pursued in a purely linear manner. It was not simply a question of proceeding from proposition to conclusion, or of weeding out the less likely hypotheses. It was a process also of meditation, which involves inwardness—and openness to the divine light."

Openness to the divine light. I glanced up and spotted a large crucifix hanging on the wall, and remembered once again why I was even in this room, Preternatural Illuminations or not.

Hastings seemed to be addressing a certain section of the room. "You are not going to be obliged to pray in this class. Nor will you be required even to believe in divine illumination. But it is as important to remember this 'mythos' of intellection, as it would be to understand that for the ancients, a poet was a poet by virtue of the muse. We find this idea appealing and quaint, perhaps. And perhaps some of us may find the notion of the muse intriguing, but call the philosophy of illumination mere superstition. However," — he looked pointedly at Nat — "such prejudices are puerile."

I was pleased to see that Hastings seemed quite prepared to put the annoying bald atheist in his place.

"Yet, this means we have a futile task ahead of us, because I am essentially inviting you to try to become a thirteenth-century monastic scholar, and this is quite impossible. For some of us" — and here he glanced at me, "it would have been impossible even then. But for all of us, we cannot even begin to imagine the separate set of assumptions and prejudices that would be guiding that reason which we would be so certain was objective." He smiled and cleared his throat.

"This does not mean that we should fall into radical skepticism, or despair. But we should try as much as possible to be aware of the variables — or, perhaps, if we think we are arguing from first principles, to examine our principles and make sure they are really foundational."

He looked around the class. "Can you give me an example of one self-evident truth that was taken for granted in Aquinas's day?"

Several hands went up, but Sean's had gone up first, so Hastings nodded to him.

"That women are naturally inferior to men." He grinned at me.

My eyes widened. Clearly, I thought, this is deliberate provocation. Well, bring it on!

"Can you give me an example of this kind of prejudice, Sean, or are you just speaking out of your own predetermined modern prejudice against the Middle Ages?"

"Why do you call it a prejudice? I would call that a universal constant," Michael said, with his baby-face grin. Hastings glared at him. "Okay, sorry. Too much levity?"

"Too much idiocy," said Hastings. I agreed.

"By levity Christ ascended," added Che in his Mexican accent, but to my surprise Hastings did not reprove him and even seemed to find this funny.

"I can give you an example," said Sean, flipping through his paperback copy of the Summa, "just give me a minute so I can find it...it's that bit about being misbegotten..."

"Part I, Question 92, Article 1, Objection 1," said Hastings drily.

Michael found the section first, and interrupted Sean, reading in surprisingly precise tones: "'It would seem that woman should not have been made in the first production of things. For the Philosopher says that the female is a misbegotten male. But nothing misbegotten or defective should have been made in the first production of things. Therefore women should not have been made at that first production.'"

I was smarting at Michael's rudeness, when I remembered that it was St. Thomas, not Michael, who had originally said it: I felt a sinking feeling within, almost as though I had caught a boyfriend cheating. How could my own Angelic Doctor have said such a thing? Then, a thought occurred to me.

"Ah," said Hastings, in what seemed a vaguely mocking sort of way. "Yes, Catelyn?"

My hand had gone up even before I willed it, it seemed. "Yes," I said, "that excerpt was taken from Objection 1, right? He is simply restating a prejudice that Aristotle held, not necessarily stating his own view."

"Quite right," said the professor, "Michael, be careful not to quote out of context. It's a bad habit we have gotten into, in this fragmentary age."

"But read on ahead," said Sean, "See, in the reply to that objection, he agrees with that part—'for the active power in the male seed tends to a perfect likeness according to the masculine sex; while the production of woman comes from some defect in the active power, or'—get this!—'from some material indisposition, or even from some external influence, such as that of a south wind, which is moist, as the Philosopher observes.'"

"Gotta love that Aristotelian biology," said Nat, running a hand over his shaven head.

"So it is to be deduced from this," said Michael, "that if one chooses to, hmm, consummate the sacrament, so to speak, while a moist southern wind is blowing…one will thus have the misfortune to beget a girl?"

"And what is meant by 'material indisposition?' I'd like to know," said Che. Now his Mexican accent was starting to annoy me. I couldn't help it, I almost smirked.

"Oh, I think you know," said Sean.

"There's no need to be crass," said the Perfect Man, Justin, nodding in my direction. "There are ladies present."

Well. On one hand, I could appreciate the consideration—but on the other, I had no desire to be viewed as some Dickensian fainting wisp of a maiden. Not that there is anything notably wispy about me. "Please, it's not the Victorian period," I said, "I think we can discuss philosophy without shame."

"Can we?" said Garrett moodily, "isn't philosophy all about shame? Metaphysics speaks to us of the origins of things. The dark loins of being. That is why we are ashamed of metaphysics."

Everyone ignored him. I guessed that this sort of gnomic utterance was common with him. But I had no idea what he thought he was talking about.

"What I object to," I said, "is not the inherent vulgarity in certain varieties of low humor. That is beneath my notice. I am more concerned with this assumption of his that Aquinas considered women inferior."

"Sorry, but it's right there in front of you," said Sean, with an engaging shrug. "Hey, don't glare at me, I didn't say it."

"Okay," I said, "but look here, later on..." I loved this passage, and read it aloud in a clear voice.

"Article 3: 'It was right for woman to be made from a rib of man. First, to signify the social union of man and woman, for the woman should neither use authority over man, and so she was not made from his head; nor was it right for her to be subject to man's contempt as his slave, and so she was not made from his feet.'"

I looked around at my classmates. But they were less than impressed. "Rrrrrrrigght," said Sean, "so, woman is not to be man's slave. It doesn't say she's not to be his servant."

Oh, wouldn't you just love that, I thought—a little woman always waiting on you hand and foot. Inadvertently, I thought of the character Gaston, from Disney's *Beauty and the Beast*.

"It says social union, Sean," I said. "Now, maybe you are unacquainted with the nuances of social ranks but it is quite out of the question that a master would ever consider his servant in any way in 'social union' with him." *And a social union with someone like you is out of the question. Adorable brown curls or not.*

"Catelyn is right," said Hastings. "Unfortunately, in our democratic civilization, we forget the weight that such words would have had, in an aristocratic age—and coming from an aristocrat. Remember that Aquinas came from titled family. Inequality of human beings was one self-evident assumption."

"Although Aquinas rejected his titles to become a lowly friar," said Bartholomew. It was the first time I had heard him speak, and I was surprised to hear such a rich, lush Southern drawl: straight off the plantation.

"But friars were not so lowly," said Justin. "Remember, the Church was a source of tremendous power."

"You mean political power?" asked Michael.

"Political power, yes—but only by way of spiritual authority. Think of King Henry IV doing penance in the snows of Canossa, humbling himself before Pope Gregory VII. That was the power of excommunication: a spiritual power that could translate into worldly power."

"But the Dominicans turned away from worldly goods and offices," I pointed out. "They were a begging order."

"Still, they were immensely influential within the Church," Justin argued, looking intent. "Just think: in 1276 the first Dominican Pope, Blessed Innocent V, was elected to the chair of Peter. Just two years after the death of St Thomas Aquinas. Innocent had been a pupil of Thomas, too."

I was a little astonished at Justin's knowledge of Church history, not to mention dates and persons. Tall, dark, handsome, and brilliant? I was beginning to get intimidated.

"This is getting off topic," said Hastings. "I believe the question is, whether or not Aquinas' choice to become a Dominican friar is enough to qualify him as a social egalitarian. If it is, then 'social union' has less weight to it. However, I am afraid the question is anachronistic. The choice to abandon riches and titles for a mendicant's robe was not necessarily a social gesture; moreover, there is as much hierarchy within the Church as there ever was in civil society. Indeed, if we keep in mind the etymology of the word, only the Church has true hierarchy."

"*Hierarchia*," said Nat. Justin and Hastings both looked at him in some surprise. "Greek," he went on, "for High Priest. A hierarchy is a priestly order, not just any old order." Well. So maybe there was a reason the pagan had gotten into this class.

I focused on the argument. Restate your opponent's position. "What you are saying," I said, "is that while Aquinas may have believed in a true hierarchy, it doesn't mean that he despised social order. He would have considered social ranks as essential to natural order and natural right—is that correct?"

"That is correct," said Hastings.

"But," Sean cut in, "within that social order marriage could easily be called a 'social union' without meaning actual social equality." He leaned forward and his brown eyes twinkled.

"Also correct," said Hastings, who was clearly enjoying this. I was starting to feel strangely hemmed in, however.

I took a deep breath, trying not to lose my cool. "But marriage is also a sacrament." I said.

"Yes, representing the unity of Christ and the Church. Is the Church equal with Christ?" Sean asked me.

"What do you mean by 'equal'?" I countered, but with some desperation. Falling back on the Bill Clinton defense? Yikes!

"Is there any possible meaning of the word 'equal' that would allow anyone to ever say that Christ and the Church are equal?" asked Justin slowly.

"Well, marriage," I said, and then realized to my horror what I had just done.

"Circular reasoning!" Sean exclaimed.

"*Feminine* reasoning," added Michael, "just kidding," he added hastily. But I glared at him all the same.

To my amazement Hastings came to my rescue: "I told you Natural Theology didn't have to be linear," he said. "Cool off, folks. We can come back to this topic later. Right now we need to discuss the nature of sacred doctrine. It is devoutly to be wished that this topic will be less…incendiary?"

I looked coolly past Sean's ear, off into the remote distance. Sean grinned. Justin looked troubled. Michael leaned over and whispered something to Justin, which made him frown more deeply. Che raised his eyebrows suggestively at me. Bart stared at his own bicep. Garrett pouted. Nat appeared to be doodling, and ignoring us all.

I sat up straight in my chair and even felt my nostrils flare a bit: maybe Hastings had called a draw, but at least as far as I was concerned, the battle was still on.

That was when the juxtaposition of my Private Sense of Destiny and my current Mental Outrage hit me. Me, end up with one of these men? Inconceivable! Jewish grandmother or not, my Tingling was apparently a false beacon.

I groaned. It was clear that I had even more discernment ahead of me. For instance, discerning whether or not I was crazy.

10

Sic et Non?

Let us consider the matter of my sanity, my supposed private revelation, and what this means for my future interactions with my Suminar classmates.

Question One: Am I insane?

Article 1: Does my life history suggest that I am generally more or less together?

Objection 1: It would seem that I do not have it together. When I fret about my weight, I rush immediately to devour cinnabons, buttery muffins, doughnuts, and other things of that nature. Whereas, if I were sane, worries about my weight should drive me to diet and exercise.

Objection 2: Furthermore, I gave up a high-paying job with a good career path, in order to come to Texas and get a PhD in philosophy. My parents suspect that I am insane, for this reason.

Objection 3: Considering the way I behaved my first couple of years in college, and the situations I put myself in – especially with totally repulsive and idiotic guys – I must be not only insane but bonkers, crackers, off my rocker, out of my gourd, and so forth.

On the contrary, my behavior in the past, although eccentric, is in no way compatible with typically mad behavior (doing the same thing repeatedly while expecting different results, indulging in conspiracy theories about the Masons or the Templars, inventing imaginary friends, refusing to bathe for fear of diluting one's vital essence, etc. etc.).

I answer that, therefore I am, in fact, sane. Weird, maybe, but still sane. In spite of having entertained, even for a brief time, a private revelation regarding the marriageability of any one of seven philosophical misogynists.

Reply to Objection 1: It is a well-known but unfortunate fact that women under stress tend to turn to food to self-medicate. And I am a woman who loves food. So eating the cinnabon may not have been a good idea, but it was normal.

Reply to Objection 2: Money isn't everything. Neither is success. Those are both finite goods. Mistaking the finite for the infinite is actually far more insane than giving up temporal values to pursue eternal ones. Besides, I am going to be a rich and famous philosopher (fingers crossed), so I'm not even necessarily giving up finite goods, either.

Reply to Objection 3: Shut up. I was confused back then.

Article 2: Whether it is possible for a sane woman to think she is getting a "Tingling"?

Objection 1: If I really had a supernatural power of this sort, shouldn't it have come into play earlier in my life, maybe as a warning to stay out of trouble (see Article 1, Objection 3)?

Objection 2: I am an enlightened, rational person with very well-developed powers of skepticism. I don't believe in bizarre powers of prescience, nor in ESP, nor in astrology, nor in most of those goofy things that were probably invented by pre-feminist-era women to keep them occupied since they weren't allowed to study real stuff like philosophy or theology.

On the Contrary, there are more things in heaven and earth than are dreamt of in philosophy — even Thomistic philosophy.

I answer that: It is entirely possible, then, that I did indeed inherit some sort of vague prescient sensibility from my grandmother. So thinking that I am experiencing it doesn't make me insane. And if it is for real – if it is something that is actually happening to me – then I guess this means I'm not so much crazy as blessed. I guess.

Reply to Objection 1: Perhaps God wanted to let me to do dumb things and make mistakes, for some reason. To teach me to be humble maybe (humility is not my strong point).

Reply to Objection 2: History is full of rational, enlightened individuals who also believed in the supernatural — and not just the "official" supernatural, either. I mean, Rene Descartes, the great rationalist and skeptic, got his idea for *Meditations on First Philosophy* from a dream in which Our Lady appeared to him! So, put that in your Enlightenment pipe and smoke it!

Question Two: How am I going to deal with those guys???

Article 1: It seems to be out of the question that I would be "destined" to be with any of those chauvinistic pigs.

Objection 1: But some of them were rather nice. The Mexican guy, Che, was actually apologetic. I should have been nicer to him.

Objection 2. And then, Sean may be patriarchal, but maybe he is just doing it to put on an act?

Also — not that this is relevant, of course — he is pretty easy on the eyes.

Objection 3. Justin. Enough said.

Objection 4. If having a Tingling doesn't make you crazy, then the Tingling must be for real. Take your pick: either you are crazy, or you are destined to end up for ever and ever, till death do you part, with one of the guys in the Suminar. Principle of Non-Contradiction!

On the Contrary, it is utterly ridiculous to think that you are destined to be with any of them. Tinglings are well and good, but it is entirely possible for a premonition to be wrong. Private revelation, duh!

I answer that: Whatever the future may have in store for me, there is no way I can really be sure. And it is also very, very unlikely that my future would entail a romance with Sean, Justin, Che, Nat, Michael, Garrett, or Bartholomew. Even my fairly lively imagination can't quite see ANYTHING like that unfolding. So, better not to even think of it.

Reply to Objection 1: Che may have been nice enough…but that doesn't mean niceness is enough. Besides, skinny jeans on men? I think not.

Reply to Objection 2: I've had three encounters now with Sean, and on no occasion has he led me to believe that it's just an act. I bet he gets a lot of female attention and likes it. He thinks it's his due. Well, no doubt there are gaggles of undergrad girls to swarm all over him, if that's what he likes. Not me. The Next Great Catholic Philosopher does not swarm.

Reply to Objection 3. Just stop thinking about it, get over it, why would the Perfect Man ever even look at me? Besides, despite his great looks, he might well be just as snotty as the rest of them. And no, that is not sour grapes talking!

Reply to Objection 4. Like I said before: private revelation! I might have such a faculty, but that doesn't mean it's infallible. Maybe the Tingling is trying to tell me something totally different—like, that one of those guys is going to end up editing a journal with me, or something. And, being a pathetic frivolous blob of romantic blubber, my mind immediately turned to marriage. So there's no contradiction.

Thus I concluded my Thomistic disputation, conducted in front of the statue of Aquinas in the chapel (I had my face in my hands, grateful for the semi-darkness, and the candles, and the faint aroma of lingering incense). I could not tell if Thomas himself approved, but he seemed to be at least entertained by my exercise.

On finishing the laying out of my thoughts, I experienced a strange relief, a kind of clarity, almost as though I was watching the debate unfold outside of myself. Oh blessed, blessed philosophy!

No, I was not crazy. I had just gotten derailed from my purpose, worrying about a totally hypothetical vocation to marry a totally improbable male. I had let the stress and excitement go to my head.

From now on, Tingling or no, I would proceed with my eyes fixed on the goal: doing fabulously in the class — despite whatever obstacles presented by woman-disdaining males or the ominous pricklings of destiny.

11 ⤳

Exercitia Spiritualia

Now that I had a plan, or at least a mindset for dealing with uncomfortable implausible personal revelations, I was back to the mundane. It was the Morning of Unhappy Realizations. My boxes had arrived, and my initial hurrah at thinking now I would be reunited with my wardrobe was cut short when it dawned on me that, back in Philly, I had packed with a different notion of "dorm room" in mind.

Surrounded by clothes and shoes and purses and scarves, staring sadly at the microscopic closet that was already half-full, I could no longer deny the inevitable: I was going to have to get rid of some of this, or at least send it home. I thought about the Dominicans and the Franciscans, the mendicant orders committed to lives of poverty, or at least detachment from earthly things. Probably I had something to learn from them. At the very least, I should ditch my back issues of Italian *Vogue* which wasn't fitting on the shallow bookcases provided by the college.

I hurriedly repacked, as I had two classes to attend: Ethics and Early Modern. I dressed quickly, taking advantage of my new abundance of outfit options…and then had the next Unhappy Realization of the morning: my clothes were tight. It wasn't just the clothes I had taken with me: all, every single one of them, had done the Incredible Shrinking Trick. No matter what I put on, I bulged. Had I been bulging like this in class? Gazing with horror and disgust upon the grotesque spectacle of a doctoral student oozing out of a blood-red silk tank-top, looking like a squashed tomato, I had my final realization of the morning: diet alone would not suffice; I was going to have to start exercising. After all, if I was actually in the presence of my Destiny during this class…no, no, I had to stop thinking this way!

I had already mapped out the best place to run, so when I set out that evening, surreptitious as a spy in enemy territory, I was able to creep along a wooded path hoping no one would see me in my horrendous running clothes—actually, not horrendous in themselves—just horrendous on me. Also, it was important that anyone who DID see me, would see me running, as opposed to waddling along energetically, so no one would think that this was a pathetic first-time effort.

As I power-walked along, warming up and feeling my flesh jiggle, I tried to comfort myself with the reminder that Aquinas had not been known for his slim girth—but somehow this didn't quite help. Suddenly I remembered Nat, the irritating bald bearded boy, mentioning "fat Aquinas" outside the chapel. Had he spoken with a double meaning? Had he been insinuating that my devotion to Aquinas had something to do with a common weight issue? Rage seethed up in me, and I began to jog with all the feverish intensity of the Light Brigade on their final charge.

Did I mention that it was hot in Houston? I was dripping before I even started running. Then I was out of breath. Then I started to have stomach cramps. Alone on the trail I stopped and took rapid desperate gulps of air. Then to my horror I heard pounding rhythmic feet behind me. No! Not other runners—athletic runners, who would now see that I was not running: I was standing gasping like a fish on the path.

"Hey!"

It was Danielle: pretty, slim Danielle in a sports top and sleek grey running pants. I remembered hearing once that in the South, ladies never sweat: they only glow. Danielle was glowing. Her companion, olive-skinned and black-haired, who was running in place and seemed to be counting to herself, was glowing too, in a pair of spandex calf-length running pants and a spandex sports bra—impossible that anyone would look good in such an outfit! But she did.

"Can't stop," said the spandex girl, "sorry!"

"Oh, honestly, Felicity, it's not the end of the world," said Danielle. "How's it going, Cate? I saw you joined the FPV group, cool!"

"Yep, it looks like you've got a good number of people involved. I'm impressed."

Danielle made a face. "That's the problem. A lot of people joined in the virtual world, sure'" she said, "but I wouldn't exactly say they were involved. You know how it goes…"

"I do," I said, "I plead guilty myself. I join Facebook groups sometimes just to annoy my peers. Good thing I'm not going into politics."

"Well, we need someone to keep things shook up, right?"

"Danielle," said her friend, still jogging disconsolately in place, "I am going to run on. I have to keep my heart rate up! Sorry…but…"

"Go ahead, Felicity," said Danielle cheerfully, "I can't really keep up with you anyway. Meet you back at the dorm later, then?"

Felicity looked a little miffed, but forced a grin and said, "Sure." And she was gone. Danielle and I settled in at a more comfortable pace that allowed one to chat without hyperventilating.

"Did you check your Facebook today?" Danielle asked.

"Believe it or not, no," I said. "Which is weird and strange. Usually I'm such a slave to my social networking…but that's one of those things I'm working on changing." I grimaced a bit. "Sort of like my physical fitness."

"Oh, aren't we all?" Danielle laughed. "When you do check it though—I sent out a message about an event—our first meeting, actually, since we got approved on campus! It's Saturday night which might be a hassle for some people but I figure, if we go out for drinks afterwards, we can mix business and pleasure, right?"

"I hate to have to confess it, but I don't exactly have any hot dates planned for Saturday night," I said, "I mean, not to insinuate that if I did I'd stop caring about social justice…"

We started on together, at what struck me as an eminently reasonable pace. And since Danielle was with me, and Danielle was the image of fitness, no one could accuse us of sloth. We chatted about pro-life work, about our respective backgrounds, my old job, her D.C. internship, and from there we went into the wonderfully engaging subject of Catholicism and feminism and how the former enriched the latter. In other words, precisely the sort of conversation I could only have with another intellectual woman. Precisely NOT the sort of conversation I could picture having with any of my Suminar classmates.

I was grateful to be single and a student and able to be thinking about higher things and temporarily free from care. Ah, no wonder the medievals found the monastic life of study and disputation to be heaven on earth! What a change from the rat race of subsistence living and turf wars! Even if they were engaged in such activities in shaded stone monasteries, and I was engaged in such pursuits on a hot gravel trail with the sun relentlessly beating down on my forehead...

By the time we circled back to the personal, to the question of the future and vocations, we were shamelessly walking on the jogging trail. Danielle's heart rate was probably back to normal; mine wasn't, but walking suited me fine.

"I don't know yet if I'm called to marriage or the single life," Danielle said. "That's partly why I'm here. Sort of a respite, a chance to think it all out. I'd like to get married, but I still feel called to work in politics. It's a mess. Sometimes I think that we should imitate the Chinese. Their mandarins were celibate: they understood that a life in politics didn't mesh well with family life."

"I can understand that," I agreed. "No wonder so many politicians have awful marriages."

"Plus it was supposed to help their government officials to be more objective," Danielle said. "You know, they weren't always putting their sons in key positions and giving family members cushy jobs. Kind of the same reason why the Roman Rite Church settled on celibacy. Bureaucracies can be so easy to manipulate. If you minimize the chance for nepotism, you minimize corruption."

"Wow, that's a really good point," I said appreciatively.

"So I can see it would make sense for me to be single." Danielle sighed. "But when I meet some really cool guy...or, believe it or not, when I see some perfectly adorable baby..."

I groaned. "I *so* agree. The flesh has a way of rushing in where angels fear to tread, doesn't it?"

"But remember, God Himself became flesh…so maybe that's okay," Danielle said.

"Wow, well, there's a metaphysical twist! One that makes me feel better, actually."

We were now at the end of the trail and my much-vaunted run had turned into a cerebral discussion, but I was not disappointed.

"Felicity is going to kill me," Danielle said. "She's my roommate. She's super into fitness."

"I'm sorry I disrupted your run," I said.

"No, it's fine! Personally, I think she's addicted to workouts. She's a nursing student, so she says she does it to relieve stress, but if she keeps dragging me on these runs, I'm going to check her into a twelve-step group."

I smirked. "I could run such a group. Overexercisers Anonymous? Lead them back to the way of sanity…But I suppose I'd just be trading one set of inordinate desires for another."

Danielle laughed. "So thanks for rescuing me! Anyway, you HAVE to come to the meeting Saturday. You are like totally my answer to prayer…I need someone else who's passionate about pro-life work. Right now I'm carrying the whole thing myself and it's hard to be the rah-rah squad all the time."

"I'll be there with my pompoms," I promised, and we parted ways. I was insufficiently exercised, but happy for all that. Until I recalled that I had a paper due—the first paper of the semester!—for Hastings the following Tuesday, not to mention studying in my other classes. But my pride wanted to make sure that first paper was perfect. I wanted the whole weekend to work on it. I tried to power-walk back to the dorm, promising my aching thighs that I would shower, slip into comfortable clothes, make coffee, and then cloister myself in my dorm room with books for the next forty-eight hours.

To my horror, I realized that my sanctum had been violated in my absence. The door was open, and voices resonated loudly, raucously: Kimmy and Co. Suddenly reluctant to enter my own room, I stopped in the hallway, making a pretense of being deeply interested in a Calvin and Hobbes cut-out some girl had taped to her door.

"Well, your roommate may be a total snot but at least you don't have to have Jesus crap all over your room."

I recognized the voice of the girl whose posterior one was invited to look at but not touch: she had a twangy Southern accent, maybe East Texas?

Kimmy: "Omigawd, you mean like that picture of Jesus? With the heart showing? Creeeee-py!"

Hot pants: "No, it's worse than that. You don't even KNOW. She has this one picture over her bed, and it's all these huge fat naked people, up in the clouds or something. I was like, hello, that's a cool thing to have over your bed. NOT."

A third voice said, "Okay, that's just wrong."

"She said one of the naked people was Jesus too, but I don't know, he didn't have a beard, so I'm all, what is this, some sort of fat fetish or something? I mean, I didn't say that but I was thinking, you know, awesome, now I have to see that every time I come into my room?"

Third voice: "Well, go easy on her. She can't help it. She's like, from the dark ages or something. I saw her coming down the hallway and I was like, omigawd, did I like, walk onto the set of Little House on the Prairie, or what?"

Kimmy: "That is SO what she looks like. I wanted to be like, get out to the Mall ASAP or something. I mean, this chick I have to live with, she might be totally stuck up and weird, but at least her clothes aren't like borrowed from the Beverly Hillbillies."

Hot pants: "Yeah, but she's like what, thirty? And she lives in a dorm? That's not normal."

Thirty! I wanted to march in with a blaze of vengeance, but I realized that, sweaty and bulging out of my running clothes, I probably *looked* thirty. I decided I needed to use the bathroom, so I crept past the door as swiftly as I could. I thought one of them saw me, but I was walking quickly, head in the air, so as to not give any sign that I'd been driven away from my own room.

The girl with the purple teddy-bear nightgown was in the bathroom brushing her hair — not wearing purple teddy-bears this time, at least. She had on a long denim skirt that bunched in the middle, under a button-down plaid shirt that was too baggy for her. I had a sudden suspicion that she was the girl I had overheard mentioned as hanging up pictures of naked people and channeling Little House on the Prairie — and thus my heart warmed to her, in spite of her admittedly dingy clothes. I also noticed that, bad outfit or not, she had gorgeous hair, thick and long and honey-gold.

"You have amazing hair," I said.

"Oh...thanks," she seemed perturbed at being complimented. "Actually, I was noticing your hair the other day. I was wishing mine were like yours. Mine takes so long to brush."

"Well, it's the curse of Eve," I said. "You know, like it says in Genesis. 'You shall bring forth children in pain, and no matter what your hair is, you will hate it.'"

The girl did a double take, and laughed. "That's not in the Bible! But it should be! It's so true!"

"My grandmother used to say that," I confessed. That same Jewish grandmother whose genes I had inherited.

"Well, I love *your* hair. You're so stylish."

"Thanks..." I couldn't very well return the compliment, unfortunately. On an impulse I said, "I don't know about you, but this dorm life gets on my nerves a bit. Maybe I'm too old and set in my ways...it's just weird sharing a room and all that."

"Oh, well, I always had to share a room with my sisters at home. So it's not that bad. I mean, sharing a room isn't that bad..."

I deduced from this the unspoken caveat: it depends on who you're sharing a room with.

"What year are you?"

"Actually, I'm here for my MA." She smiled as though this were something to be ashamed of. She was actually quite pretty—in a rosy German tavern-wench sort of way, though you wouldn't notice it, really, with the horrendous clothes she wore.

"Really, seriously? I thought I was the only grad student in the entire building! What are you studying?"

"Literature. What about you?"

"Philosophy." I was curious to know if this was the poor girl who was sharing a room with Hot Pants but couldn't figure out how to say this. Asking her if she had paintings of naked people in her room sounded way to invasive, not to mention misleading. I decided to stick with formalities. "I'm Catelyn Frank."

"Mary-Clare Watkins." We shook hands. I hesitated, trying to figure out what else I could say to her, but then decided I should start finding a new haven for studying, so long as my room was commandeered for a gabfest. "I'd better go find someplace to study. I'll see you around!"

"See you!" the girl said cheerfully, but she looked a bit sad.

It was only after I headed to the showers that I realized I should have invited her to Danielle's FPV meeting. But maybe that wouldn't be Mary-Clare's thing. She looked a bit too sheltered and other-worldly for political activism.

12 ～

The Maid in Battle

I set up camp in the library for the weekend, and set out to do my paper, which involved a good amount of strategizing. After several classes now of raging debates, I decided that my destiny in the program was going to be that of a kind of Joan of Arc, a lone female warrior against a host of unsympathetic males.

As I began my studying session with a prayer to Joan of Arc—I follow the "it's all about who you know" philosophy when it comes to getting heavenly help—I thought over Friday's Suminar debate.

At the beginning of each class, we would take turns reading aloud from one of the Questions in the Summa, and then Hastings would present a brief analysis, and invite us to discuss certain points. We had been discussing the "Goodness of God" (Question 6) and Michael and Nat had gotten into a heated argument over "Whether all things are good by the Divine Goodness" (Article 4). We started to discuss participation in the Divine

Goodness, but after my classmates degenerated into
ad hominem attacks on each other, Michael calling
Nat a polytheist, and Nat coming back at Michael
with the accusation that his definition of 'substance'
was as bad as Spinoza's so HE was actually the
polytheist and just didn't know it, I tried to bring
them back to the matter at hand by pointing out that
we needed to clarify what was meant by 'participation'
before the conversation could go any further...and
they just looked at me.

"Participation is not the point," said Michael.

"Unless you're a Platonist," said Nat. "Aren't
Platonists extinct?"

"No, only Logical Positivists are extinct," said
Sean. "The last living Logical Positivist was shot by
his own student."

"He was shot for political reasons," said Che.
"Not because of the stupid Verifiability Criterion. The
assassin was an anti-Semite."

"Well, he still did the world a service," said
Michael.

I couldn't believe he would say such a thing—
even if it was a comment on Logical Positivism and
not Semitism, it sounded incredibly insensitive. Did
he not realize I was Jewish? Like most Jews among
the Gentiles, I seldom bring up my ancestry, except
in dire straits. But this comment was sending me
close. "That remark doesn't need to be dignified
with a response," I snapped. "Back on track. We're
talking about participation here, right, not philosopher
celebrity gossip? If you look back at the text, Aquinas

actually defines 'participation' so there's no need for us to quarrel over it!"

Sean waved his hand at me impatiently. "That's just splitting hairs."

"Hello, this is a PHILOSOPHY CLASS, right?" I exclaimed. "Isn't that kind of what we're supposed to be doing?"

"Yes, but we're not supposed to admit it," said Nat. "We're supposed to be pretending that what we're doing is actually important." I was getting really sick of Nat's sneering cynicism of all things Catholic.

"Bifurcatory diaeresis is what it's called, actually," said Hastings. Michael, Che and Sean all started laughing at this point, and I blushed because I didn't know what they were talking about, or whether I was being insulted.

Now in the library, I typed "bifurcatory diaeresis" and through the wonders of Google, discovered that actually it is pretty much the art of splitting hairs, and has nothing to do with digestive malfunctions. But either way, I felt annoyed that Hastings hadn't backed me up more.

I was deducing that these guys were well used to gloves-off combat, and that they were mostly familiar with one another's arguments. I didn't mind the heated debate. What I minded was that they seldom even acknowledged my arguments. It would be one thing if they proved my arguments were faulty — not that I would enjoy that, either, but at least it would not be unjust.

But as it was, the guys always seemed to be pretending they didn't hear me. Or, worse yet, responding as though whatever I had said was sort of cute. Sometimes, too, one of them would see fit to educate me on some point of Thomism that any freshman would know: "The Privation Theory of evil was developed so that God couldn't be held responsible for creating evil," Sean had informed me. Well!

I was reminded of Virginia Woolf's quotation from Dr. Johnson: "a woman's composing is like a dog's walking on its hind legs. It is not well done, but you are surprised to find it done at all." Was this what they thought of a woman philosophizing?

Maybe my knowledge of Thomistic debate was abecedarian, but didn't I at least understand the ground rules? I knew that Hastings supported me, but even he appeared to be amused more than impressed.

Gnawing my fingernails, I mentally compared the way I was treated to the way the other new student in the classroom was treated, Nat the pagan. True, Nat was aggravating to the extreme, but it was clear he was accepted as a worthy opponent. I wasn't sure I was making the cut.

Well, I *had* to make the cut. I was going to be graded on my contributions to the class discussion, so by Jove, I'd better have something worthwhile to contribute. I booted up a fresh page on my laptop and began typing an outline of my response to the Friday debate in earnest. If I was going to be Joan of Arc, I was going to battle full-throttle for Orleans.

But by Saturday night, I was exhausted. My original vision of burning my way through till the early hours of Monday was decimated. After all, I told myself, closing my laptop at 8 PM, as a fulfilled Jew, I needed to respect the Sabbath. Apparently my mind needed a Sabbath, too. I was thinking of whether or not reading the Summa would count now as menial work, whereas before it had been recreational reading for me? — when I comprehended the time and remembered, with a start, my promise to attend Danielle's meeting, which started in fifteen minutes!

Ah, frailty, thy name is exercising female! While my heart had every intention of attending, my body had apparently wanted to banish the memory of that failed exercise attempt by giving me temporary amnesia.

In a sweat, I packed everything up, ran back to my room. I switched my ochre leather bag for my apple-green one, added studded ankle boots to glam up my otherwise-casual attire, touched up my makeup, and high-tailed it over to the building where the meeting was being held.

By the time I arrived, I found that the meeting had barely started. Danielle was sitting behind a small table, looking nervous, and the ample conference room with rust-colored padded chairs was sadly vacant. Three other girls were there — one of them was Felicity, Danielle's roommate. She looked sulky: doing her duty as roommate and friend, but clearly not enjoying it. When I walked in,

Danielle brightened in relief: I realized with a pang she was wondering if I had ditched her like most of the virtual members of the group. If only she knew how close I had come...!

In situations like this, I kick into social-butterfly mode: not that I am naturally gregarious, but back when I was working in journalism I learned to be. I gaily greeted Danielle and then introduced myself to the rest of the group. The other two girls were undergraduates, of course, majoring in theology and education. We talked about what had led us to join Feministas Pro Vita, and I told them how I used to be a mentor in a support group for abused women (long story) when I first encountered the fact that there was something weird and self-contradictory in the attitude of some feminists towards abortion.

"There was this one girl, kind of a Goth type, really young. Oh, the story was so sad: she said she just felt completely worthless all her life so she started dating all these loser guys, and one of them was a cokehead. There was so much abuse involved, it was really intense hearing about it. And then she got pregnant and her boyfriend made her get an abortion. But the thing was, the woman who was leading the group, she was really nice and sympathetic and strong and all, but it was like she'd been trained to not even admit that guilt for abortion could even exist. She just kind of parroted a lot of stuff like 'it should have been your choice, not his choice,' and the girl was like 'no, it shouldn't have been anyone's choice, I'm awful, I'm evil,' and the leader just didn't seem to get how the girl was feeling, or why she was feeling that way."

"Wow," one of the undergraduates said.

"I know! Then this other woman in the group started telling the Goth girl it wasn't a baby, it was just a part of her body, and she had a right to do what she wanted with it. And the Goth girl started crying and kind of went hysterical. She left and didn't come back. That made me start thinking — because, it seemed so odd to me, that even though they were really welcoming to people in general, they wouldn't validate this one person's experience."

"Well, isn't that just like feminists?" Felicity said. "In my experience, they really just don't get women at all. I mean, no wonder this group is so small on this campus. It's because most feminists are out of touch with reality."

Danielle looked at her roommate with a slightly exasperated we've-had-this-conversation-before look. "Look, just because most women don't understand what it means to be a feminist…"

"It's not just about understanding, it's about reality!" Felicity said. "Hey, if I go around advertising that I'm a feminist, I'll never get a date!"

"Hey! I had a date…three years ago!" said Danielle brightly. She seemed determined to play the politician. "But it *is* true. About this campus, I mean. And probably among conservative Catholics in general. Most of the girls here, let's face it, are here to get their M.R.S. degrees."

I colored and the other two girls giggled. "Hey, I'm here to study educational theory," one said.

"But if I happen to meet the perfect guy here, I'm not complaining!"

"Well, I'm here to get equipped," Danielle said and caught my eye. "Even though—like you said—if Mr. Right came along, I wouldn't complain."

"So why aren't we just a regular pro-life group? Why do we have to drag feminism into it?" Felicity asked resentfully.

"Because there's a whole range of issues connected to women that need work, not just abortion," Danielle said. "Although obviously, that one's the most important. Cate mentioned working with abused women. There's sex trafficking. Human rights violations. Lots of these issues are connected to abortion, though not as obviously. And secular feminists are concerned—or should be concerned—about defending the rights of women everywhere. There's a lot we have to do. And this is one way we can bridge the gap and find common ground."

"We need more guy members," one of the undergraduates said idly. "That one Hispanic boy who came last semester—what was his name? Hector?"

"Do you mean Che?" I asked, surprised. "Dresses well? But with a kind of obnoxious attitude?"

Felicity snorted. "That's the one!" she said. "How do you know him?"

"He's in my Suminar class," I said. Che, a pro-feminist? But then, I thought, he's got to be nicknamed after a Marxist revolutionary for a reason. The whole liberation-theology thing had some overlaps with feminism. Still, it was puzzling.

Suddenly the door to the room banged open, and everyone jumped. There, striking a dramatic pose, her hand laid across her brow in an attitude of distress, the other arched behind her, stood the tall red-haired girl I had noticed outside the English department offices. She wore a loose-fitting one-shoulder dress that looked vaguely Grecian, and she was actually barefoot.

"Portia!" one of the girls exclaimed. "What happened? How did the audition go?"

Portia threw herself down on the back of a chair. "I don't want to talk about it at all," she said melodramatically, "I'm here to drown my woes in serious social issues." She glanced up, saw me, and then looked away. "Danielle, give me something grim and solemn to look at, I don't know, statistics about something horrible in some third-world slum."

Danielle tossed her a folder of papers with a grin. Here," she said, "plenty of grim statistics. You've given me a great lead-in to tonight's presentation on the situation in the Middle East and FGM."

So the FPV meeting commenced. A few other girls trickled in while Danielle showed us a power point and played an audio clip of some interviewers. Then we discussed some action that could be taken on campus. It was the typical activist group, one of the many such groups I'd been a part of throughout my educational career, but it was good to stretch those social-justice muscles. A good regimen to keep someone as introspective as myself from solipsism and despair.

I confess I was also just the smallest bit smug when I caught Portia glancing appraisingly at my studded boots during one part of the presentation. Apparently they met with her approval.

"Now, for the nuts and bolts: fundraising!" Danielle said. "The annual campus Mardi Gras Funds Fair will be next semester, and we're allowed to have a booth now that we're approved on campus by student government. So what are we going to do? We're a new group, so we've got to come up with something unexpected and really cool, so we get a lot of funds AND publicity."

Felicity wanted to know what we were going to raise money for.

"Bread and circuses, obviously," said Portia, who also seemed annoyed with Felicity, but was not bothering to disguise it. "Getting us all plastic surgery so we can catch us some men." The other girls laughed. I didn't.

"Raising awareness, bringing in some great speakers—I'd kill to get Immaculée Ilibagiza to come in—maybe doing a mission trip..."Danielle sighed.

"And bumper stickers," said one girl. "We definitely need cool bumper stickers. I used to have one that said, 'Real Feminists Don't Kill Babies.'"

"So we need to raise funds," Danielle said, doing a great job keeping the discussion on track. I wished I could have her in the Suminar. "We need something that gets the whole campus involved. It's sort of our debut here at Dominican, so we want to make our mark in style!"

"We could do a bake sale!" said one of the girls who did pregnancy counseling, "It's a great money-maker, because you just have to buy a bunch of packages of brownie mix and things like that, and they're so easy to make, but you can sell each brownie for a dollar—pure profit! And guys love them."

"Ha! Feminists who make brownies for guys: got to love the irony," Felicity said.

"Those packaged brownie mixes are full of artificial ingredients and trans fats," said Portia.

"Oh, who cares," said the other girl. "They're just brownies! It's not like heroin, or anything. Geez, you natural food freaks."

"I'd rather take heroin than trans fats," said Portia melodramatically. Again, Danielle re-focused the discussion.

"A bake sale," she said. "Well, everyone loves sweets. We could have a few all-natural options, too." But she didn't sound too enthused. Nor did I blame her. While it's only too obvious that I loved baked goods of all sorts, a bake sale just seemed *so* high-school. "Any other ideas?"

"How about selling t-shirts," said one of the girls, "we could print up cool pro-life logos on cheap t-shirts. There's a great place online you can get it done."

"I'd rather take heroin than wear a cheap t-shirt with a cheesy pro-life logo," said Portia.

"Um... that's a tad bit fringe," Danielle said. "But on the other hand, printing tees might get expensive.

Unless we could find a printing company that would want to donate its services to our cause…"

No one spoke. Silence ruled the room. I could see Danielle beginning to get more uncomfortable. Suddenly, I had a flash of revelation.

"Here's an idea," I said slowly, "at my school Amnesty International did this fundraiser every year for political prisoners. It was hugely popular… everyone got involved, the campus would almost shut down for the weekend, while it was going on. It was called the Freedom Prison, and the premise was that, the group set up a kind of little play dungeon, with guards and everything, and you could pay them to track down anyone you wanted, and have that person locked up in their dungeon. The person could get out by bribing the guards, though, so there was even more money in it. The awesome thing was that it involved people on so many different levels. You might have someone locked up because you had a crush on them — then you'd visit them in prison and make them kiss you for you to pay for their release. Sometimes people had their sports rivals locked up. Even some professors got kidnapped — which everyone loved, because whole classes would be canceled! There were a lot of rules about how to proceed safely, no one got hurt, and it was always a blast."

"That actually sounds really fun," said one undergraduate.

"You could have some cool sinister costumes for the guards and jailers," said Portia, apparently amazed that a stuffy grad student like me could have thought of something so subversive. I admit I was pleased.

"Cate, that's a great idea!" said Danielle.

We discussed the pros and cons. A few people seemed to think it could be potentially dangerous, or that it promoted violence or frivolity, or that kissing to earn one's release would be contrary to Catholic sexual ethics, or that we wouldn't want to use a method employed by a left-wing group like Amnesty—but in general the group was unanimous in its approval. "We'll just need to get permission from Student Life," said Danielle, "and write up a list of guidelines. Cate, can you help with that?"

"No problem," I said, "I can write to the Amnesty group at school, even, and ask them to send us the guidelines they used."

"We'll need a jail, too," said Danielle, "any carpenters here?"

"Oh, I can talk to the set designers at the theatre," said Portia, "Malvolio's prison from *Twelfth Night* might still be intact."

"We can call it Kidnap for Life," said Danielle "I think this is going to be a big hit!"

So the meeting ended on a high note for the future of the feminists cause at Dominican, and afterwards I went out with Danielle and her friends for celebratory drinks. I seemed to be well on my way to impressing Portia, but that wasn't to last long.

13 ～

Petitio Principii

"Once upon a midnight dreary, where I pondered weak and weary..." Portia murmured throatily, peering at the olive in the depth of her dirty martini. Our party, at a 50's style restaurant half a mile from the university, consisted of Danielle, a still-disgruntled Felicity, Portia, and me.

I was curious as to the connection between Danielle and Portia, who seemed to be good friends. But perhaps there's an inherent sympathy between actors and politicians? At least in today's climate, starting with Ronald Reagan and on to Arnold Schwarzenegger and beyond. Sometimes in my cynicism I think there's not much difference between being president and playing one on TV.

It should have been fun to talk with Portia, but she turned out to have a lot to say to Felicity, of all people. Danielle and I compared FPV stories and talked about our other classes. One of my theology courses was one she had audited just for fun last year. Then Portia looked up, halting in mid-sentence.

Danielle rolled her eyes at me and Felicity. A young man had slouched into the vicinity and was whispering something in Portia's ear. To my surprise I recognized him as Garrett, the hipster guru from the Suminar.

Garrett had never struck me as the brightest fluorescent light tube in the classroom light socket, to put it mildly. Actually, that's a horrendous analogy but apt: like said tube, he seemed perpetually dim, occasionally flickered on and off, and never really shed much light on any subject. And yet he always seemed to be deeply pleased with himself.

When I saw the dewy-eyed look Portia gave him, I confess I snorted my Shiraz.

That would have been bad enough under any circumstance, but as I was sitting right across from Portia, she noticed.

"God bless me," I said, trying to pretend I had sneezed, and tried to mop myself up, but Portia could apparently detect bad acting when she saw it.

She got up at once and walked over to another table with Garrett, where they proceeded to have an intense tête-a-tête. She didn't look at me for the rest of the evening.

Considering how hard Portia took my faux pas, Garrett was surprisingly oblique about it. But as I said, viz. fluorescent light tube.

By this time in the semester we had established a regular seating pattern in the classroom. I sat on the south side of the room, an island of estrogen in a sea of testosterone. I remember my mother telling me once that the developing male embryo in the womb starts producing testosterone; it basically destroys half the embryo's brain cells. If this is true, that means these guy had been racing to catch up with me intellectually since before we were all born. So, I should have an advantage on them in quality even if they beat me in quantity.

Sean, disconcertingly, always sat across the table, directly in front of me, so he was constantly in my vision. I had no idea why he did this, but I admitted that it was nice to have him at a good vantage point.

I wished I could have a better view of Justin. Justin tended to sit at the right hand of his teacher, thus he was blocked much of the time. If I wanted to look at him, I had to look through Hastings. Not a big deal, but do you blame me for wishing that Sean and Justin would switch places, just once?

Baby-faced Michael, as usual, was Sean's right hand man, and big, silent Bart sat in the far corner of the classroom.

I sat between Garrett who seldom said anything, to me or to anyone else, and Che. Che was not my enemy, in spite of his brain-damaging testosterone. He occasionally passed me notes in class, making vulgar but clever witticisms about Latin phrases, sharing tidbits of philosophical gossip. I had a feeling that he was just a jester by nature and would have passed notes to anyone he sat next to, so long as no one discouraged him—but all the same, I appreciated his friendliness. Sometimes his witticisms were directed—without malice—at others in the class, and this, also, I appreciated.

Unfortunately, he appeared to have chosen Justin in particular as an object of mockery. I thought this might be some sort of latent envy of Justin's amazing good looks. Che wore bohemian clothes and lounged insouciantly, playing up his Latin blood. But he couldn't compete with Justin, who, in impeccable sartorial style, wore beautifully tailored shirts with cufflinks—cufflinks!—and sported sweet Italian leather shoes, but he didn't lounge. Even when he was sitting back, supposedly at ease, his posture resembled that of a model on a Tessori Uomo photo shoot. He could be a politician, or a top salesman plotting to land his largest contract.

Dr. Hastings, with a look of sardonic amusement that was typical of him when reminding us of his power over us, passed us back our most recent writing assignment.

"Whatdja get?" Che whispered.

I was reluctant to show him my A-. He had a B himself, though, so I felt better.

"Moderation is the key," Che intoned in a sing-song. "Aim too high, and you'll fall like, you know, that dude who tried to fly…whatever."

Nat, who sat on the left side of the classroom, was holding a paper that had been so dramatically marked with red pen as to vaguely look ornamented, like a medieval illumination. Glancing at it, I smirked in spite of myself, and he saw me and glared from beneath his gleaming shaven head. Why would anyone with his looks deliberately wear that hairstyle, if you could call it a style and not a travesty?

Hastings liked to start class sometimes by shooting a series of questions at us, and calling upon us to resolve them on the basis of the material just read. The reading for today's class was Question 16, "On Truth." Good and general and likely to provoke a fight.

"Aquinas asserts in the first article," Hastings said, "that 'the true is in the intellect so far as the intellect is conformed to the thing understood." His clipped pleasant tones were just a tad pompous.

"So, our minds can understand the true insofar as we ourselves are conformed to the true. Well and good, a basic simple statement of what is often called the "correspondence theory' of truth. But then he goes on to say this:" he pointed to the next sentence. "'since this is true, the aspect of the true must needs pass from the intellect to the thing understood, so that the thing understood is said to be true insofar as it has some relation to the intellect.' Do you see the problem here?"

Justin, Sean and Nat all raised their hands simultaneously. Hastings nodded at Sean.

"It's circular," Sean said. "Intellect depends on things for truth, truth depends on things for intellect. Circular reasoning." He shrugged a bit, spreading his big hands, and smiled, as though he couldn't be held responsible for attacking Aquinas.

Justin leaned forward and, with an air of being driven to it against his will, spoke without being called upon: "That's only if you take this quotation out of context," he said. "Aquinas goes on to explain the difference between an accidental relation and an essential relation of a thing to an intellect. I think that clears it all up." He raised one of his swoon-worthy eyebrows and I really wanted to agree with him—but I couldn't.

Hastings nodded at Nat, who was grimacing as though in pain.

"What Aquinas does," Nat said, "is that he seems to address the issue of circularity by setting up a distinction as a sort of Trojan Horse. You get all distracted by the distinction but you don't notice that either way the circularity still stands. Clever Thomas. If you think he's the best thing since sliced bread you'll get all quivery with excitement no matter what he says, and look for any possible way to excuse him of logical error."

"The point," I said drily—at least, I hoped my tones were dry, cold, etc.—"is the reasoning inherent in the text, not an analysis of people who like the text. Can you demonstrate that the circularity stands, or are you just going to do the ad hominem thing and try to get us distracted?"

Nat glared at me again. "Well, it worked, didn't it? Getting you distracted, that is."

"Well?" Hastings put in. "What do you think? Is it or is it not circular?"

"Why don't we have a show of hands," Che murmured. "Philosophy by popular vote."

Nat said, with the air of one trying to perpetuate chaos: "Isn't that the way it works these days? One dude writes something, and a bunch of other dudes say it works, or something, so it gets published. Then the dudes who agree with the first dude get hired by someone else who agrees with the first dude, and publishes more of the same sh—stuff, I mean. And so, whatever's popularly decided on is the philosophy that goes."

Hastings said, "Your account, Nat, marred as it is by the deplorable inelegance of your diction, is, alas, correct." His lean pared face radiated irony.

"But," I said, "is that really true of Catholic scholarship? I mean, Thomism isn't popular anymore. Metaphysics isn't really done, outside a few select circles. So you can say that most of the wide world is functioning on the basis of these, um, popularity contests. But in our world, aren't we still trying to figure out what is in fact true?"

"That's what we were discussing, yes," Hastings said, "before Nat succeeded in briefly derailing the discussion. Don't look smug, Nat. Derailing a discussion is about the easiest thing there is to accomplish, especially in philosophy class."

"You can tell yourself that," said Nat to me, ignoring the professor. "Tell yourself that you're some special little band of blessed martyrs, heroically pursuing True Philosophy in a world of darkness. That's what DU is always congratulating itself on. It's a kind of desperate congratulation, isn't it? Do you think that at Oxford the dons get up and congratulate themselves on being at Oxford? No, they don't have to, because it's self-evident."

"Did you notice that?" I asked Nat, "The last time you were at Oxford?"

I thought he would be abashed — especially before Hastings, who *had* been at Oxford — but he merely sneered the more.

"This," he said, "is just a smaller and less successful popularity club. You're not recognized as important by the big bad world, so you pride yourselves on that. *Ressentiment*, Nietzsche calls it — resentment and envy for what you can't have, so you blow up whatever you do have, pitiful as it may be, into a kind of virtue. The world reviles you? Okay, so it's now a virtue to be reviled by the world."

"Nietzsche's observations," I pointed out, "might more succinctly be summed up in the term 'sour grapes.' And it might more accurately be applied to you than to us."

"Equally accurately to all of us," Nat said. "We're all equally pathetic. As Hobbes stated." He slouched in his chair, the light gleaming from his bald dome — a dome just begging for me to thwack it with my big hefty Summa.

"Can you really follow Hobbes and Nietzsche at the same time?" I asked.

Che quoted, in a silly campy sort of voice: "Do I contradict myself? Very well, I contradict myself. I am large. I contain multitudes."

Hastings, with one of his brief and surprising bursts of levity, asked, "Are you channeling Aquinas here, Che? The Large Doctor? Is that your solution to the problem of circularity?"

"That would be too easy a way out," said Sean.

"Dude," said Che. "I wasn't being serious."

"Well, let's be serious again, shall we?" Hastings suggested.

We returned to the topic at hand, but I was still hankering to pulverize Nat. From the look that he gave me before he settled down into his characteristic anarchist's slouch, he wouldn't have much minded pulverizing me, either.

14 ～

Honora Matrem Tuam

Some two weeks later, I lay on my stomach on my bed with Aquinas prone in front of me, a cup of coffee in arm's reach on my desk, and several pieces of baklava on a plate, seducing me to take nibble after honey-dripping nibble, my stubborn waistline forgotten for the moment. Bach in all his ordered perfection danced in my ears: bliss. Kimmy was out — had been out for several days, as far as I could tell; at any rate, her heap of smoke-smelling miniscule sparkly bits of club-wear had not noticeably increased or transmogrified in any way since Monday.

It was strong in my mind that things were going well. On one hand, I had only lost three pounds since I started running/walking with Danielle, and had gained at least one pound back when Portia talked a group of FPV folks into going out for White Russians — but on the other hand I had gotten a decent tan in the hot Texas sun. My roommate was a little snit, but on the level of the divine I could accept that as a lesson in charity, and on the level of the practical I could always escape her and go hang out with real, live, interesting, intelligent people like Danielle.

The guys in the Suminar were still aggressive and chauvinistic, but I had gotten an A- on my last paper (as far as I could tell, Hastings never gave A's, so that was as good as it could get) and Hastings had congratulated my reasoning! I had Bach and baklava. Yes, things were good.

Just as I was letting these thoughts distract me from the pages of the Summa, a less pleasant distraction came crashing through the door: Kimmy.

"*You* used my hairbrush!" she exclaimed.

"What?"

"My friggin hairbrush!" She brandished it before me.

"Why would I want to use your hairbrush?" I asked, refraining from adding that I wouldn't use her brush in a million years because I'd be afraid of catching the stupid germ from her hair follicles. (Spirit of sarcasm, begone!)

"Yeah, I don't know, you tell me."

"Well, I didn't, so it's not really an issue."

"Oh, yeah? Look!" she shoved it under my nose, this time yanking a handful of hair out of it: curly brown hair. Mine. Then I suddenly remembered the previous morning: the power had gone out briefly in the dorm, due to a thunderstorm. I had showered, come back to the room and dressed in semi-darkness, then grabbed from the table under the mirror the hairbrush I thought was mine, dragged it through my damp locks a few times, and then darted out to breakfast.

"Oh," I said, "right…" I started to explain, but she just tossed the brush at me and said, "Why don't you keep it now? I don't want to use it anymore."

I just stared at her. Various things I wanted to say flitted through my head, but all I did was silently place the hairbrush back on the vanity, and shake my head a little. Getting into a fracas with the Sassy Goddess was beneath the dignity of the world's next famous Catholic philosopher. But said Catholic philosopher's peace was nonetheless effectively shattered.

Kimmy was also silent as she rooted through her mess of a wardrobe for a few minutes. But silence, alas, was not really her forte: in a few minutes she started griping about my music.

"What is this, the friggin Mormon Tabernacle Choir?"

"It's Bach," I said, "Johann Sebastian." Then, completely succumbing to my worse side, I added "you probably pronounce it 'batch.'" I went on, feeling evil, "Now, yesterday I was listening to Chopin. Kind of like choppin' broccoli, only not."

"You know what?" Kimmy asked, and then she proceeded to tell me what she thought of me in words of four letters. Her diatribe was neither complimentary nor ladylike, and despite the fact that I scarcely valued her opinion, it was still kind of upsetting.

"Shut up, you little brat," I said abruptly. To my surprise, Kimmy had worked herself to such a pitch that she was nearly in tears; now, she flung down the tiny scrap of a glittery tank-top she'd been holding, and went wailing out of the room, slamming the door behind her.

I was immediately swamped with remorse. Some Christian I am, I thought. Some great Catholic philosopher. I asked myself: what would Thomas Aquinas do? But then suddenly there arose in my mind the image of him—fat and magnificent in Dominican robes—chasing Kimmy (in her Sassy Goddess shirt) out of the room with a poker, and I started giggling to myself, a little hysterically. I have really got to go to confession SOON, I thought.

My phone bleeped—I had been waiting on a call from Danielle, so I grabbed it without looking at who was calling.

"Well, HELLO there, stranger!" It was my mother. Not a relief. Instead, a whole new wave of guilt swept over me: I had not called my parents since my first week at the U. They had left me several messages; I had ignored one call from my mother while in the library; I had texted each of them once with a vague sense of half-satisfying my filial duty…but really, I had been avoiding talking to them.

There was just too much on my mind that would just be foreign to them, impossible to explain. Leaving aside altogether the matter of my Premonition of Destiny. From the start they had tolerated my decision to go back to school as a bizarre whim from which they hoped I would quickly recover. Now, if I had gone to law school…or med school...or even started an MBA, any of those would have been understandable, if signifying a failure to plan my career adequately on my part. But a PhD in philosophy from a university in Texas they had never heard of — this, I could tell, was not part of their Big Plan for Cate. I was supposed to be a success in the milieu they had chosen, not in some different, eccentric world of Catholic scholarship. Of course, they would be proud of me if I did well. My parents are not the quintessential pushy types who are determined to design their kids in a pre-ordained image, or else disown them. But there was a gulf between us, a gulf made up of different choices, different understandings of life, even of the meanings of words.

If I said "Dr. Hastings," for instance, they would immediately think "medical doctor." If I said "philosophy," they would think: useless, theoretical, wishy-washy, impractical, the sort of thing that absent-minded intellectual types worry about; they would probably imagine some faux-eastern guru type with robes and a beard saying faux-Zen things like "the truth is in yourself, seek within and find" or "the universe is woven out of the dreams of those who dare to dream."

I was certain that hard solid First Principles like "a thing cannot both be and not be at the same time and in the same respect," which gave me a feeling of ecstatic intellectual delight, would be, to their pragmatic minds, indistinguishable from the fluff uttered by the imaginary faux guru.

"Hey, Mom," I said, "I've been meaning to call you for days! I've just been so busy lately…I had a presentation to prepare." Presentations were good things. People in business do presentations.

"Well, well, so, how did it go?"

"Oh, it went really well. No problems. I think the professor is really happy with my work. You know he's a big name? He's a young guy, but he already has an international reputation. But anyway, Mom, it's good to hear from you. How's everything?"

"Everything's fine, Cate, same as always. Your father got really badly sunburned on the golf course but he's better now. I tell him and tell him, he has to put sunscreen on, he doesn't have our dark complexion—you're lucky you got that from me, dear, even if you didn't get my height. But he never listens to me. Well, what do you expect? Men!" She was adopting a deliberately conspiratorial tone with me, and I knew what the next question would be.

"So, dear, have you met some nice friends?" Translation: have you met a nice, rich young man with a good career ahead of him, a young man who knows how to play golf and already has a retirement fund?

"I've met some awesome girls." I went on to describe Danielle and Portia, emphasizing their strengths and glossing over their eccentricities: Danielle had been an intern in DC, Portia was a promising actress, etc. Then I added, "I've met a lot of interesting guys, too—in fact, I'm the only girl in one of my classes. Got to love that gender diversity, huh?" Mom is hip enough to know how to talk about things like gender diversity.

"Well, that's nice, dear. Maybe I'll get to meet some of them?"

I thought she was suggesting that she would be meeting some of them if I started dating some of them, and was racking my brain for the right response to this, when Mom forestalled me by adding, "When I come to visit! Parents' Weekend! We got the flyer in the mail and decided we'd come down as a nice surprise for you."

A surprise? A *nice* surprise? I suddenly realized how frequently the word "nice" appeared in my mother's discourse. Then I remembered I'd better sound nicely surprised, in a hurry. "Mom, that's awesome," I said. "I had totally forgotten about Parents' Weekend—but yeah, that will be great!" It was not strictly true that I had forgotten about Parents' Weekend: I had, in fact, never even thought about it. Wasn't that sort of thing for undergraduates? Would I be the only grad student trotting about campus with parental units in tow? How mortifying. "When is that, in two weeks, I forget?"

"No, dear, it's this coming weekend!"

My mind boggled. My parents would be here in a couple days! I needed to go to the chapel, or something, and beg for the fortitude to endure this. The prospect of showing my folks about the place, introducing them to my friends, filled me with a vague sense of panic. Not that I thought my parents would embarrass me or anything. Nor did I think my friends would embarrass me (Portia's eccentricities could be explained by her being an actress — and besides, she was thin: being thin is big in Mom's book). It was just that problem with the gap in understanding. The prospect of trying to bridge it for a whole weekend was distressing. Not to mention the whole seeming-like-an-undergrad thing.

"Mom, that's awesome. I guess I'll have to put together an itinerary for you. Places to go, things to see. When are you getting in?"

"Friday night. We'll rent a car, of course, and find a nice hotel near campus. You know, we've never been to Houston before. I suppose it's pretty horrible — the heat?"

"Tolerable," I said. "Everything's air conditioned, though, so it's not a big deal. It's too bad you won't be able to sit in on some of the classes. You might find them amusing." (Actually I was thinking: *thank the Lord* they won't be able to come to my classes!)

"Well, that's okay, dear. Philosophy — that's what you're studying, right? — philosophy was never exactly my thing. I think I had to take one philosophy class at Columbia; I don't remember it one bit. No, I'd be more interested to just look around the place. Meet your friends, see your room."

A little spark of rage flared up in my soul. Her condescending tone towards philosophy was so typical! Out of sheer spite, I went on. "Of course, if you're here on Sunday, you'll want to go to Mass with me."

"Oh yes, your Catholic service. Well, I have seen one before. Remember my friend Clara, she's a Catholic, she had a Catholic wedding. She was brought up that way, though, of course. It seems to me it makes sense to stick with the traditions you were brought up with."

I gritted my teeth. We'd been down this path before. "Mom, I haven't stopped being Jewish just because I'm Catholic."

"I never said you had, dear, of course not. I just don't see why you have to be Catholic at all. I suppose it's a phase you are going through. Your father went through a phase in the sixties where he decided to be a communist. I think he even marched with signs once, can you imagine? I can't. He told me about it and I just laughed, it's so unlike him. But he got over it quickly."

The implication was that I would get over being Catholic quickly. I was angry but did not want to show it, so I changed the subject: what sort of restaurant would they like to eat at? I could go ahead and make reservations.

I said all the right things, and, I hope, gave a general impression of bubbling over with glee.

But when I hung up and returned to Bach, baklava and Aquinas, things were dampened. I sighed and glared at the plate. "Oh vile baklava," I apostrophized it, "you will make me fat!" The spell of benevolence that had lain over the afternoon was broken.

I got up. I had to escape: escape from the problems of the world into the problems of philosophy. Not that one is more soluble than the other, but if I didn't figure out the Problem of Evil, well, I was no worse than anyone else — whereas, the problem of Parents' Weekend…that one, I actually had to deal with.

15 ᔈ

Fashionista Agonista

I decided to change, put on some make-up and wander down to the library, putter around a bit before class, in hopes that maybe I would run into…no, never mind, scratch that. I kept sort of wanting to run into Justin. He seemed perennially understanding, and, I thought hopefully, he was so handsome that if he happened to meet my parents, my mother might actually approve of him, philosophy major or not. But it was hard to locate him outside of class. Maybe he was one of those grad students who held down an outside job, and when not in class, he was working in some posh office, or sitting in some café trading stocks via iPhone?

I started up to the library by the back way, because it allowed me to amble through a pleasant little wooded area, rather than past lounging, smoking undergraduates. There I could worry over the next Suminar class in peace. Really, I thought, the way it gets me all riled up, I OUGHT to be burning calories, just by *sitting* in Suminar! Maybe I would start weighing myself before and after class? If I discovered any actual weight loss, wouldn't that be a fantastic diet: lose weight through Thomistic disputation?

As I walked down the winding concrete path past the shrubberies, the little rock garden, and the park benches, I heard a strange snuffling sound from behind a large bush up on a landscaped slope. It sounded vaguely like a wounded animal, so I craned my neck to see.

I could just catch a glimpse of a blond girl in braids and a broomstick skirt, sitting behind an ornamental cherry bush in the midst of the rock garden, weeping: it was the Little House on the Prairie girl from my dorm, Mary-Clare.

It dawned on me that she had been seeking out a private place to be alone with whatever was bothering her, so hastily I ducked back and started on. I'm not really the sympathetic, maternal type: and if I'm bawling my eyes out, I'd rather that no one saw me for several hours until I'm done and have fixed my makeup. But as I started to hurry away, it occurred to me that not everyone was as skittish as I am. Maybe she needed—maybe she *wanted* someone to happen upon her.

I retraced my steps and looked hesitantly at the shrubbery and the powdery black mulch. Of course I was dressed for Suminar success as usual, and that meant I was wearing immaculate beige capris with a retro brown-and-magenta shell and my prized ivory Jimmy Choo wedges. Oh dear…

My fashionista superego immediately began murmuring in my ear: remember how much you paid for those shoes! Why don't you just go back and pray a few Hail Marys for her? She probably doesn't want to be bothered anyway. I had noticed that my baser side had become remarkably adept at hijacking Catholic piety when making its arguments. But I had failed so miserably this morning with Kimmy...

Mortifying my inner shopper, I put a foot into the flaking black mulch and started towards the distressed girl, trying to worm between shrubs without slipping or catching my outfit on one of the prickly decorative cacti. "Uh—Mary-Clare?" I called out as I came. I had to do a bit of a limbo bend to get around the decorative cherry and ended up nearly stepping on her.

"Oh—hi Cate!" she said awkwardly, sitting up and dashing away a tear.

"I—uh—couldn't help noticing—uh—are you okay?"

"Um, sure, I'm okay, thanks," Mary-Clare said, though it was clear she wasn't, with her red eyes and nose. I fumbled in my purse for a tissue, found a napkin I had used to sneak some Oreo cookies (now gone) out of the cafeteria yesterday, shook it out, and handed it over.

She blew her nose and wiped her eyes and tried to smile. "It's really a silly thing."

"What is?" I asked.

She sighed. "It's Parents' Weekend this weekend."

"Oh," I said, remembering my own parental problem, and was about to launch into a tirade of joint sympathy when she brought me up short by saying, "And it made me realize I miss my parents so much."

"Oh," I said, in an altered tone of voice. Different problem. "Well, aren't they coming to see you?"

"Well, I'm a graduate student. I should be grown up by now, not wishing I were back home. I guess I must sound pretty pathetic to you."

"Not at all," I said. "Everyone gets homesick from time to time," I said, determined to take a stab at being sympathetic. I hadn't been homesick since I was seven when I went off to music camp for a weekend. But I got over it quickly, and had a good time, even though musically the camp was a total waste. But not everyone was like me. "Where are you from again?"

"Oh, they're just a couple of hours away. But they're farmers and this is a really busy season for them. I don't want to bother them, and I really want them to feel I'm succeeding at being on my own. Anyway, like I said, it's the busy time of year: they're in the middle of harvesting tomatoes and peppers and okra and – well, everything!""

"You live on a farm?" I asked, suddenly understanding the pioneer-gal getup.

"Yes," she sighed. "I miss the garden, and the horses, and even my little brothers! The latter I never would have thought possible. I guess that's the big thing that was bothering me. But, oh, I don't know, I'm shy, and I really don't fit in here. I'm just a country bumpkin."

"Your parents are farmers? That's awesome."

"Isn't it impossibly gauche?"

"Uh, no, hardly! Farming is so hip these days. It's very 'green,' you know. What sort of stuff do they raise?"

"Oh, they mostly grow organic vegetables, also some chickens. We sell free-range chicken to yuppies."

I laughed. "If my parents lived near yours, they'd be the yuppies who ate your chickens. Where are you located?"

She dug into her backpack and pulled out a little wallet that looked handmade from faded green velvet. Handing me a business card, a little frayed on the edges, she said "this is us."

Innisfree Farm – Jewett, TX. It was a pretty card, with curlicue script and stylized pictures of squash vines or something horticultural like that. There was a list of produce items, a P.O. Box, and a phone number.

"Do you have other cards? Can I keep this? In case I need to order cucumbers or something?" I hastily added, to explain myself. "I cook a lot. I like ethnic and vegetarian cuisine, though I'm definitely not a vegetarian myself. But I can't always find fresh stuff so easily."

"Well, Jewett's kind of a drive from here, but if ever you're in the area, Papa loves to show people around. He's not shy like me. I don't know where I get it from."

"I'm not shy," I said, "but almost every day this place intimidates me."

"Really? You seem so elegant and put-together," she said.

"Well, I'm new to this whole Catholic thing," I said. "I'm a convert. A baby Christian, only two years old."

"And you're studying philosophy? You must have had a stimulating life," Mary-Clare said. "I've never left the Catholic hothouse before. We were all home-schooled, and then I did my undergrad work at this tiny little liberal arts school where we lived in little apartments in this row of old houses, and went to class in an old elementary school building. The melancholy truth of the matter is that it wasn't a very good school. We didn't read very much good stuff, no original source material. It was really strict, too—not that I was a rebel, but it had a kind of convent aura...nothing against convents, of course, but I was going there for erudition, not a vocation! After that, I just went back home to live. I couldn't think of what else to do with my life, so I applied for a scholarship to come here, and so here I am. I guess," she said, looking around a bit sorrowfully, "this is just a slightly larger hothouse. I'm not very brave, am I?"

"Oh, I wouldn't call it a hothouse...well, except for in a literal sense, it seems I am ALWAYS sweating! But really—I've been surprised by the diversity here. It's a pretty challenging place to be, in a lot of ways. Trust me!"

"I guess it is pretty different, in a lot of ways," Mary-Clare said thoughtfully. "Maybe not so much academically, but socially? They have open hours, and my roommate has a boyfriend, and she went to a party with him over the weekend and never came home! I was really worried. But apparently that is the norm in what they call the 'real world'?"

"One of many norms," I said with a sigh. "My roommate has disappeared to several parties, too," I added. "To be honest, it's kind of a relief. I'm an only child. I like my space."

"I'm not an only child...but there are circumstances under which space is eminently desirable."

I looked down at my pants and winced. Sure enough, I had snagged my knee on the bush and pulled a thread. Another sacrifice to the cause of charity...

"Well, thanks for listening," Mary-Clare said, wiping her eyes. She really did look better.

"Any time," I said. It occurred to me that for all her dowdiness and shyness, this girl was extremely intelligent—at any rate, she had a rare sophistication of diction. It was easy to see that she had spent a lot of time with good books.

"Hey, I've got to go to class, but do you want to meet for coffee later?" I asked.

"Sure, that would be fun!" she said. "If you don't have other plans..."

I *did* have other plans, but I wasn't going to let her in on those—yet.

16 ⌇

Texas Gothic

"Cate! This HEAT! How can you stand it?"

That, after an engulfing hug and a quick kiss, was my mother's greeting to me—in her usual strident, somewhat nasal East Coast tones. As usual, she was elegantly bronzed, gold-bangled, her greying hair spiked so that her head looked vaguely like a hedgehog. She wore a little white jacket and black capris, and was sweating into them even more copiously than I had sweated into my clothes, my first day in Texas. My father, shorter and stockier and balding, with reddish brown hair and skin—sunburned as Mom had said—smiled benevolently behind her.

"This is nothing, Mom," I said. "This is blessed autumn coolness."

"George, did you get my red bag? All my pills are in there!" Mom is a medical doctor—a fertility specialist, actually—and a bit of a hypochondriac. Dad nodded, holding up the red bag, and kissed me on the cheek in an embarrassed sort of way. He always gives the impression of being a little henpecked, but really he has plenty of confidence: he's a CFO, after all. You'd never guess it at home, though, not from the way Mom bosses him around— nor from his love of music and books.

"Well, this is it!" I said, spreading my arm dramatically. They had rented a car and come straight from the airport without checking in yet at their hotel. The plan was that I would show them around campus, and then we'd go find some place to eat.

"Do you think that cross is big enough?" Mom asked, pointing to the large steel crucifix in the middle of the quad. I think it had been set there in hopes that it would inspire a spirit of reverence and sobriety in the students who lived here. It worked, sort of.

"Big enough for what?" I asked.

"Oh, I know you *like* that sort of thing," she said impatiently, "but I just think, isn't that going a little too far?"

"It's very seventies," said Dad. "I didn't realize this place was so...recent." He stared around, openly gawking, in fact.

Of course, he had gone to Georgetown, and Mom to Columbia, and goodness, they had sent me to an Ivy League school back in the day, before I Got Religion and came to Texas...I could just see them thinking how far their little apple had fallen from the tree. I decided to take them to the fountain, and then to the little Mediterranean-inspired Espresso bar—not that they'd really be impressed. The reasons why Dominican was home to me—the

Chapel, the Suminar—I could hardly expect them to understand.

"A lot of it was added in the seventies," I said.

"Bad 70's art. And yet you study...medieval philosophy. Is that right?" Dad asked.

"Thomas Aquinas, actually," I said.

"So they updated the art, but they won't update the subject matter?" He laughed at his own joke. A few boys who were smoking near the crucifix—in a respectful manner, no doubt—and discussing whether Plato was really a Theist, stared at us. I looked away. My parents were so obviously *not* Texan, *not* Dominican U, so *not* people who worried about whether or not Plato was a Theist. I sighed to myself: probably few parents were, really. But university was supposed to be a place where one could forge oneself anew, not be reminded of one's origins.

I hoped the weekend would pass quickly.

I helped Mom and Dad carry their luggage into their hotel, and then we went out to eat: Danielle had recommended a good curry house—"we're sweating already, might as well go whole hog," Dad declared, as he ordered a vindaloo "hot enough to make my ears burn."

I paused a moment over my tikka masala, poised for the sign of the cross. Mom gave me a lovingly exasperated look, twisting her lipsticked mouth.

I went through the motions quickly, muttering to myself:

"BlessusoLordinthesethygiftswhichwereboutorecei
vethroughthybountythroughChristourLordamen."

"Got the hiccups?" Dad said mildly. Dad was brought up a good Jewish agnostic and finds religious display to be a bit ridiculous. I wondered: should I perhaps have been more forthright in my piety? Was I embarrassed to pray over my food, in front of my parents? What Would Thomas Aquinas Do? I remembered the story about how they had to cut a piece out of the table, for him to fit in, and looked down at my plate: Thomas Aquinas, I thought, would probably enjoy his curry, for the greater glory of God. So, that's what I did.

"Do you really think it's wise to have the naan AND the rice?" Mom asked, looking with lips pursed at my plate. "Carbs, dear."

"You're here! I'm celebrating," I said, inwardly fuming. Being thin is such a big thing for Mom. Easy for her: she hardly ever has any appetite, anyway, her job gives her a lot of stress, and she's so nervous, she scarcely needs to work out; she gets thin just by worrying. But my naan was less tasty now that it had been filed under the dreaded heading FATTENING CARBS. I tried to change the subject:

"What's new back home, Mom? Any gossip?"

This got Mom going, happily recounting: who had a new job, who was pregnant, who was getting a divorce, who was out of the closet, etc.

"Seems like forever since I've been home," I said truthfully, neglecting to qualify whether this was negative or positive.

"Seems like forever to us, too, Cate," said Dad.

"I asked for hot, but I think they gave me extra hot," Mom complained. "I can just feel it eating away at my stomach lining." Her voice carried across the room and several diners glanced at us.

"Annie, you've gone and given yourself indigestion again," said my dad. Why had I never before noticed how LOUDLY my parents both spoke? And about indigestion! I supposed the whole restaurant would now be treated with the tales of my mother's digestive organs, complete with accurate medical terminology.

"Well, we're going to eat ice cream back at school," I said quietly, hoping to give them a cue to lower their voices. "That'll make you feel better."

"Ice cream! You can't eat ice cream after all that bread and rice." She groaned—loudly, of course. "Give me my red bag!"

"I don't have it," Dad mumbled.

"WHAT??? HOW could you forget my red bag?"

"I thought you had it."

The ensuing altercation was loud and boring at the same time. I wanted to hide under the table. At last it turned out that Mom had a few extra pills in her regular handbag, so she popped these with the look of an expiring martyr, and many audible groans.

I am lucky to have inherited my father's iron stomach; I can eat just about anything…or is that luck? Maybe a more delicate digestive tract would result in a smaller waistline. Ah well. At any rate, I guess I don't have quite enough pity for people who do get heartburn and upset stomachs; I felt impatient with my mother, as though her discomfort was all her fault. I looked at my watch: I had to be back at campus by seven, so I told Mom and Dad that it was time to pay up and go. At least, with Dad being in finance, he never gets flustered over a bill: he just works the whole thing out quietly in his head, tip, tax, and all, and off we go.

We were supposed to meet Mary-Clare over at the cafeteria, where the school was hosting an ice cream social. I had told Mom and Dad about the plan, but I was still uncomfortable about how it would all work out. I wondered what they would think of Mary-Clare. Mom was so fussy about Keeping Up With the Fashions and Looking Good — and about assertiveness, empowerment, etc. etc. Mary-Clare, as far as I could see, was usually dressed for a visit to the henhouse. Well, why not? I thought. Her thrift store garments were, really, more practical than all Mom's boutique fripperies. More ethical, too. In close proximity to the Philadelphia parental contingent, Mary-Clare with her homespun sensibilities suddenly seemed less weird to me, more endearing.

She was waiting for us in the foyer, predictably dressed in a denim skirt that buttoned down the front, a baggy plaid blouse, and sensible sandals. She looked pretty, though, as usual. I could see my mother mentally re-dressing her in the latest styles from Sak's.

"So nice to meet you, dear," Mom said. "So, you're Cate's roommate?"

I laughed. "I wish," I said. "No, my roommate is Kimmy. I never see her. Mary-Clare lives on my wing in the dorm—the only other grad student there, I think."

"Yes, I think so," Mary-Clare said, and she and I looked at one another. I realized that it would make sense—way more sense—for her and me to live together, instead of sharing rooms with Sassy Goddess and Hot Pants. But—Mary-Clare was so— *frumpy*—and aside from being smart, did we really have anything else in common? I pushed the thought from my mind.

"You're really kind to bring me along," Mary-Clare said to me in a low voice as we walked out of the dorm. (My parents were bickering over whether to bring the red bag again.)

"You're kind to come," I whispered. "I love my parents, but I find it difficult to have a conversation that's more than three minutes long with either of them. They're all about the practical. They don't understand philosophy at all. Just help me fill in the conversational gaps."

"If that's what you asked me for, I warn you, I'm not much of a conversationalist. Did you say your mother is a doctor?"

"Yes, but don't worry, she's harmless."

Mary-Clare didn't look less worried.

Having been warned earlier, I was not allowed to indulge in the free ice cream as wildly as I would have liked: I had a modest scoop of vanilla with a tiny dollop of fudge sauce, and that, alas, was all. Mom's gimlet eye on me made me want to run off to the bathroom with a gallon of ice cream and gobble it up in secret…but instead I sat down and began to eat with sad little nibbles.

"So are you another philosophy student?" Dad asked Mary-Clare.

She shook her head over her (happily heaped-up) dish of ice cream. "English Lit," she said. "Just as impractical as philosophy, though." Then she added quickly: "I mean, impractical like it's not going to help fix the plumbing or anything. There're all sorts of great jobs you can get out there, in liberal arts."

Well, that was stretching it a bit, but I smiled at her anyway.

"So, what classes are you taking?" Dad asked her. They began discussing, of all things, Faulkner.

Dad said, "I know he's a modernist, but I've always thought Faulkner's view of the South was more romantic than realistic."

"I would say, classical, not romantic," said Mary-Clare. "Though to the modern mind, it's often hard to see the difference—OH MY GOODNESS!!!"

I had seen them come in, a split second before Mary-Clare jumped up in surprise and spilled her ice cream all over the table…all over me, over Dad's lap, over Mom's precious red bag. So there we all were assuring her it was okay, wiping ice cream off everything, and trying to nod and smile at the two strangers who were now hovering over us, who were handing us napkins and helping sop up the mess.

"I am so sorry…so sorry…" Mary-Clare kept babbling. She looked like she was going to cry.

"Don't worry, it's fine, ice cream doesn't stain," I said. Mom, though, was wiping it off her red bag as though it were some sort of radioactive sludge. I could see that she was trying to be gracious, but...

"Cooled us off," said Dad, trying also to be gracious, and succeeding.

"Mama! Papa!" said Mary-Clare, finally managing to get a chance to hug them. "I can't believe...I mean, you see how surprised I was?" she indicated the heap of crumpled ice-cream-sopping napkins on the table.

"You can thank your friend Cate for the surprise," said her mother. "Or blame her, maybe," but she smiled as she said it.

I don't know what I had been expecting Mary-Clare's parents to be like. I think I'd had a sort of American Gothic image of a couple of long dour faces, overalls, calico, and pitchforks. But believe it or not, Mary-Clare's mom and dad were...hot. Well, hot for a mom and dad—in a farmer sort of way. Her dad wore boots, true, and blue jeans—but he was tall and craggy with pleasantly messy thick grey hair, and clear blue eyes. She wore a plain heather-colored cotton dress, that looked handmade, but it perfectly showed off her statuesque shoulders and graceful arms. Her hair was reddish-blond with streaks of silver, long, thick, swept back into a ballerina's bun.

We all introduced ourselves, then they got some ice cream, and Mary-Clare replenished her bowl, and we all sat sort of exchanging friendly glances.

I was at a loss, conversationally. The one flaw in my plan: I had conspired to bring the Watkins down here but the plan would have worked more splendidly if my parents hadn't been involved. People milled about us laughing and talking, but we all seemed to have been struck dumb.

"Those poor girls," said Mary-Clare's mom—Lina Watkins, as she had introduced herself. I followed her glance and observed a gaggle of undergrads of the Kimmy variety, all short-shorted and tanned and tube-topped.

"Why?" asked Mom. I could see she was thinking Mrs. Watkins must know something about those girls in particular: a tragic accident? Illness in the family? Her nose for gossip was (metaphorically) quivering.

"They look so lost, so lost."

Mom was clearly confused, but I had spent enough time at Dominican to get an inkling of what Mrs. Watkins was on to.

"They remind me of my roommate," I said. "Same fashion sense, at any rate."

"Fashion sense? Fashion *non*sense!" snapped Mrs. Watkins. "That's what happens at public schools. No education, just a lot of pressure to follow these silly fashions."

"It *is* silly for educated college girls to dress like teeny-boppers. But they always grow out of it," said my mom.

"Dressed like prostitutes, is more like it," said Mrs. Watkins. "Every year, the girls wear less. I suppose before we know it, America will be a nudist colony."

Dad, trying to relax the atmosphere, said: "I guess it's this global warming. Every year it gets hotter, people wear fewer clothes. Not in Philadelphia, though. Winter's still too cold for nudism there."

"Of course, global warming is all a hoax." Mrs. Watkins said.

"'Climate change,'" her husband corrected. "Climate change is for real. We just don't know exactly what causes it."

Mary-Clare and I sat, not looking at one another, or at our parents. A general miasma of awkwardness prevailed. Our ice cream dishes were empty so we couldn't blame our silence on having our mouths full.

"Mr. Watkins," I said, in a desperate attempt, "I wish I had thought, I would have asked you to bring some fresh produce for me to buy. The salads in the cafe aren't exactly gourmet. It must be great to have fresh vegetables all the time."

"You have a garden?" Mom asked them.

"A whole lot of gardens," said Mr. Watkins. "It's how we scrape by. I write for a living, theoretically, but really we're organic farmers."

"You're CERTIFIED organic?" Mom asked.

"Certified, and probably certifiable," Mr. Watkins's eyes twinkled.

"Isn't it a lot of work, the certification process?" asked Dad.

"It's a bit of a nuisance," said Mr. Watkins, "but it pays off, after the initial trouble and expenditure. People will pay more for organic, if you're in the right demographic. But it's about sustainability, really. Saves a lot of money. Fertility comes from the farm, instead of costing us: compost, manure, good stuff like that." He grinned.

"You are an answer to prayer. I need," Mom said firmly. "To know about compost. Worms. I saw they have those kits advertised. Is that the best way to compost?"

I stared at her. Mom? Worms? Compost? This was a new development.

"Garden club, dear," said Mom, noticing my gawk. "We have prizes every year. This year I'm determined to win the Great Compost Contest. They're bringing in a soil scientist to judge, and a luncheon with all local food."

"Oh," I said.

"So, do you homeschool, then?" Dad was asking Mrs. Watkins.

"We unschool," she said. I had no idea what she was talking about, but apparently Dad had read an article about it.

"I can see that from a purely pedagogical perspective it might be effective," he said. "But there are other angles to consider. What about preparedness for the world?"

"Socialization," sighed Mrs. Watkins. "Everyone's always going on about—"

"No, no, I'm not going to go off about socialization…I know homeschooled students have a lot of opportunities these days, sports and all that. I'm looking at the issue of being prepared for a world that requires…well, more structure…"

Mary-Clare leaned over and gave me a side hug. "Thank you so much! I can't believe you did this! It's great to see them here. It makes the place feel more real, somehow."

I glanced around, and lowered my voice: "I'm afraid having my parents here is having the opposite effect on me. I don't feel like I'm real, or the university, or them, or anything, really."

"Your mother is so classy."

"Yes, it's a thorn in my side. She expects me to be classy, too, which in her book means thin, and there's no way I'll ever be thin enough for her to be happy, unless I join a convent and take a vow to abstain from food or something."

"I think you look great," said Mary-Clare. "People put too much emphasis on being thin. I always wonder, do men really like women to be skinny?"

"Some men do," I sighed, wishing she had said, not "you look great," but "you look thin." Then, wishing not to sound whiny, I added: "Your mom's elegant, too — she looks like a dancer."

"Actually her parents forced her to take ballet. But she turned out to be quite good, I believe. Then she ran off and made money doing medieval dancing with a group of street performers, and Grandma and Grandpa never forgave her. For turning out weird, that is."

I said, "Hm, I bet my mom and dad would sympathize with them."

We glanced over at the elder contingent: they were all talking at once, with great and improbable gusto. Mom and Mrs. Watkins were discussing factory farming, and Dad and Mr. Watkins were exchanging Sixties wacko stories; apparently they had both once almost witnessed the same riot at the same place.

"Amazing," I said. "We usually have to BEG him to tell that story. Well, I do. Mom's not so big on it."

"Papa's always as eager as can be to tell any of his stories—He's got tons of them. He comes from a family of intellectuals."

"That sounds wonderful." I was in earnest.

"Oh, no, really it's awkward at times. If my two sets of grandparents get together they have nothing to talk about. I think they sneer at each other a bit, behind each other's backs."

"Families can be so difficult," I sighed. "I've spent my whole life trying to create my own identity, over and against what Mom and Dad want me to be. I suppose I'm doomed to have kids who, when I try to teach them to love philosophy and ideas and beauty, will rebel and become rich and respectable like my parents."

"Well, maybe they won't. I haven't rebelled," said Mary-Clare. "I hope you don't despise me for that."

"No—maybe you didn't need to rebel, to find what you were looking for."

"But I HAVEN'T found what I'm looking for. I don't even know what it is."

"*Can* you know what it is?" I asked, "If you haven't found it? You know, I've always loved that song by U2. I sometimes think it's kind of Augustinian...you know, beauty ever-ancient and ever-new, I forget how it goes?"

To my surprise, Mary-Clare lifted her eyes, as though looking off to the horizon, and began to recite:

"Late have I loved you, O Beauty ever ancient, ever new, late have I loved you! You were within me, but I was outside, and it was there that I searched for you... You flashed, you shone, and you dispelled my blindness. You breathed your fragrance on me; I drew in breath and now I pant for you. I have tasted you, now I hunger and thirst for more. You touched me, and I burned for your peace."

"Wow," I said. Rather ineptly.

Mary-Clare continued the conversation as though it were normal to quote from the writings of the saints at length. "But Augustine was talking about God. We've found God, right? So what IS it we're looking for?"

"Well, it sounds pretty banal to say I'm looking for a man," I said, "but..."

She giggled, "I know..."

"Banal and pathetic," I said, and sighed, thinking of Justin. But he kept himself so aloof: did I really have any hope at all of attracting his notice?

"Is it just me, or does it seem as though too many of the Catholic men around here are scared of women?" I asked aloud.

Mary-Clare said meditatively, "I suppose any decent man *would* be scared of a woman as a matter of course. G. K. Chesterton said something like that."

"No, I mean—maybe it's their reaction against radical feminism: they're scared of a bunch of raging Amazons coming to emasculate them or something, so they get scared of the idea of women THINKING at all."

"Well, I suppose we *are* rather intimidating."

"I just wish they would accept me," I said. "It's almost making me feel as though I have to choose between a vocation as an intellectual, and a vocation as wife and mother. But really! The last thing I need is a man who thinks my sex prevents me from practicing philosophy. These guys are all looking for some little fluffy thing in pink who will bake them pies and coo at them and praise their superior masculine intelligence."

I stopped suddenly, forgetting that I was talking to Mary-Clare who, for all I knew, was adept at pies and sometimes wore pink. "Not that I'm opposed to pie—or masculine intelligence," I added quickly, "but cooing is just not in my repertoire."

"Nor mine," she said, cheerfully. She was more of a kindred soul than I had expected.

"So how do you earn respect?" I asked. "Do we really have to beat them at their own game? Whatever can we do to have them both respect our intellect and—I don't know, allow us to be women at the same time? I suppose that's what most feminists are still so mad about. And I can appreciate that anger. But I don't see any way out."

Mary-Clare said slowly, "I suppose it sounds facile to say this, but maybe we have to be patient. Don't you ever feel as though...I don't quite know how to say it...it's like you're in a valley, and you know if you keep climbing, you'll reach the top of the mountain, and everything will be clear? Or is that just an evasion?"

"Cate," said Mom, interrupting us without warning. "I just completely lost track of the time! If only you hadn't left my red bag at the hotel!" she scowled, but semi-jokingly, at Dad. "I should have taken my pills half an hour ago! But we've been having such a nice talk!"

Well, *that* was something. It looked like I was going to survive parents' weekend after all. I had thought I was doing Mary-Clare a favor, but as it turned out, it was her family who was doing one for me. I grinned at Mary-Clare, and she smiled back.

17 ～

Vita Brevis, Ars Longa

It turned out that Mary-Clare and I had class schedules that were very similar, so we started meeting for breakfast on most mornings. But both of us had similar feelings about the cafeteria food—I from a fattening-carbs point of view, and her from a whole-foods point of view. So Mary-Clare had an inspiration. She talked her parents into sending up care packages of some of her mother's homemade bread, and even, on occasion, fresh fruits and vegetables well-packaged enough to withstand the journey. I contributed my French-press coffeemaker, so in our dorm kitchenette we had all the makings of a daily continental breakfast that was pleasurable without being inordinate.

We were enjoying ourselves one morning with blueberries and sour cream (not the nonfat kind—Mary-Clare had this thing about certain fats being good for you) when Danielle came by. She looked a bit hassled, but brightened when she saw us.

"Ooh, blueberries!" she said. "Are there any more where they came from?"

"Help yourself," I said, pulling out a chair.

"I can only stop a moment," Danielle said regretfully. "Paper due today. Plus I have to go and make flyers for our Mardi Gras Fund Fair event…how do you like this, Cate? Remember Lauren who was going to make all the flyers for us? Turns out she has this art final that she's supposedly soooo busy on—so she backed out!"

"What kind of flyers do you need?" Mary-Clare asked. She'd never been to a FPV meeting, but she'd heard enough on the subject from me.

"Oh, I guess I could just print it out in Times New Roman sized 72 point," Danielle said, "but you know, this was supposed to be the fundraiser that showed the campus how cool we were…it must be my pride, but I really wanted to have something really awesome…"

"Well, why don't we have a flyer-making party tomorrow?" I asked without thinking. After the words had left my mouth, I remembered that I had three papers due, including the next Suminar paper.

"I'll help!" Mary-Clare said.

"I'm sure Portia will help too…if we go out for drinks afterwards, of course," Danielle said reflectively. "Actually, that might just work…"

I was formulating an excuse to back out when Mary-Clare said, blushing, "Can we really? I mean…I can come, too? To go out for drinks?"

"Of course," I said, a bit surprised at this reaction.

She twisted her napkin, all red. "It's just that…well, you're not going to believe this, but I've never been out for drinks before."

Danielle and I both stared at her, as though we were regarding some freak of nature. "What? Really? How old are you?"

"Twenty-two."

"And you didn't even go out for your twenty-first birthday? Are you kidding me?" I asked.

"No. I mean, I *have* had alcohol before. When we turn sixteen we get to have some with dinner, just a small glass. But I've never been out, as in 'going out.'"

"Well, that settles it," I said. "We'll have two parties: a flyer-making party, and then your belated twenty-first birthday party."

So it was that we ended up sitting in the common room of my hall the following evening, staring stupidly at a pile of papers. We were racking our brains trying to come up with something catchy but not too cutesy to attract volunteers for our Kidnap for Life fundraiser. Although we had decided it was more amusing and retro to do hand-made flyers, I was wondering if that had been a good idea. The blank sheets of paper seemed to condemn our mental vacuity.

"Good thing we're in liberal arts and not marketing," said Portia, trying to be upbeat. She was in a better mood, but still did not seem to be very warmly inclined towards me.

"Actually, I used to be in marketing. But obviously philosophy is sucking the capacity for duplicity out of my soul."

"It's not duplicity," said Danielle. "We believe in what we're doing!"

"We don't even *know* what we're doing," said Portia. "But I suppose if we knew, we would believe in it." She put her bare feet up on the table and tossed her long red hair in petulance.

"Let's brainstorm!" Danielle commanded, in a slightly unconvincing tone of command, pounding one small fist on the table. I had to smirk. Danielle was not really effective as a tyrant; it was her air of decency and sincerity that inspired people to do what she wanted them to do. But brain storms are not to be summoned so easily.

"Okay, okay...free association game," said Mary-Clare, sitting up, trying her best to seem intensely interested: "Feministas Pro Vita...Vita, life. Life...Game of Life, life or death, Life cereal, life is short..."

"Kidnap for Life," I murmured. "Kidnapping. Stockholm Syndrome. Stockholm, Sweden. Swedish meatballs...no, no, no good." I sighed. "Swedish meatballs sound good right now."

"Focus!" said Danielle.

"Kidnapped. Abducted. Alien abduction," said Portia hopelessly. We all sat there, like brain-wiped victims of alien abduction. "Look, let's go out now and get some drinks, and maybe it will come to us when the pressure is off."

Danielle looked irritated. Her straight dark brows were knitted in a frown. "We are not going ANYWHERE until we figure this out."

"I take it we are to regard ourselves as hostages, kidnapped for life," I said, in a pathetic attempt at humor. Danielle did not smile. Portia rolled her eyes. Mary-Clare flashed me a conspiratorial grin.

"Ooookayyyyy…" I said, trying to communicate that I was less than thrilled with Danielle's attitude. We were doing our best, after all.

"Why don't we just print out something simple on the computer, just a big black and white sign, stating it like it is and asking for help?" Mary-Clare suggested. "I feel like we're making this a bigger issue than it needs to be."

"But it needs to stand out!" Danielle said. "Haven't you seen how many flyers are already out on campus typed up exactly like that? Scads of them! We'll just blend right in—unless we do something unexpected…"

"Kidnapped by pirates. Kidnapped by bandits. Kidnapped by one's ex-husband…okay, now I'm thinking movie plots or something." In desperation, I started writing the words "Kidnap for Life" at the top of a sheet of paper along with the information. Then I pushed it aside and started writing it again, in another handwriting style on another sheet of paper. "Help me out!" I said. "Just grab some paper and start writing, or we'll be here until midterms are over!"

Obediently, Danielle and Mary-Clare started lettering. But Portia, being Portia, started doodling instead. I ignored her. Five minutes later, we each had a small heap of flyers, but she only had one, with a rather romantic-looking pirate face in the corner, with Charles II curls and a swashbuckling hat. She drew quite well.

"That's a hot pirate," I said. "I don't suppose you know anyone with bones like that you could introduce me to?"

"Don't get sidetracked!" Danielle admonished, working hurriedly.

"Well, he *is* a hot pirate," I said. "Look what a good artist Portia is."

Danielle finally paused and stared at the pirate for a long moment. "I wish he'd kidnap me," she said. "And you did NOT hear me say that!"

"Ooh! Nailed!" I said in my best news anchor voice. "President of Dominican Chapter of Feministas Pro Vita caught swooning in arms of lusty pirate! Scandal rocks Catholic university! Feminists everywhere rise up in protest."

"Feminists are ALWAYS rising up in protest," said Mary-Clare. "That's not news."

"The pro-life movement is alerted to the dangers that pirates pose to life, from conception to natural death," I went on. "Oh, the humanity! The irony!" Then I resumed a more sensible tone. "We should definitely do Portia's pirates."

Danielle bit her lip thoughtfully. "Irony is good," she said. "At least, at Dominican, it is. Let's do a pirate theme," she said. "Instead of a jail, it will be a pirate ship. We'll have jailers dressed as pirates. I bet you can nab some costumes from the *Tempest,* Portia — there're pirates in that, right? Sort of?"

"No, not in this version. It's guys on a yacht, in annoying preppy outfits, with tennis rackets for some damned reason. And I have to wear a sweater vest. A *sweater vest.* With my bosom bound...not that there's much to bind, but still, it makes breathing a pain."

"Never mind, we can make our own costumes," said Danielle, hastily. We were all learning how to deflect Portia's theatre diatribes.

"Can you draw some more pirates?" I asked Portia.

"I can draw tons of pirates," said Portia, warming to the idea. "Pirates and horses and ladies fair are about the only things I can draw. It's very limiting, unless I get a job as an illustrator for adventure stories."

"Limiting or not, you're great at it," I said. She seemed to give me a smile that wasn't completely frosty.

"Well, let's have horses and ladies fair, too," said Danielle. "Who cares whether it makes sense or not? Irony and absurdity…very hip and intellectual. And people will notice flyers like that. It works for me!"

"What an avant-garde politician you are going to be," I said.

"It's you guys' influence, I swear," said Danielle. "Better stop, or I'll end up being too interesting to go into politics at all!"

In the end our flyers looked intriguing and cryptic, but not too cryptic. "Volunteers needed. Save lives," they said, obliquely. "Get on the ship. Kidnap for Life." Portia's drawings were eye-grabbing. We included contact information for Danielle, in big block-letters, then set off for the library to make copies and then start papering the campus.

18 ～

Delenda est Carthago

About an hour and a half later, Mary-Clare and I were busy taping several flyers to the big wall near the fountain, when I glanced up and happened to see a bald head shining in the lamplight. Nat was smoking, of course, and looking—with one eyebrow raised—at our flyer.

"What's that all about?"

"It's a fundraiser we're planning," I said evenly.

"Pro-life stuff, huh? That's all you ever see around here. By 'pro-life' meaning 'anti-abortion', of course."

"I suppose social justice would make little or no sense to a nihilist," I said. "So I'm sorry if you're having difficulty wrapping your brain around the concept that life has inherent dignity."

"You should look up words before you use them, Frank," said Nat. He had recently adopted this habit of addressing me by my last name, and I hated it. Which was odd, because I didn't mind it when Hastings, getting all Oxonian and bombastic, addressed us by our surnames. In Nat's case it felt as though he were weirdly denying me my femininity.

"Why? If nothing means anything, who cares, *Santorini*?"

"Precisely my point," he said. Then he gave the flyer another long stare, and grinned. "What is it with women and pirates? Do you secretly desire to be kidnapped by some big brute? What happened to honor and equality and dignity?"

"Oh, quit with the Freudian code," I said, more than a little annoyed.

Nat blew smoke out of the corner of his mouth. "When you're not in touch with your superego, it's amazing what can be sublimated. The so-called Catholic faith—"

"Oh good Lord, not sublimation again," I shook my head. "You'll do anything to try to destroy Aquinas via Freud."

Nat tapped the butt of his scrawny cigarette on the top of the fountain wall. "If you ever graduate from the fourteenth century, you'll be amazed at the things you'll learn. Such as why you insist that you're a moral Catholic feminist while swooning over pirates. Who are really nothing more than brutal terrorists. Read the international news lately?" And he gave a small, sardonic flap of his hand in farewell and then slouched off. I wanted to throw things at him.

'One of the awful guys from your class?" asked Mary-Clare who, during this altercation, had quietly taped up the last flyers, not glancing at Nat even once.

"The worst of the lot," I said. "The others are just chauvinist, for the most part—or else amused and gratified at having me in the class since I'm just a token female body, I guess. But this guy...I really don't know what he's doing at this school at all! It really mystifies me, he's an agnostic or maybe an atheist, he has nothing but contempt for the Catholic intellectual tradition and moreover he's a jerk! I wonder, did Dominican give him a secret scholarship so he could come here and play devil's advocate?"

'Maybe he's just searching for the truth. He might be really unhappy, that could be what's making him act the way he does."

"He seems unhappy. I don't know. But I wouldn't say he's searching. That would be too human. Unless you mean search as in 'search and destroy.' He's here to destroy. I just know it."

"We should probably pray for him then," Mary-Clare said. And although I'd heard other students end conversations with that glib subjunctive, she said it thoughtfully, as though she was actually going to do it.

"Talking of sublimation," Mary-Clare went on, as we walked back towards the dorm to meet up with Danielle and Portia—"There's something that occurred to me. All these theories I keep hearing about...about how romantic love is just a sublimated sex drive—that religious experience is just a sublimated feeling of inadequacy or need—they say that just to convince us we're on level with the animals, right? Is that what it's all about?"

"Yes—it's sort of like they're trying to undermine the idea of the soul. I guess it's a denial of transcendence. A kind of naturalism... that's the gist of it."

"Right, well, here's what I was thinking: would an animal sublimate a sex drive into romantic love? How do the sublimation theorists explain sublimation?" She stopped and held out her hands at her side, palms up, questioning. "Does that make sense?"

I stared at her. "That's great, Mary-Clare," I said. "You should have said that to Nat."

"Oh, I couldn't. I can't argue with people who aren't friends or family. I mean, what's the point? I'll never convince people who aren't my friends."

"Just imagine that they're friends, too. In a way they are. There are degrees of friendship, Aristotle said. In some sense almost everyone here is a friend of yours."

"Not my roommate," said Mary-Clare quietly.

I sighed. "Not mine either."

So much for Aristotle. For some people, you need the grace of God to deal with them; natural philosophy just won't cut it.

Danielle and Portia were waiting for us by the dorm in Danielle's small sensible Honda. "Jump in!" Danielle called. "The night is still young!"

"I can't go out in this," I said, "I need to change!" I grimaced down at my faded boot-cut denim, and plain black t-shirt.

"What's wrong with that? You look great!" said Portia—who was wearing black skinny jeans with gladiator sandals, and a blue velvet mini-dress for a shirt—"Anyway, we're not going anywhere fancy—we're going to the Dump."

"What's that?"

"I just discovered it. Ancient moldering cowboys and young doctoral candidates all cheek to jowl drinking beer out of buckets. It's got an awesome jukebox. And pool tables."

"Beer out of buckets?" I marveled. After a small hesitation, I got in the car. It didn't sound like the sort of place where I was likely to meet anyone I knew.

"Did you say it was called the Dump?" Mary-Clare looked back at us, dubious. As the honorary birthday girl, we insisted that she sit up front, while Portia and I were in the back. Mary-Clare had traded her skirt for jeans for the evening—high-waisted, but otherwise okay—with a plain blue fleece, and the most scuffed and distressed looking cowboy boots I had ever seen. Danielle wore green corduroys and an oversized black blazer.

"Oh, it doesn't have a name. Not that anyone knows of. But everyone calls it the Dump." Portia smiled a little coyly as she added: "Garrett took me there."

I tried to think of something pleasant to say, and said, "He's a nice guy. Quite the rockstar look about him."

"I like musicians," Portia sighed. "It's my doom."

"You can have them," said Danielle, putting on her seatbelt. "The artistic temperament makes me want to scream."

As we all buckled up, I noticed that Portia's un-dressed-up look seemed to have been carefully planned out, even if it was ostensibly as casual as ours — her eye makeup was even more lavish and dramatic than usual, and she wore enormous beaten-copper earrings. But I didn't really put two and two together, yet.

"Put some music on!" I said as Danielle pulled into reverse.

"My iPod's in the glovebox, Mary-Clare," said Danielle. "How about Sinatra?"

We whirled on past the never-ending strip-malls out into a more industrial area. The lights glowed yellow over warehouses and factories, but in the darkness the whole grimy metropolis seemed transformed, even magical.

"I'm ridiculously excited," Mary-Clare said. "I know going out for drinks isn't a big deal — everyone does it —"

" — except for Baptists," I put in.

"No, the Baptists sneak in through the back doors," said Portia. "I grew up here. Trust me, when there's a Baptist convention in this town, the liquor stores do a booming business!"

"I know how it is, Mary-Clare," said Danielle. "It's like learning to drive. Everyone does it, so it shouldn't seem that special — it's not like climbing Mt. Everest or something — but when you do it, it IS special."

"Or like getting married," said Mary-Clare. "I mean, I know that's more important than driving a car or going out but — you know, everyone does it, and it's no big deal. But if you don't get married…then it IS a big deal. And it also seems like impossible to imagine that you'll ever meet anyone who will want to marry you."

"Or who you'll want to marry," I added, thinking uncomfortably of my Personal Revelation.

"Have any of you ever met someone that you thought you could marry?"? Danielle asked.

"Well, when I was seven, I was sure I was going to marry this kid who was the star of the Pop Warner football team. Seriously," I said.

"When I was thirteen I wanted to marry Orlando Bloom," said Portia. "How's that for embarrassing?"

"Pretty pedestrian," I agreed. "How about you, Mary-Clare?"

"I wanted to be a nun when I was six," she said. "I used to dress up with a sheet over my head and a rosary and run across the fields singing like I was in *The Sound of Music*. Too bad nuns never actually do that."

"I bet you were cute," said Danielle.

"You were spared a lot of anguish," said Portia. "The pangs of pre-teen love are so very sick-making."

"Oh, no," said Mary-Clare, grinning sheepishly. "When I was ten I had a crush on the vet. I was always happy when one of the animals got sick so we'd have to call him. Isn't that awful?"

"Did you read the James Herriot books?" Portia asked.

"Yes, of course! That had a lot to do with it."

We started on a discussion of teenage favorites we had or had not read, and as far as I could tell, both Portia and Mary-Clare had read *everything*. They started off with *Anne of Green Gables*, which Portia said wasn't as good as *I Capture the Castle*, but Mary-Clare disagreed. They went on to E.B. White, Rowling, Margery Sharp, Charles Dickens, Thackeray, Poe, L'Engle... It struck me as ironic that, despite my being in advanced academic classes in ultra-expensive schools all my life, these two unconventionally brought-up girls could blow me away with their reading prowess. I was also happy Mary-Clare was getting along so unexpectedly well, even with Portia.

"Oh, I totally forgot," Mary-Clare said. "I'm going to this really amazing silent retreat the first week of January—do any of you want to come? It's at this beautiful old convent that was modeled on a Spanish convent. They do candlelight processions, and Taize, and it's not at all stuffy or sappy, but just—well, beautiful, I've heard. I really want to go but I'm terrified to go alone. Do you think any of you all would be up for it? It's really neat: you get to stay in a cloister—not the part with the nuns, but a different part—and there're all sorts of cool and interesting talks—and plus the singing is just really beautiful."

I guess I spoke too soon about Mary-Clare fitting in. "Oh, I wish I could," said Portia, though I sensed an air of falseness in her voice. "But right now...I don't know, I'm so tied up with this bloody play, I can't think of anything else right now. Which is kind of scary because I know I have finals coming up— and then I'll really have to apply my nose to the grindstone! Which," she added, with humor, "might make it smaller and more piquant and better for the securing of Leading Lady roles."

"Your nose is very pretty, actually," said Mary-Clare.

"I think I'd like to give the retreat a try," I said slowly. "I wouldn't mind coming back from break early — I've been wondering what on earth I'd do with my month off — but is it one of those things where they try to kidnap you and make you become a nun?"

"Oh, no, nothing like that," Mary-Clare said. "Actually it's co-ed — guys can come too. They usually bring in these theologians from the Vatican and very interesting speakers to lead the retreat."

It actually did sound interesting: though since I had never been on a retreat before, I wouldn't be a good judge. "Sounds great," I said. "Where do I sign up?"

"I'll sign us both up! Danielle, how about you?"

"Oh...I don't know...right now, everything's so crazy, I probably NEED a retreat but...Okay, I hate to change the subject," said Danielle, "but where in the world ARE we?"

We were in a region of town I mentally put down as "the other side of the tracks." Danielle, following Portia's directions turned dubiously down what appeared to be a dirt road into nowhere. Visions of toothless slavering hicks wielding firearms, or inbred one-eyed, five-legged hound dogs, flitted through my head. I realized that really, for all the time I'd been at Dominican, I really didn't know all that much about Texas or Texans.

"Are you SURE this is right, Portia?"

"Oh, yeah, this is totally the right way. I recognize that—" she pointed to a large, faded, wooden sign nailed to a stricken tree. The sign bore faint indications of having once advertised some brand of chewing tobacco. Woods loomed in around us, and I saw that mist was gathering.

"Portia," I said quietly. "Are those BULLET HOLES in that sign?"

"Probably," she answered with sang-froid.

"Just from a .22, though, it looks like," said Mary-Clare. Portia and I gazed at her with new respect; Danielle, however, did not, since she was too busy peering through the mist and trying to avoid massive potholes.

We pulled up to what looked like a rundown shack. It had no windows, and a tin roof, and I was pretty sure we were all done for—but then I noticed that the other cars in the parking lot were more or less respectable. To my surprise, I saw that one even had a Dominican bumper sticker. Of course, Portia had told us it was a grad student hang-out, but the mist and the bullet holes and the general ambience, if you could call it ambience, had led me to suspect that we had come into *Deliverance* territory, and would next be heard of as a horrible tabloid headline.

The room inside was fairly smoky, as was right and proper for a place that looked like the favorite hangout of Butch Cassidy and the Sundance Kid—but quickly my vision cleared and I saw that the place was not peopled with toothless slavering hicks. No, it was peopled with two harmless-looking old men smoking cheap cigars in the corner and—*and*— about half the guys from the Suminar.

19 ❧

In Taberna Texan

For a moment I was filled with horror and mortification, and then I heard Portia cheerily greeting Garrett, and I knew we'd been tricked. I wanted to give her a swift kick in the seat of her carefully-chosen-to-be-casual-but-still-glamorous jeans. And then it occurred to me that probably she hadn't known they would be there, but had just hoped that they—no, not *they*, just Garrett—would be there, and had kept her mouth shut for fear of my mockery.

I could see where she'd been coming from—but *still!* It was supposed to be girls' night out, after all.

There was Michael, banging a beer bottle on the table, trying to make some esoteric point, his baby-face crinkled in a wide grin to show how innocent and good-humored he was, in spite of the table-pounding; there was Garrett, who was looking moody and remote as usual; there was Che, in a bright red cowboy shirt and purple neckerchief; and there was Sean, gesticulating with a pool cue and exclaiming to me, "What are you doing here? You're supposed to be locked up in your Ivory Tower!"

"They let me out for the night," I said coldly. But there was nothing for it: I had to introduce my friends to the guys, and Girl's Night Out had officially become Co-ed.

If Justin had been there, I might not have minded. But of course, he wasn't. To tell the truth, I couldn't imagine someone like Justin in a dive like this one.

And also, thanks to Danielle and Portia rushing me, I was dressed entirely unglamorously. If Portia had given me a heads-up, or if I had deciphered her own dress code, I might have blinged up a bit, or at least touched up my makeup. But here I was, in my hanging-out jeans, which were comfy but made my hips look like a pair of battleships and my hair in a tumbling ponytail, not even wearing lipstick, and feeling utterly gauche.

Oddly, the guys all seemed genuinely pleased to see me. Not thrilled, but not un-thrilled. I was starting to wonder about this when I realized it could have something to do with the fact that I had some attractive friends with me. Jealousy, be thou banished! I vowed to relax and just enjoy the evening.

Che expansively announced without preamble that he would buy a round of beers for everyone. So we all had one, except Danielle, who didn't like cheap beer and had opted to be the designated driver, anyway.

The guys chivalrously pulled out chairs for us near the door to the pool table room (Che had just finished beating Sean at the game).

"Cate, if we thought you ever went out, we would have invited you to come here long ago," Che said. "This is the official philosophical hang-out. The New Academy."

"The Stoa," Mike suggested.

"So what brings you ladies all the way out here?" Sean asked.

"Garrett!" said Portia. "Help me pick something out on the jukebox!" She pulled the lanky blond guru to his feet and off they went. Danielle, Mary-Clare and I all exchanged glances. I rolled my eyes, and they grinned: they were on to her, too. I could see that Sean had picked it up too.

"We're celebrating Mary-Clare's birthday, retroactively," I said quickly. Portia might be chasing a guy, but I didn't want Sean to think that I would be engaging in any such pursuit.

"Wow, congrats," Sean said to Mary-Clare. "How old are you?"

"Twenty-one," she said, flushing. I hadn't mentioned that it was Mary-Clare's first night out, because I didn't want the guys teasing her, but now the secret was out.

An ancient barmaid, who vaguely resembled the Cumaean Sybil in modern garb, brought us two tin buckets filled with PBR bottles nestled in ice. Ah—I understood now: beer in a bucket. I was a little disappointed. For some reason I had imagined medieval wooden buckets sloshing with foam.

"Well, hey, have your first official one," Sean said heartily, and popped open the frosty bottle. He handed it to her ceremonially.

Mary-Clare took her first sip—and made a face. I winced for her.

"Not a beer drinker?" Sean asked. "Not everyone cares for the taste. Maybe we should have gotten you a wine cooler...?"

"Oh! No—" she blushed prettily. "It's not that. My father makes his own beer. It's just that this tastes—really different." She scrutinized the label for a minute, as though she didn't really believe this was beer she was drinking. "It's really on the light, watery side, isn't it?"

The guys thought this was funny, and Mary-Clare blushed even more. I felt suddenly protective—wished I could whisk her away to some remote glamorous cocktail lounge, where no Neanderthal quasi-academics could annoy and embarrass her. But it was too late for that; we'd have to make the best of where we were.

"European beer tastes different," I said in her defense. "They say our beer tastes like water."

"Yes, that's what I was thinking," Mary-Clare confessed. "My father makes a dark lager."

"Watery darkness," Garrett murmured, reminding me oddly of the Dormouse from *Alice in Wonderland.* He and Portia had just sauntered back from the jukebox, which had begun to play "Ring of Fire."

"Any of you ladies up for a game of pool?" Che asked. "I know I shouldn't ask—it goes against the grain of my innate chivalry to even think about it—because I know I'm going to win. But you all are post-modern enlightened liberated women, right, and won't mind being treated as equals?"

"Who said anything about us being your equals?" I asked. "Why should we lower ourselves?"

"Because you can't resist our charm," Che said. He waved his pool cue in the air and struck a few poses, miming a Hollywood version of swordplay, jabbing and brandishing. Sean reached out a long arm and poked him under the ribs with his own pool cue.

"Unfair advantage!" shouted Che.

"Careful!" exclaimed Danielle, her ponytail swung energetically as she ducked Che's return strike.

"Oops!" said Che, and went on poking and posturing.

Sean and Che jousted ineptly for a few seconds, but then the Cumaean Sybil hollered over, in a voice that grated over years of cigarettes and rough living: "Okay, that's enough, boys!"

To my surprise they immediately stopped, and Sean even squirmed a little, shame-faced. "Sorry Cora," he called.

"You don't mess with Cora," said Che to us. "She was chasing 'em off back when our dads were still in diapers. The stories that lady has! Man! She's seen it all, I'm telling you."

I found it strangely touching that the guys were so respectful to the aged barmaid, whom a lot of young men might have just written off as a dried-up old crone.

"Well, so, how about that pool game?" Mary-Clare asked, to my surprise.

"Guys against girls?" Sean suggested wickedly, brown eyes glinting.

"Sure," I said, resigned. I'm no good at pool—never have been. I thought Danielle might be, what with her drive and athleticism, but I could see that Portia was too busy flirting with Garrett to focus on the game, and as for Mary-Clare—well, I would try to guide her as best I could, but I foresaw humiliation ahead.

"You're not too proud to play with us, are you?" Sean asked me, apparently catching on to my expression.

"I'm not afraid of you, if that's what you mean," I said, and tried hard to tell myself it was just a game. Everything those days was so wrapped up with my struggle to hold my own against the guys in the Suminar, I felt that this game had some deep significance—even theological import—like ancient jousts, or playing chess with Death, or something. Why was I making such a big deal out of this? I am afraid I blamed my Jewish grandmother, and the Tingling.

The pool-room was filled with battered old posters advertising beer, NASCAR, cigarettes and, apparently, scantily clad females. In a similar though different degree from our Suminar classroom, it seemed to me to be another atmosphere rife with male chauvinism. Women here were objects—or worse yet, just props for certain anatomical parts that were the really prized objects. Danielle glanced around and rolled her eyes.

"An almost Elizabethan vulgarity," Che noted, with a gesture towards one of the posters. He seemed to be neither enthralled nor distressed by it: just sort of vaguely amused. Civilized of him, really.

"And they say women in America are empowered," I said.

"Advertising is the new art form for the twenty-first century," said Garrett, still channeling the Dormouse. I just looked at him. I've never been one for those creative types who exude mystery; often enough, the thing they're trying to exude just isn't there. It's like those ideologies that are all about obscurity, just to conceal the vacuum in the middle. Completely the opposite of Catholicism, whatever cynics like Nat might say.

"I don't think it's so new," said Portia, who—like me—seemed to enjoy carrying on a flirtation by way of argument. "Look at the posters in Paris in La Belle Epoque—absinthe ads, and all that. I think those were a lot more artistic than posters you see today."

Garrett gave her a long look, and said sadly, "it's a matter of grasping how we've had this total shifting of parameters and really a whole new concept of space..." And I stopped listening, because when an artist or wannabe-artist starts going on about space, well, it's time to turn one's attention elsewhere.

The pool game began.

Michael broke, and balls ricocheted everywhere— none of them sinking. Now it was Danielle's turn. She aimed a careful but not very imaginative long shot at the seven, into a corner pocket, and missed by a hair.

"Hey, almost!" said Sean, cheerily. It was his turn; he called and sunk the nine.

"A nine," said Michael. "What's that mean?"

"I'm sorry, what?" I asked.

"Dantesque significance!" exclaimed Che. "We were just discussing the typological significance of numbers when you ladies joined us. The nine — the number of Beatrice — remember? In *La Vita Nuova*? Beatrice is compared to the number nine. Three represents the Trinity, and three times three is nine, so, I forget why, that means…Beatrice."

"So, if I sunk the nine, I guess that means I'm going to go on a world tour of the afterlife and end up in Paradise with some old Italian dude lecturing me on Florentine politics?" asked Sean.

"No, it means you're going to meet your Beatrice," said Che, solemnly. "And fall at her feet."

He winked at us girls when he said it. Oh, these winking guys! Even Che, who typically didn't annoy me, had caught the virus.

Sean scratched on his next shot, so it was my turn. I called the seven that Danielle had hit into a frozen position in the corner, and tried for an incredibly complicated shot off the wall, so as to cover the fact that there was no way I would sink even the easiest shot. But it ran wild, hit the one ball, and amazingly knocked it in.

"Cate got the one!" exclaimed Che. "One! Oh, the numerological significance!"

"Yes, but she hit it by accident," said Michael, "so does it count?"

"So," said Mary-Clare, who had been watching and listening closely. "You guys analyze your shots…numerologically?"

"Yeah, it makes the game more fun, I guess. I mean...we don't do it systematically...it's just, a sort of joke." Sean said.

"Well, number one ought to be pretty loaded with meaning," said Danielle. 'One God. One truth. All that."

"Plato argues that one isn't even really a number," said Michael.

"Ooh! Good! Then my scratch wasn't really a scratch," I said.

"No such luck," said Sean, grinning.

Che sunk the twelve. "The twelve tribes of Israel," I said, falling in with the game—which was, I could see, really an excuse to keep everyone talking and showing off his erudition.

"Or the twelve apostles," said Sean. "So, what does that mean?"

"It means I'm one of the elect, sucker!" said Che, cheerily, and pocketed the fifteen, with a neat bank shot. "Oh, yeah, baby!" He scratched on the thirteen, though. "Unlucky number. The number of Judas. So passé. Whatever," he said.

It would have been Portia's turn, but she was too busy gazing at Garrett, who was drawing strange designs on the bar table with a broken piece of blue chalk. It seemed Garrett was rather the odd man out in this party. I wondered whether he actually hung out with the other guys very often at all.

So Mary-Clare said she'd go. I deftly chalked the tip for her before she took the cue, since I wasn't sure she would know to do it.

"Thanks," she said. She positioned herself at the cue ball, took careful aim at the three—and with a loud, satisfying "click" they kissed, and in the ball went, incredibly, in a neat angle shot.

"Oh my, that was lucky!" she said.

"Three," said Michael, "for the Trinity. For Hegelian Dialectic, too."

"And the square root of Beatrice," added Che.

"You get another turn, since you got that one," I murmured. She nodded, and called the seven. I started to point out that there was no way; the six was in the way—but before I could say anything she BOUNCED the cue ball over the six, hit the seven, and pocketed it.

"Holy crow!" Sean exclaimed.

"That was...wow," Michael said.

"Mary-Clare, you rock!" exclaimed Portia, who had suddenly become interested enough in the game to stop contemplating Garrett.

"I'm sorry, I just can't even begin to analyze that one numerologically," said Che. "If I had a hat, mademoiselle, it would be off to you. I am struck dumb."

"And that," added Sean, "is a miracle in itself."

It occurred to me that maybe, just maybe Mary-Clare had played pool before—so I kept my mouth shut and watched as she sunk the two with a fairly easy straight shot, pocketed the five with a long shot, and then finally, attempting to put some major English on the six, scratched.

"I have a sneaking suspicion," said Che, "that we've got a hustler on our hands."

Mary-Clare looked blank, not recognizing the reference. Garrett took his turn, pocketed the eleven, and missed the thirteen, without comment. Only two of our balls remained on the table, and three of theirs.

"Okay, I am not even going to BEGIN to try to out-hustle Mary-Clare," said Portia, "but I just really, really want to try something crazy. Okay?"

She leaned back against the pool table with the cue behind her back, bridged it unsteadily, smiled archly—I noticed that the position accentuated the grace of her figure, even if she was a shoddy player—and shot, totally ineptly. The cue ball woggled off into nowhere. Portia made a face. "Ugh. That was even worse than I expected."

Michael took his turn, and finally sunk the elusive thirteen. Then Danielle sunk the four—and now, only one of ours remained, the six.

"That's even worse than the thirteen, the six," said Michael, "it's the number of the beast."

"Well, then, I hope I don't get it," said Danielle, smiling sweetly—and she didn't.

"Well played," said Michael, "since that's what you were going for."

Sean was looking slightly less cocky than usual. I guess the prospect of losing the game to a gang of females was undoing his masculine grandeur— besides which, the table was totally wretched; I couldn't see the prospect of a shot for him anywhere.

"It looks pretty grim, doesn't it?" I asked, with feigned sympathy.

He shrugged, tried an impossible—for him, probably not for Mary-Clare—bank shot. "Ah well," he said. "A man's reach should exceed his grasp, or what's a heaven for?" For a moment he seemed genuinely charming—ironically, while he was losing. But losing graciously, for all that.

It was my turn, and I gazed at the table. I was faced with an amazingly easy shot: the cue ball hovered enticingly a few inches from the six.

It hit me suddenly that I should not even try to take this shot—after all, six was the number of the beast. Perhaps no one should take it. Perhaps I might have some strange bad luck if I pocketed the six? Would I have some terrible fall from grace?

No, this was crazy thinking—numerology was making me crazy. Numerology *always* makes people crazy. Thomas Aquinas, even though he admired Biblical numerology, drew the line at superstition. "Just as religion is due worship, so is superstition undue worship," he wrote in the Summa.

Fortified with Thomas, I aimed—quieting my shaking elbow—I shot—

—and in went the six. We had won!

The guys took their loss with surprisingly good grace, and Sean bought everyone another round. Though I had sunk the closing shot, Mary-Clare was the real winner of the game. We all toasted her, and then, when "I've got Friends in Low Places" came on the jukebox ("This is SO delightfully lowbrow, I LOVE it," said Portia to Garrett) Sean grabbed her and began two-stepping her around the room.

"Oh my!" Mary-Clare gasped. "Stop, I don't know HOW to dance!"

"Whatever!" Sean exclaimed. "You have the perfect boots for it."

I noticed that, in spite of his stocky build and his large, rambling feet in work boots, he danced decently. And for one brief, inexplicable moment, I envied Mary-Clare. But I didn't have long to stew. After he had made several rounds with her, he passed her to Che and — to my astonishment — seized me.

Before I knew it, we were whirling around the floor together. Part of me was ecstatic because I was close to Sean, and it was fun to be caught up in his reeling masculine energy. The other part of me — well, I was going to ignore that part and just relish the fun. I just hoped those giant boots of his had steel toes, because I think I kept stepping on them.

20 ⌒

The Outrage of the Appetitive Power

When the song ended, I wondered whether we were going to segregate now, having done our duty and mingled with the Enemy. Though—even if it was the effect of the beer—I was feeling less animosity towards them at that moment, I couldn't help but wonder if professional tensions would break in soon.

But no—we all sort of gravitated towards a large table in the other room, and soon were sitting and talking. Michael asked us all what we were planning to do for Christmas break.

"Work," said Danielle, "I always help out at this flower shop when I'm home for Christmas. It's so depressing. They sell all these DYED flowers. I hate that…they're so garish; they might as well be plastic. Oh, and grave blankets. I had never even heard of grave blankets…"

"Grave blankets? To keep graves warm?" I asked.

"It's a kind of ornamentation. So beyond tacky," she sighed. "Depressing, like I said."

"I'll probably try to pick up some construction work," said Sean, "or lie in bed all day and make my siblings feed me grapes. Haven't decided yet."

"Aren't you coming back early to—" Michael began to ask, but Sean cut in.

"So spill the beans, Mary-Clare. Are you some kind of national pool champion or what?"

"Noooo," said Mary-Clare quickly. "But—well, my grandfather was. He has a pool table in his basement—he taught me to play when I was really little, and every time we visited we'd all play—really vicious, cutthroat games."

"Like the one you just played," said Sean, admiringly.

We drove home in that condition which Aquinas would clearly recognize as the "point of hilarity"—even Danielle, who was capable of a kind of emotional sympathy with our high spirits.

"What a fun evening! You know, I LIKE country music!" said Mary-Clare.

"You're a country girl," I said. "And a totally rocking pool-player. That was AWESOME the way you demolished them!"

"So?" Danielle asked Portia, suddenly. "Was your plan successful?"

"What plan?"

"You know exactly what plan," Danielle spoke pleasantly, but there was a touch of pique in her voice, and in the stern hold of her hands on the steering wheel.

Portia tossed her head, and said, meaningfully, "Cate didn't seem to mind having the guys there...did you, Cate?"

Again, I just wasn't quite sure.

I wondered whether my next Suminar class would clarify anything for me in this respect. Would their attitudes change towards me, after our night outside of the academic bubble? They seemed more human to me now — even like people I could truly be friends with. And so, I hoped that they were feeling similarly towards me.

I arrived a little late to class, coming in just as Hastings was beginning to speak. This was a faux pas, and put me at a disadvantage — but I had been stupid enough to paint my nails fifteen minutes before class, and of course the polish hadn't dried, and I had waited and waited before daring to smudge it by putting my books in my bag — and then had smudged it anyway.

Che glanced up and made a "tsk, tsk" face at me, shaking his head at my lateness. I had a sudden impulse to stick my tongue out at him but instead I kept my composure and sat down under Hastings' cold stare. None of the other guys acknowledged my entry at all.

Back to being invisible again?

Hastings had just finished asking a question, and I listened intently, trying mentally to catch up.

Apparently we were discussing the powers of the soul — that much I picked up. Michael said:

"I just don't get why Aquinas says that only the three parts of the soul are commonly assigned—why just the vegetative, and the appetitive, and the intellectual? Why does he leave out the...let me see here...the sensitive and the locomotive?"

Che whispered in my ear, barely audibly: "Choo chooooo." It was silly, but I still had to suppress a giggle.

Justin responded, with a graceful stab into the text with a manicured index finger (why did he always look like a model from a Valentino ad striking an attitude? Poetry in non-motion...), "Aquinas answers that himself. He says that there are five parts, yes, but only three of them are properly called souls. The other two he terms 'modes of living.' Read right ahead there, into the 'I answer that,' and it's quite clear."

"Oh," said Michael. "Yeah..." he scrutinized the page, looking confused.

Nat rolled his eyes. "Why can't he make up his mind? Three parts of the soul? Three powers of the soul? Three souls? What is this, like, multiple personality disorder?"

"It's meant to be an image of the Trinity," I snapped back, having found the place in the text, and quickly picked up the gist of the discussion.

"So God has multiple personality disorder?" Nat asked.

"Don't you think that's a bit irreverent?" Justin gave Nat a cold look. I was grateful to him for saying what I was thinking.

"My issue here," Sean said slowly, "is that I don't know why he switches back from talking about powers of the soul, and parts of the soul, and actual souls. It would be easier if he would choose one terminology and stick with it."

"Yeah, it's sort of mechanistic to be talking about 'parts' of the soul. It makes it seem as though we're discussing a power tool or something." Che agreed.

"It's a metaphor," said Hastings. "When you look at the history of philosophy, you can view it as a long, slow process of trying to understand what we mean by 'psyche'—mind, or soul—without having recourse to material metaphors."

Garrett, staring off into the air, murmured, "When you really stop and think about it, you can sort of see how a metaphor always just transcends all those distinctions, material or immaterial, you know?"

Hastings seemed, almost imperceptibly, to glance up at the ceiling in amused exasperation.

"That doesn't make much sense, dude," said Che.

"According to Nietzsche, all language is metaphor...*die Wahrheiten sind illusionen, von denen man vergissen hat*," Nat said. "But as for transcending? I don't think so."

"Maybe we're the ones bringing the materialism to the table," I said. "Maybe for Aquinas, the idea of 'parts' wasn't conceived mechanically at all? We might be thinking anachronistically here, because of our post-enlightenment prejudices."

Hastings turned and looked at me with an actual smile of delight. So everyone else had to look at me too, whether they liked it or not. "That is exactly right, Cate! Exactly! *That* is the way we need to be thinking, in a class like this; otherwise language ends up becoming restrictive, when in reality it should be freeing."

I think I may have blushed beneath such unexpected and fulsome praise. It seemed silly to say "thank you" so instead I said, rather foolishly, "Yes, that's right, language SHOULD be freeing."

I noticed that Justin gave me a long gaze out of those incredible pale-blue eyes of his, for just a moment longer than everyone else. It seemed, at least to him, as though I was anything but invisible. Perhaps the others were just too insecure to accept me as intelligent. But Justin, certainly, had nothing to be insecure about! So, could it be that he…?

No. This thought was ridiculous to entertain. I sternly turned my thoughts back to the arcane matters at hand, and away from any silly girlish speculation.

I was so determined not to dwell on Justin and to keep my mind on Higher Things that I walked back to my dorm thinking fervently about St. Thomas' theories on the soul—giving my Intellectual powers a free run, keeping the Appetitive and Vegetative well reined in. This could be a good philosophy of dieting, I reflected, as I marched into my room and dumped my bookbag on my desk.

Then I realized I had dumped it right on top of a mess of crumpled paper and greasy napkins, which I had certainly never left there. I am not tidy, but even I have my standards.

I removed the bag, and investigated. Kimmy had clearly left the remnants of a fast-food feast on my desk. At the bottom of the heap, facing downwards on top of my hitherto-glossy new copy of *The Consolation of Philosophy*, was half a cheeseburger. Semi-melted processed cheese food was smeared liberally over the title. Mustard and ketchup too, apparently. And grease. My book was defiled. My Appetitive powers were outraged.

I gingerly picked up the whole mess and dumped it into the trashcan, wondering all the while whether Kimmy had left a half-eaten burger on my desk by accident, or on purpose. Both options were plausible.

Fuming inwardly, I took *The Consolation of Philosophy* down to the bathroom and, with a lot of soap and paper towels, tried to clean it up without getting it too wet. A lot of the gunk came off, but the cover still looked greasy and smelled vile.

Kimmy was just coming down the hallway as I went back to the room—she was ripe for a "worst dressed" tabloid spread, wearing cut-off shorts with knee-high red plasticene open-toed boots.

I went in ahead of her and then turned to confront her with my book. "You left a cheeseburger on my desk," I said, "Right on top of Boethius."

Kimmy actually burst out laughing. "Right on top of Bo Who?" she asked. "That is so LOL worthy. I thought you would have eaten it."

"Processed cheese food on greasy dog meat? I don't think so."

"Really? From the way you look, I just figured you'd eat anything."

I opened my mouth. I was fully prepared to retort: "From the way you look, I just figured you'd sleep with anything." But I managed to stop myself just in time. Unregenerate Cate had a tendency to rear her ugly head in Kimmy's presence, and it was getting harder and harder for me to control my tongue.

I grabbed my bag, and marched out of the room. I was angry—and also filled with a familiar loathing for my fat, angry self. My beaten Intellectual powers were curled up whimpering in a corner, while my Appetitive powers were shaking their fists and stomping about, swearing.

I knew I needed some serious chapel time with St Thomas Aquinas.

Pax et Bonum

Post-Christmas break. Retreat-ward-bound.

As I had never been on retreat before, I was both interested and hesitant about what it would be like. Would we be called from our beds in the dark of the night, for the liturgy of the hours? Would it be like living in a convent? Or would it be more like a kind of girl-scout camp for Catholics—would we be made to sing songs or hold hands or play little games or—please, Lord, no!—introduce ourselves with our favorite flavor of ice cream? Would it be boring or silly or solemn or uplifting or what?

I was at that stage of my spirituality when I felt compelled to hurl myself passionately into everything the Church had to offer—but at the same time I was sensitive to anything foreign or false that I sensed in certain displays of certain types of people. I also found that my initial enthusiasm could very quickly dwindle into disinterest or even total boredom: this was unnerving, because I realized that I truly was the product of a post-modern, instant-gratification, technological culture; and just as basically ADHD as everyone else. I often sadly realized that I wouldn't have lasted an hour sitting about in a medieval scriptorium.

So after my return to Texas, it was with some trepidation that I got into the campus van and traveled to the secluded monastery for the weekend, together with Mary-Clare and a handful of other Dominican students.

But the retreat ended up being delightfully simple — and, as Mary-Clare had promised, beautiful. We had our freedom most of the time, and everything was very quiet, unobtrusive but welcoming. We kept silence, and it was a relief to be in the presence of a handful of fellow believers, both men and women and not feel any compulsion to chat. The contemplative nuns who ran the retreat reminded me of the sort of magical servants one reads about in fairy tales: coming in silently to place meals on the table or to ring a small bell, and then vanishing. I had the feeling that I had come to rest for a moment in a secret sanctuary.

On the first evening, we all went to Benediction in a lovely old mission-style chapel, with radiant stained glass. There were wooden choir stalls facing a center aisle leading up to the altar with the Blessed Sacrament. Kneeling in the dim light, contemplating the rainbow of colors thrown randomly around the room by the afternoon light, I remembered something Chesterton had said somewhere, about how in order to appreciate stained glass you have to stand inside the church: from the outside, all you see is a few dull colors against the dark interior. A few years ago, that's all Christianity would have seemed to me—something, dull, dark, outmoded, far from the pulsing reality of exultant life. I knew better now.

I reminded myself that I should perhaps be more considerate to others who still saw it that way…Nat, for instance? No, somehow I could not make myself reach out to him. He wasn't just seeing things differently; he was openly hostile, malicious. I could try to see things from his angle, but there was no way he would do me a similar courtesy.

But fortunately Nat did not cross my mind again for the remainder of the retreat. Mostly because on the second day of the retreat, as I was kneeling devoutly at the choir, thinking about my vocation, and wondering idly about my irritating Personal Revelation, I looked up as the chapel door opened and saw Sean walk in.

He had a breviary in his hand and he did not look at me: just genuflected to the Real Presence and joined the men's side of the choir. I sat back on my pew with astonishment. How did *he* get to be here?

Fortunately a bell rang somewhere in the monastery halls, and I decided to take it as my personal signal to return to my room.

After that, I found my thoughts mingled with interest and worry, but Sean did not appear again. I did not see him at Benediction that evening, and went to bed that night thinking, well, maybe I just hadn't looked hard enough? Though why I would have wanted to looked hard was a mystery.

We were free to walk a while in the lovely old gardens—blooming, in January! Should one be delighted or appalled? I was adapting rapidly to the Texas climate, and thus settled for delight. Once while walking in the gardens, I came across a nun in a white habit and a black veil sitting on a stone bench in a sheltered nook by a freesia bush. She was reading a thick book: I wasn't sure, but it certainly looked like a copy of the *Summa*.

Thinking that, being a nun, she must be rapt in prayer, I quickly started to turn around. She looked up at me, and smiled in a friendly way, then went back to her reading. I went on my way.

The gesture was so offhand and normal, so much like the accidental meeting of glances that happens at a New York café—that I was struck. A phrase came into my mind: ordinary holiness. Perhaps I had been too occupied in the pursuit of the extraordinary: being an amazing philosopher, finding the perfect man. But then, perhaps, there is something extraordinary at the heart of even the most seemingly ordinary life. Something to think about.

"I'm so glad you wanted to come with me!" Mary-Clare said. It was the morning of the third day, and we would be leaving in the next hour or so—but we had found the atmosphere of the gardens so salutary, we didn't want to leave. We lounged side by side on a wooden garden bench, close by a small goldfish pond beside a tiny, but beautifully rustic shrine to the Holy Family. I had managed to sneak out some strong coffee in a chipped pottery mug which I had rescued from being thrown in the trash bin the one night we helped with dishes. I was thinking of taking it with me as a memento of the retreat. Our bags—Mary-Clare's meager, mine overstuffed—lay at our feet. It would be easy to slip the mug in.

"Me too," I said, "I'd like to come again, I think. It would be interesting to talk with the nuns sometime."

"I think we have a lot of wrong ideas about nuns in convents," said Mary-Clare. "I imagine they have a lot more freedom in some ways than we do."

"It seems so foreign to me. If ever I were to consider a religious vocation, it would have to be in one of those really active orders. Teaching, probably. But I guess…I'm so frivolous, it's hard to imagine a world where you don't have to worry about what to wear every morning, you just put on the same thing every day. Or worry about boys. Or whether or not to go out, or stay in, or go running…"

"Nuns can go running. At least, some can. They have special habits for it."

"Seriously?" I paused for a moment to consider this fashion anomaly—and grin a little at the image of a jogging nun. "Well, that eliminates one argument for a religious vocation. I was thinking, if I were a nun, I wouldn't have to run again…I could just get hugely, magnificently fat and billow about in my robes, maybe tending herb gardens or poring over ancient manuscripts." I sighed. "Incidentally, did you see Sean on the retreat?"

"Sean? Oh, I saw him a lot."

"Really? When?"

"He was at breakfast the same time I was every morning. Plus I saw him in the chapel…"

"Oh." I was taken aback. Mary-Clare and I had kept very different schedules during the retreat, even though our single rooms had been next to one another. "Did you guys talk?"

"No." Mary-Clare gave me a look. "It was a silent retreat. Remember?"

"Right," I said, not sure whether to feel relived or not that I had been able to spend the retreat quite Sean-free, at least physically, if not mentally.

Distractions had been relatively rare, I admitted. I had had time to sit by myself in the chapel or the garden, and to feel integrated, at peace—no need to look to the horizon. At least, that's how I had been feeling for most of the weekend. The weekend was now over; we were just waiting for the retreat leaders to come tell us when the vans from school arrived.

"Let's walk down and look at the waterfall again," I said "I really want to take a picture of it."

"Yes, but won't the vans be here? It's almost time to leave."

"Not for another half hour, at least. It's only nine, see?" I held up my Anne Klein watch—in an attempt to flee the world for the weekend, I had left my cell phone in my dormitory.

"It seemed later to me."

"That's because we've gotten used to getting up early."

"Ummm, Cate. It's only been two days. And on neither of them did you get up early."

"Okay, okay," I admitted. "You know what I mean, it's the AURA of getting up early that has beguiled us."

We were now in the woods—a sweet, quiet green light prevailed, and the sound of running water. It would have been a romantic place for a tryst—if one had anyone to tryst with—almost like a scene in a movie set. Yes, I am a city girl: can't even look at a piece of unblemished nature without thinking of something artificial and contrived.

We sat down on the rocks near the waterfall, but then quickly jumped up, since they were damp.

"Here, spread a towel out," I said.

"You brought towels? To a retreat?"

"I always overpack. Look!" I pulled out a long, white silk scarf I had brought with me for...well, Lord only knows what for. So I could dress up as a forties film vixen in the artificial little world I had conjured for myself? A film vixen finding religion?

"How pretty!" said Mary-Clare. She swathed it around her head; it was so long she could drape it over her shoulder like a semi-toga.

"Wait!" I said, rummaging in my bag for my camera. "Go back on that rock, there! What a great shot!"

Mary-Clare looked sheepish, but she climbed up onto a flat rock behind her. My eye had not deceived me: a shaft of light fell through the half-formed leaves, catching a strand of her honey-gold hair that had escaped from the scarf. "Awesome!" I said, clicking away, "it's so...Joan of Arc!"

"I think she was actually kind of a stocky plain peasant girl."

"Well, this is an artistic interpretation. Hey, can you lean out over that other rock? I mean, put your arms on it, like you're resting on it, with the fabric hanging down…no, on that side…turn your face…no, down a bit. Look at the water. No, just eeeeevver so slightly…"

Mary-Clare obliged me, but it was clear that she was uncomfortable posing: the one shot I had gotten, with the natural turn of her face and the beneficent light, had been a mere chance. "Your turn, Cate!" she said, "I'm not going to be the only one immortalized playing dress-up on retreat."

"I don't want any body shots, though!" I said. "Only my face."

"Put that red one on!" she said, pointing at my other scarf, which had fallen out of my bag—an Indian woven one, with threads of gold. I draped it over my head like a veil. "Do I look like I'm contemplating a religious vocation?"

"No, I'm afraid you look waaaay too alluring for that," said Mary-Clare. "If I'm Joan of Arc you look more like one of the Old Testament women, Judith or Rebecca or Bathsheba, maybe."

"Yeah, right. If anyone sees me bathing on my roof, they won't fall madly into a wicked passion for me, I can tell you that. They'll just call the cops."

"No, really, Cate. You look—glamorous."

"I'd rather be Judith though. Slaying the enemy. Suits my present situation better."

Mary-Clare skipped lightly from the rock across the stepping stones and back onto the bank. "You should go over on the other bank, and get behind that rock, so you can be sort of peering over it," she said.

I did — with far less ease than she had demonstrated; slithering about on wet mossy rocks is not one of my skills. She took a few tentative pictures, but I started to feel very silly. "That's enough, I feel like an idiot," I said. I'd been present at fashion shoots before — shoots with slinky emaciated models looking drugged in their make-up, contorting themselves into edgy post-modern poses. My place in that world had, thank God, been more along the lines of hiding behind a computer as opposed to flaunting myself before a camera.

Mary-Clare asked again, squinting through the trees, "What time is it? The sun looks awfully high."

I glanced at my watch. "Nine," I said, automatically, and then realized with horror that my watch had stopped. I had no idea what time it was.

Mary-Clare's eyes widened. "Uh-oh…" she murmured.

"The van!"

"We'd better hurry!" She began scraping together my clothes, towels, and make-up satchels which had tumbled out of my bag.

"Okay!" And with hurrying foremost in my mind, I wrapped my Old Testament trappings about me, and took a daring leap from the bank onto the rock Mary-Clare had been standing on — and, hitting it, felt my feet flying out from underneath me, and then there was a crack, and a splash, and an explosion of stars, and next thing I knew I was lying on my back in the stream, with water in my nose and mouth, and my head pounding.

Mary-Clare screamed, "CATE!!!"

She leaped in, floundered about, began tugging at my arm, and helped me up to a sitting position. Now we were both in the stream, and I was still sitting there stupidly, half-shrouded in my finery. Mary-Clare had tangled herself up in my white scarf so that she looked less like Jean d'Arc now, and more like a soggy mummy.

"I'm alright," I said. "But we had better get going. We may have already missed the van! But...I'm not sure I want to NOT miss the van. I mean, look at us? What are we going to tell them—?"

"Hey there!"

We looked up and—there, strolling down into the ravine, was Sean.

22 ～

Eques Ad Liberandum

Mary-Clare, who had been holding me up—I was still a little dizzy—gave another shriek, which started on a note of surprise and ended in total dismay. Staggering in the water, I found myself biting back a stream of uncouth words: the pain had jolted my old unladylike self into an unpleasant resurrection.

Sean was dressed, not in his usual baggy jeans and t-shirt, but in immaculate slacks in what looked like raw cotton—a slightly faded but beautifully tailored sky-blue shirt—and of course the ubiquitous boots. But they looked strangely debonair, now that the rest of his clothes fit him properly. He stood staring at us with a mixture of concern and amusement—really, it was hard to guess what he might think we were doing, half-shrouded in scarves, soaking wet, grappling in the water. Some sort of weird Wiccan baptismal rite, maybe?

"There you two are!" he said. "Did you know the van left a while ago?"

"Did it?" I asked, my heart sinking.

"It's nearly eleven," he said. "And I didn't see you two getting into the van, so I thought I'd check to make sure everything was okay."

He was looking for us? Checking around for us? Checking us out? Right? But I had just banged my head on a rock and wasn't thinking straight.

He held out his hand and hoisted Mary-Clare back up onto the bank; the two of them together then hoisted me. We stood there dripping and absurd.

"Are you ladies okay?" he asked, looking back and forth from one of us to the other.

"Yes, we were just having a refreshing bath before heading back to school," I said. "Communing with nature and all that." I hoped my sarcasm was biting. No, scratch that: I just hoped my sarcasm was DISCERNIBLE. I was feeling very strange.

Mary-Clare was blushing and obviously incapable of speech.

"How were you planning on getting back to campus? Or does communing with nature give you special powers? Levitation—flying—bilocation?"

I started to say something unladylike again, caught myself, and settled for stamping my foot. "Well, this is just great," I said. "I probably have a concussion, and we're stranded here, to boot. And I suppose you find this incredibly amusing, too? Of course, it is amusing. This will make a great story to tell the guys in Suminar." I wasn't sure whether I was serious or not.

Sean stared at me, looking mildly concerned. "I can drive you back to campus. But I think maybe Cate should go to the ER or something?" he glanced at Mary-Clare. I wondered whether I was acting strangely, and decided to just shut my mouth and leave it to the two people who hadn't recently had their brains addled.

Fortunately the convent hadn't re-cloistered itself yet, and we were able to go inside with our bags and change into dry clothes. We thanked the nun who had let us back in, returned to where Sean was waiting for us in the garden.

"How you feeling, Cate?"

"Better," I said. "I don't think I'll need to go to the ER. I've got a big bump on my head, and that's supposed to be a good thing: if the bump is visible, that means it's on the outside, not the inside, so it's not dangerous."

"Are you sure about that?" asked Mary-Clare.

"Cate's always sure about everything," said Sean. I think he winked, but I was ignoring him.

"No," I admitted.

"Okay, well then—we'll just keep an eye on her," he grinned at Mary-Clare in an encouraging sort of way, and then patted me on the shoulder—it was a sort of fraternal gesture, but it was kind. "Good thing I went looking for you ladies!"

I swallowed the impulse to retort that we didn't need looking after: given the circumstances, it might be less than convincing.

I should have said something earlier about Sean's car, because it was such a significant motif on campus—an enormous gas-guzzling yellow Chevy

Impala from the seventies, a giant pimped-out banana; it rumbled when it drove, and I had once seen a couple of undergrad girls perched on its hood, trying to get his attention. Yes, it did seem that the girls liked Sean, at least girls who were undergraduates. Whatever!

I had seen him driving it around so often—more often than necessary—cruising campus, really, sometimes with Che and Michael, blasting eighties rock or classic country. I guess I had always wanted to ride in it—and now my chance had come. But it was a mortifying chance.

"So, how did you like the retreat?" Mary-Clare managed to ask. She was in the back seat—she had dived in there, literally, before I could offer her shotgun. There was nothing for it but for me to take the passenger front. So there I sat next to Sean. Luckily there seemed to be several miles or so of beat-up vinyl seat between us.

"Oh, love it. It's my third year going. I'm kinda at home there. And when I go, I kind of like to have time to myself. I need that, you know." He seemed sheepish, shrugging his big shoulders a bit as he pulled out of the convent's long driveway. "I spend so much time with people—socializing, studying. Sometimes I need to...whatchamacallit...listen to the still small voice within? Nothing against people of course!" He looked even more sheepish now.

I was really surprised to hear him talking this way. It made him seem more vulnerable. "I can see that," I said. "I really enjoyed it."

"So did I," Mary-Clare added.

"Well, back to the real world for us!" Sean said. "You're both living on campus, right?"

"Right," I said gloomily. I had spent most of break, outside of Christmas weekend, on campus in my dorm room which at least was blessedly Kimmy-free. But when I returned, it was only a matter of days before the Sassy Goddess returned to her domain. I was getting to the point at which even the thought of dealing with her gave me a weird twist of anxiety in the pit of my stomach.

"It's been great spending the weekend with you," I said to Mary-Clare.

She sighed, apparently thinking the same thing. "Yes, back to the normal trials—such as our roommates!"

Sean gave us a confused glance. "Wait…what? You two aren't roommates?"

"I wish," I said, without thinking.

Mary-Clare, leaning forward with her chin right behind my shoulder, giggled. "Everyone always thinks we are!"

"Maybe we should be," I said, and immediately regretted it—not that I regretted suggesting to Mary-Clare that we should be roommates, but regretting that I had broached it in front of Sean. If there were reasons why Mary-Clare couldn't or wouldn't want to room with me, she might feel uncomfortable addressing them in front of a third party.

But my regret was unfounded. "Ooh!" she exclaimed. "Why didn't we think of that before? Do you think it's too late? I mean, classes start in…what, five days?"

"Six days!" I said. "There is TOTALLY time."

"Are you sure Kimmy will want to switch?" Mary-Clare said innocently, and I started to reply before I saw her mischievous expression.

"Why don't you guys just room off campus?" Sean asked. "I mean, it's so much cheaper."

"But—I thought—we already put our housing deposits down—" Mary-Clare said.

"No, listen!" I said, "That's a really great idea. You and I should look for an apartment together off campus! I'm sure we can find something!"

"But what about my deposit?"

"They'll give it back. And anyway, I can put down a security deposit or whatever on an apartment, so don't worry about that, if it takes a while to get it back." I wanted to say: I'll pay for it! But I didn't want to make her look like an object of charity. Still, I would do what I could.

Sean said, "It's a great idea. Trust me; I have not once regretted living off campus. No annoying roommates, no annoying drunks puking in the hall, no annoying rules…"

"Do you have any recommendations?"

"Why not try Three Chokes? It's nothing fancy, but you'll be close by school, so you won't have to worry about transportation."

The apartment complex near campus was actually called Three Oaks, but for a variety of reasons the student body typically referred to it as "Three Chokes."

Mary-Clare looked a little disappointed. "Do we have to live there? The name is so appalling, even if it is a nice place. I know, I know, maybe I read too much *Anne of Green Gables* growing up. But still…Three Chokes?"

"The apartments aren't so bad," said Sean. "It's all about what you do with them."

"Okay," I said, "we have a week…if we can find your dream cottage by the end of next week, we'll go for it. But let me go talk to the apartment manager at Three Chokes first—just to see what the deal is—in case we can't find anything else. Don't worry, Mary-Clare! We can go out foraging at thrift stores and find all sorts of amazing things. And we'll spend our real furniture budget on getting a huge bookshelf. And I'll have Mom and Dad send my framed prints—I have one of Rembrandt's 'Aristotle Contemplating a Bust of Homer' that totally fits our ethos."

Sean said, "You sound like you're feeling better."

"I am!" I said happily, and without thinking gave him a totally, unrelievedly friendly smile. He smiled back. I noticed the warm crinkling look in his brown eyes—his long eyelashes—but then, all guys have long eyelashes. Testosterone makes them, for some reason: as inexplicable as the peacock and its tail. Or maybe not inexplicable. Women love beauty. Beauty lures us in.

"Look," I said, "we really really really appreciate how you came dashing to our rescue. And we appreciate getting to ride in this awesome car. But"— I tried to capture a tone that was coaxing without sounding wheedling—"Pleeeeease don't tell anyone back at the U about this! It's too mortifying. Even if it makes an excellent story—I KNOW the guys in class would laugh. But it's Mary-Clare's story, too. So, please, just keep it a secret?"

He nodded in a smug sort of way. "All right," he said. "But on one condition..."

"What?" I said suspiciously.

He only smiled. "Look, let me change the subject. You ladies must be hungry. There's this awesome little Mexican place coming up here — want to stop for a bite? My treat?"

"Oh, yes!" said Mary-Clare, "Chips and salsa! I LOVE chips and salsa."

Mexican restaurants in Texas are the real deal, I had discovered the previous semester: gaudy, tiny, often a little dangerous looking — but the food was authentically delicious. Sometimes these places had mariachi bands, too. And it wasn't fake, so it never seemed kitschy or overblown.

We settled down with our chips and salsa — Mary-Clare and I facing Sean. I wanted to order a margarita, stopped myself, ordered water, and then wished I'd just gone for it, when Sean ordered a Negra Modelo.

"Oh, man, if I'd known you were going to imbibe, I would have joined you."

"Oh, me too!" said Mary-Clare.

So I called the waiter back and ordered a lime margarita for me, and a strawberry one for Mary-Clare: it was my duty to initiate her into the wicked world.

The drinks were good, the chips salty and freshly-fried, the salsa swimming with fresh chilis and cilantro. "Can't stand that stuff," Sean said, at one whiff of cilantro, and confined himself to eating chips with hot sauce.

"Cilantro is the world's most loved and hated herb," I said. 'Personally I love it."

When our food came—enchiladas supreme for Sean, a shrimp quesadilla for Mary-Clare, and a *chile relleno* with a cup of tortilla soup for me—it was equally tasty. My head still hurt, and I felt strangely drained, though at peace. It was sort of like a hangover, but less traumatic.

"So what's this condition for your silence?" I said. I was determined not to let him get away with it, even if he was plying us with excellent Mexican appetizers.

"It's this," Sean leaned back in the booth. "I know you girls have got this big Kidnap-for-Life fundraiser going on, right? The whole campus is talking about it."

"Yes!" I said, happy that he was acknowledging it. And I was thrilled to think Danielle's publicity campaign was working.

"So if I get this straight, you can pay to have someone kidnapped. And the money goes to a good cause."

"Feministas Pro Vita," I said.

He waved his hand. "Whatever. It's a good cause. So you pay money to the pirates, and they kidnap whoever you want. And you don't have to give a name or anything."

"There's a form," I said. "So you can leave your name if you want."

"But you don't have to: you can do it anonymously."

"Right," I said. "How do you know all this?"

He shrugged. "Some undergraduate girl who's in your group told me."

"Oh. Okay, so what?"

"Here's the deal: Michael bet that I would be too chicken to have Hastings kidnapped—"

"WHAT??!!"

"Hastings isn't, like, a god, you know," Sean seemed a little miffed with me.

"Wait…isn't Hastings your professor?" asked Mary-Clare.

"Yes, he is, 'a man like any other,' and besides, you're doing this thing during Mardi Gras and don't they always suspend the rules during those times?"

"They do, at Dominican? Like they do at Carnivale in Europe?" I asked.

"Totally. Catholic culture, you gotta love it. So anyway, Michael bet that I was too scared to kidnap Hastings, and then I bet him that he would be too chicken to kidnap Imogene—you know, the girl in the library."

Yes, everyone knew Imogene, the girl in the library: as near a thing to an Angelina Jolie look-alike as would be allowed in the hallowed halls of academe. I said, "Yeah, so?"

"Well, so then Che bet that you would have ME kidnapped."

"What?" I exclaimed, nearly dropping my glass.

"Well he did! But don't fly at me: I bet them all that you wouldn't. So, could you please, pretty please, with all the transcendental properties of Being on top, not have me kidnapped? Because if I win all these bets I will be a very rich man."

He smiled, and took another scoop of salsa, biting into it with a satisfied crunch.

Shock on hearing of their plans regarding Hastings was now compounded with outrage. That they would think I would kidnap Sean would mean...because the context...the suggestion...the implication...no, no, they could NOT think that I had a thing for him! What a disaster.

"I had no notion of paying to have you kidnapped," I said, coldly. "So your bet is safe. But in case a rash notion seizes me in the final hour, I swear by the *Nicomachaean Ethics* and the *Metaphysics* and the *Posterior Analytics* that I will never, ever, in a million years, even consider having you kidnapped."

I regretted mentioning the *Posterior Analytics.* The guys always made dumb jokes about that one. But my point stood. Sean looked convinced—possibly even slightly disappointed? No, I was imagining things. Why, I don't know. That knock on the head, I suppose.

23 ～

Domus Dulcis Domus?

We had an agreeable enough lunch after that, full of talk of classes, books, and other pleasantries. I admit he was easy to talk to. Or perhaps it was because Mary-Clare was such a good conversationalist? Once we got back into the car, we made it back to campus in just an hour. Sean dropped us off at our dorm, where we copiously thanked him, and I again warned him to keep his mouth shut.

"Yeah, well, you just remember YOUR end of the bargain!" he said, with a mock scowl. I think he even shook his finger at me. Then he was back in his banana-boat, and rumbling away.

"Do you think he'll tell?"

"I don't know. I hope not. Hey, Mary-Clare, do you think he…saw us actually posing on the rocks? I mean, how long was he watching us?"

"I'm sure it can't have been long," she said. But she didn't sound too certain.

"Oh, well!" I said. "I'm just not going to think about it anymore. It's too silly. Home again, home again! Only, not home for long! I hope. Let's get going on this Quest for the Anne of Green Gables House. Given that this is Houston, it seems pretty futile, but I'm always up for a challenge."

And so began our quest.

Three Chokes turned out to be perfectly awful. Once I saw it was behind a strip mall (housing a frowsy hair salon, a pawnshop, and a drug store) and adjoining a supermarket, and that we would have to walk through parking lots to get home every night, I didn't even bother to see the manager. We agreed that in this case, the name spoke to the essence of the thing described.

We next visited a nearby apartment complex which, from the outside, looked romantic and Spanish, like an old mission church.

"Casa Esperanza," Mary-Clare read on the sign. "That means hope, doesn't it? That's a good sign!"

"The landscaping is pretty scary, but I guess that's not the end of the world," I said, looking dubiously at the heaps of dyed-orange mulch and a few dolorous cacti which seemed to be leaning about drunkenly.

No one was in the office, so we waited a few minutes. Then I rang the bell. Still, no one appeared.

"Let's go out into that little courtyard area," Mary-Clare said. "Even if we don't find anyone, it won't hurt to look around."

In the courtyard there was a swimming pool heavily blanketed with algae, and more drunken sad cacti. There was also a heavyset topless woman supine in a beach chair. I looked at Mary-Clare. Her eyes were as wide as saucers. We both turned and immediately headed back towards the door.

"Hey there!" the woman shouted. I had not looked at her closely, for obvious reasons. I still did not look, but we both stopped in our tracks. We didn't want to be rude. We also didn't want to stay there.

"I'm covered up now," the woman said. We turned: she was now, thank the Lord, wrapped in a towel. She was solid and middle-aged with a profusion of frizzy dyed-red hair.

"Hi there, I'm Lolita," she said, holding out a red-clawed hand. "Lookin' for a room to rent?"

"Oh no…no, no, actually…I'm an architecture student and we were admiring the imitation Mission style, I thought I'd just come in and take a look but we've seen enough, thanks!"

If this fabrication was to be counted against me in my catalogue of venial sins—well, it was worth it, just to get out of there as quickly as possible. I was sure God would understand.

I smiled a grimace at her, took Mary-Clare firmly by the elbow and steered her towards the door. We kept walking until there was what seemed like a safe distance between us and the Casa Esperanza.

"I think I am traumatized," Mary-Clare said at last. "What WAS that place?"

"I don't know. I don't think I want to know. Lolita? Her name was Lolita, to crown it all? Is it me, or is that really, really, surreal?"

"Surreal is a generous term," Mary-Clare sighed.

I sighed too. "Esperanza. Hope. If that was a sign of hope, I think I'm depressed."

I was beginning to wonder if this just wasn't meant to be. Neither Mary-Clare nor I had an automobile (in a fit of cluelessness about the nature of Texan cities, I had sold my Mini before leaving New York), so we were limited as to how far we could go from campus. But once Portia heard of our search, she donated her car and chauffer services to the cause so we could go further afield. Portia had an old gray Buick which was painted with daisies and quotations from Shakespeare. Mary-Clare and I enjoyed being driven around by her, particularly when she was blasting Vivaldi through the rolled-down windows.

Danielle also contributed her moral support by suggesting that we check out a set of row houses in a slightly more upscale area of town. It was a pleasant, sedate brownstone building with trees in the front yard and a lot of green lush ground cover.

"I could see myself living here," I said.

"Me too," said Mary-Clare, "the balconies look pretty!"

After we finally found the rental office, we sat down and waited for the harried-looking young man to pay attention to us. He was on the phone, speaking in hushed tones. Finally he hung up and looked up at us nervously through his wire-rimmed glasses. His forehead was beaded with sweat.

"Oh yeah, yeah, yeah we have rooms free," he said hurriedly. Then he bent and began rummaging through one of the open drawers. Patiently we waited.

Finally I asked, "So, can we see the apartments?"

"Oh. Yeah, yeah," the guy said. But still he didn't get up or even really look at us.

At that moment the door swung open and a very tanned, very irate looking woman in a smart suit and glossy high heels stomped in. "The exterminators STILL haven't come!" she snapped.

Mary-Clare and I glanced at each other. Exterminators?

The young man wiped his brow and ducked his head and mumbled something that sounded like "Sorry."

"I can't even live in my house. I am living out of a suitcase, like a refugee! What have you got to say to me about that?"

The young man said, "Well, we're working on it…"

The woman went up to his desk and actually slammed her thin fists down on it. "I am at my wit's end!" she shouted. She loomed over the young man, who ducked down below the desk.

As Mary-Clare and I left the building, we heard a crescendo of colorful profanities beginning to rise. I am pretty sure I heard the word "Vermin!" repeated at regular intervals.

"You can't judge a book by its cover, as they say," Mary-Clare said.

However, there seemed to be no such discrepancy in regard to Kimmy. She arrived back a few days early, still the Sassy Goddess as advertised.

"Oh, you're back already," she said looking and sounding disappointed when she came in and saw me searching online lists for apartments on my laptop. "Do you know what my favorite part of vacation was?"

"What?" I asked, distracted.

"Not seeing you!" she laughed.

Hilarious. "Well, I may just be able to make that permanent," I muttered. "I'm trying to get off."

"You're trying to what?"

"I'm looking for off-campus housing."

Kimmy snickered. "Oh! Ha! For a moment I thought you were getting 'off' with some hot guy. About time, don't you think?"

Lovely. I was more determined than ever now to find a refuge far from Kimmy and her ilk.

But after five days, we still had no luck.

Portia invited us to check out her neighborhood. She lived in a duplex in an appealing old neighborhood, far from strip malls. There were old tiled roofs, and a profusion of bright flowers in every front yard. "It probably costs an arm and a leg to live here," I said, gazing up with a sigh at the live oaks, green against the rosy evening sky. There was a good smell to the neighborhood: growing things, and garlic sautéing somewhere, and old wood, and tar, and exhaust, and cypress mulch.

"But it would be nice. It seems so much more...old south, I guess." Mary-Clare surreptitiously plucked an azalea bloom from a bush, and tucked it behind her ear.

"How do you manage, then?" I asked Portia.

"Oh! My uncle owns the duplex," Portia said with a shrug, going back to the car. "Plus I have roommates."

"It doesn't hurt to be a townie, I guess." I took another long look around and saw one of the houses had a little fence around the yard where two toddlers played. I watched their mother come out of the house with an interesting-looking book and a glass of lemonade and stretch out on a lawn chair to watch them.

Up until that moment, I hadn't warmed up much to Texas but I suddenly realized that I wished I could be that young mother living in that ample Southern house, with book and babies and time to read in the sun, and hopefully with a handsome husband coming home in the evening...

Amazing: me, the former fashion writer, the next Great Catholic Philosopher, desiring to be a wife and mother? Stranger things have happened.

I think I sighed. And then someone behind me definitely sighed. I turned to see Mary-Clare, azalea blossom behind her ear, watching the little family.

"Is biology destiny?" I asked her.

"For me, I hope it is!" she said. "Though that's a horribly fragmentary way to express it..."

"True. I can't believe you actually stole that flower!"

She flushed. "I—it was just growing here—I don't think…"

I gave her a slight nudge. "I think flowers on property-line bushes are sort of public domain, aren't they? Well, we'd better get on with house-hunting. Until our respective handsome princes turn up, I guess we must live somewhere!"

"It would be cool if it were near here. I think if Anne of Green Gables moved to Texas, she would have lived in a place like this one."

"True." I glanced around again. I knew I could probably afford the neighborhood, so long as I managed my funds carefully: Texas prices had proven to be a pleasant surprise for me. But I had noticed that Mary-Clare was a little sensitive about being helped out, and she might balk if I offered to pay more than my half of the rent. And anyway, we would have to have a car. With Portia's bizarre hours, there was no way we could rely on her for all our commuting.

So I resigned myself to finding something more affordable and closer to the school, even if with less ambience.

On our way home, we were commiserating, when Mary-Clare said, "Well, why don't we say a prayer together that we'll find one?"

Portia didn't sniff, though I could see that she wanted to. Her nose for anything that smacked of fake piety was even sharper than mine. Perhaps it had to do with her being an actress?

But she bowed her head (inasmuch as she could whilst driving) and I arranged my mind towards the devout.

"Dear Lord, please help us find a house," I said with a sigh. "Thomas Aquinas, please help us…"

"Help us to find a place where beauty can flourish." Mary-Clare said.

"And the intellect is respected," I added.

"And where we'll have FUN!" Portia interjected with a flourish.

Then she stepped on the brake, hard. The two of us were almost thrown from the car.

"What's up?" I said breathlessly.

Portia had pulled against the curb, and was pointing. "There it is," she said, as though she couldn't believe her eyes. "See?"

We squinted through the car window. It was an apartment complex of white walls and arches, and looked very uniform and uninspiring, but in the window of one square white block was posted a small sign: *Apartment for Rent*. There was a phone number beneath.

"I saw it just out of the corner of my eye," Portia said with unusual excitement. "Maybe it's a sign! Go and check it out!"

"Actually, it really *is* a sign!" I joked, but I got out of the car, and started punching in the number. Maybe the place would at least be affordable and free of vermin and semi-clad women of odd nomenclature.

We got the apartment. It was livable, right nearby campus, not in the dreaded Three Chokes complex, not exactly Anne of Green Gables—but it had a small patio with an ivy-covered wall out back, which offered "scope for the imagination," as Anne would say—and there was an appealing archway between the dining room and the kitchen. Knowing that each and every other apartment was graced with an identical archway made it seem less appealing—so we just tried to pretend the other apartments didn't exist.

On our limited budget, acquiring furniture was difficult. But we did find a bohemian orange velvet over-stuffed chair in a fanciful antique shop, and a small vintage dining room table, and I hung my framed print of Rembrandt's "Aristotle" over the futon, and the place started to become our own. It was true that Mary-Clare had rather sentimental taste in religious art, but she hung most of it in her room—except for a lovely hand-painted icon which I admired and encouraged her to hang in our kitchenette. Her voluminous image of Michelangelo's *Last Judgment* we hung over the dining room table as a conversation piece (and a not-so-subtle reminder to myself as to where dining-hour indulgence in gluttony might lead one). So our little place began to take on a bit of character, as we made ourselves somewhat at home there.

We wanted to give our place a name—to set it apart from all the other, identical (nonexistent, of course!) apartments—to stamp upon it the fact that WE lived there, not just anyone. Unfortunately, it's hard to come up with charming yet relevant names for drab apartments.

We racked our brains trying to think of a name that would conjure up a sense of academic conviviality, or lofty aesthetics, but it was futile. "The Bard's Tavern" — "Mt Parnassus" — "The Last Academy" — we couldn't do it, we just laughed ourselves out of it. Portia ended up christening it the "Wee Nooke," in friendly derision: the name was taken from a Wodehouse story which had itself been (of course) derisive.

I was happy to put Kimmy and her sparkly clothes and drunken sullen moods behind me. Uncharitable, it might be, but I hoped I would never even have to see her again.

24 ~

Ad Feminam

It was odd, but after break, in spite of the fact that I had become somewhat friendly with a few of the Suminar guys—Che and Sean, particularly—outside of class, the in-class tensions only continued to escalate. I sometimes wondered whether Hastings was egging us on. Certainly there was something sadistic in his personality that occasionally emerged. Or, it seemed sadistic to me—maybe I was just too sensitive?

As promised, the class grew less formal as the semester progressed; he called us by our first names, permitted us to go off on tangents, and even allowed snacking in class, though no one had yet had the guts to bring in a beer bottle—let alone a keg. He maintained his sardonic half-smile and cold mannerisms, his green eyes remote behind flashing wire-rimmed glasses—but in substance he was far easier to approach and even, occasionally, challenge.

I noted the Machiavellian method and thought: someday, when I'm a famous prof, I'll do like

Hastings: paralyze them with fear in the beginning, and then gradually warm up, and I'll have them all enthralled. Certainly I was enthralled, intellectually. My desire to please and impress Hastings was stressing me out.

But it was certainly strange the way he seemed to, deliberately, bring up questions from the *Summa* that were guaranteed to get us going—often on the subject of women. He also tended to encourage any tangential discussion that appeared to be most vitriolic, so long as it remained focused and well-reasoned. On one hand, he had tamed us—but on the other, we were becoming fierce philosophical beasts. Or, at any rate, we felt like we were.

We were on the section of the *Summa* that deals with virtues. Somehow, discussion of what really constitutes good character in humans had elicited some of the most contentious and least charitable arguments the class had enjoyed yet. Since then, I have observed that the nastiest ad hominem insults and fiercest tempers are generally to be found at academic conferences on lofty theological or ethical themes, hosted by Catholic universities, and teeming with renowned priests or scholars with saintly reputations. It is a strange paradox.

Michael, Sean, Justin and Nat were the worst.

Michael said, "What about these virtues that come from human nature? That sounds really vague to me. Shouldn't we clarify what is meant by nature in this bit?" I had early on noticed that his voice had a boyish squeal to it, when he got excited.

"Maybe if you actually read 'this bit'," Justin said coolly, "you would find it clear enough. You can't just skim the *Summa*, you know." He looked like a lawyer about to bring a lying witness to heel.

"Maybe if YOU read it, with your little rosy spectacles off," said Sean, leaning back with a relaxed chummy smile, "you'd find that actually he DOESN'T clarify it."

"Perhaps," said Nat, "it could reasonably be construed"—his pompous phrasing sounded vaguely like a mockery of someone else's, but I couldn't quite tell whose; he did a little sarcastic head-wiggle as he spoke—"that this resplendent virtue of which we speak...especially, the virtue of understanding what you read...just doesn't belong to everyone."

"True. One must account for superior and inferior natures," Justin murmured, fiddling with his cufflinks and staring into space. His eyebrows were very distracting.

"Yeahhhhhh. Okay. That sounds like a pretty snobbish perspective," said Che, who had been scribbling on his margins and seemingly remaining unruffled. But I had noticed that the one sure way of raising his hackles was to suggest anything like an attitude of entitlement. Che was brought up pretty much in the ghetto, and while he was intensely conservative on all matters of liturgy, he also strongly supported social justice movements: thus, his nickname.

"Well, let's keep the discussion in an arena where we can all be comfortable, then," said Justin, lifting his eyebrows mildly. "Let's not talk about better or worse. Just different. That's the way you left-wingers like it, right?"

Che opened his mouth to object—but Sean beat him to it, saying, "Different—you mean, like what? Master and slave? Jew and Greek? Man and woman?" He grinned, eyes twinkling. I figured he was up to some sort of mischief.

"According to St. Paul, in Christ all these differences are abolished," said Bart suddenly. He was usually quiet, sitting with his big arms folded, head bent over his impeccable notebook. When he spoke, though, he usually said something interesting.

Hastings looked sharply at Bart, smiled a little coldly, and asked, "Would you take this to mean, then, an abolition of nature?"

"No, not of human nature, at least..." Bart looked down at his folded, muscular arms, and his voice trailed off. I glanced at him curiously. He was a strange, silent man (I couldn't think of him as a boy).

"We keep coming back to this," Nat sneered. "This 'nature' business. What do we think we are talking about, anyway, when we talk about nature? Tree-huggers? Organic food? Heterosexual sex? Human frailty? Essences? I mean, seriously, people, you all worship this Aristotelian-Thomistic nature crap but you don't even know what your words mean."

I expected Hastings to snap at Nat, but he just gave one of his icy smiles, as though to suggest that he knew perfectly well what his own words meant but just wasn't going to bother to explain, to us lowly peons.

"I know exactly what I am talking about." Justin said evenly.

"Yeah? So, how about telling us?"

"Sorry, a nihilist like you wouldn't get it."

"Dude, I'm not the one talking about abolishing nature here. Be true to the earth, as Nietzsche said."

Nietzsche, Nietzsche, Nietzsche!

"It's not nature as such that is going to be abolished…" Sean began. He looked a little uncertain, stopped speaking, and ran his fingers through his curly hair.

"Dr. Hastings," I broke in, "I don't want to sound nitpicky, but Bart introduced the term 'abolished' and then you picked up on it with 'abolition' but neither of those ideas has to be read into St Paul's words at all."

"Very true!" he gave me a long look. "I was wondering whether someone would notice that."

I had a moment of pure joy, and hoped that all the strutting males were properly chagrined.

"Even if in the body of Christ, the unity of the Church transcends certain distinctions," said Justin, "that doesn't mean they don't still exist. I think St. Paul was saying that the sacraments are equally available to all. He wasn't saying that everyone was equal."

"But in a sense everyone is equal," said Che.

"Different but equal," said Sean, and, of course, winked at me.

"I don't really see in what sense you could argue that everyone is equal, when each person has so many distinct qualities, virtues, strengths, weaknesses …" Michael said.

"You can't reduce people to qualities!" said Che.

"Let's talk about a very simple difference, then," said Hastings. "Take men and women, for instance."

The man IS a sadist! I thought. The class was already in a raw, combative mood; bringing up the gender issue was bound to take things to new heights.

"Everyone has a vocation to virtue, regardless of gender," I said.

Michael shrugged. "Sure, but 'virtue' is a generic term. Look at the specific virtues. Some seem more specifically masculine, and others more specifically feminine."

"Oh, really?" I trusted that my tone sounded icy enough to freeze them all solid. "And which, pray tell, would you consider to be the masculine, and which the feminine virtues?"

"Well…" he sounded sheepish, as though he didn't really want to say what he was thinking, and his round boyish face reddened a bit. "Well, men are called to be, like, courageous. Women are supposed to be more—nurturing. You know." He grinned and almost shrugged, as though he couldn't really look at me and think "nurturing."

"No, I don't know," I said. "Courage? I'd like to see a man face childbirth. But usually all it takes is a little sore throat or achy head, and men are whining for Mama."

Nat looked at me from his slouching indolence, his dark eyes looking malicious. His wisp of a goatee gave him, as always, a mildly devilish look, and not in an appealing way. "Cate, you haven't faced childbirth lately, have you? Or is there something you haven't been telling us?"

I almost threw my book at him, I was so furious. How dare he! I was offended less for myself, than for any theoretical woman who might have secretly had and lost or given up a child, a theoretical woman who would surely be hurt by his flippant words.

"You revolt me," I said, and discovered in that brief moment of honesty, how rarely I was really honest in that class: my words were always a tangle of veils and subterfuges. Academics, really, is a lot like theatre.

But it seemed to me a little terrible, that we should be talking of the most important of human issues, and not really being human at all. In that moment I was struck with a profound stab of disillusionment: here, in philosophy class, where we should have been acting in the full powers of our personal being, shining with radiant real-ness, we were just as fake as could be. Except for in the brief moment when I descended to base insult.

There was a long silence. Everyone seemed embarrassed, either for Nat or for me, I couldn't tell. But I enjoyed the brief heady feeling of honest rage. Hastings quickly cleared his throat, flashed his spectacles at me, and murmured, "*Ad hominem*, Cate?" but in a chilly, casual sort of way, as though it didn't really matter.

Nat just looked at me. "Likewise, Cate. Likewise," he said.

25 〜

Bellum Omnium Contra Omnes

"Well, enmity between the sexes is always in the air," Hastings looked us all over, from left to right, as though searching for traces of enmity in our eyes. "Perhaps you can't help it. But why don't you consider whether there's some principle according to which you can make the distinction? The distinction between masculine and feminine virtues, that is. Because you can't just base the distinction on some culturally-fabricated norm."

"That should be easy," said Justin. "We need only look to the two perfect human beings who ever existed. Christ is the model for all Christian men, and the Blessed Mother is the model for all Christian women."

"That sounds banal to me, too," Hastings said with a grin. "At least, for the purposes of this class."

"You could use it, though," said Sean, "as a basis for the principles we're looking for. Christ the king, the leader. Mary the handmaid of the Lord. So men are called by nature to virtues of leadership and women are by nature called to virtues of service."

"Um, excuse me," I said, seething—with anger, and with disappointment, too, because—why? I wasn't sure. I guess I had started to trust Sean, to think he actually respected me. Ha! But I kept my outward cool: "Isn't Mary also called the Queen of Heaven? And isn't Christ also called a servant?"

"We're getting into theology here, I think," said Hastings. "How about getting back on the philosophy track? Sean, would you like to prove your point philosophically—by means of observation, deduction or intuition, that is—not through arguments from authority?"

I couldn't keep my mouth shut; I said: "If such arguments even exist…"

To my surprise, for the first time, I saw Sean flare up—I could tell he was angry because he suddenly sat up straight, and clomped his elbows down on the table; he glared at me and said, "Yeah, you're one to talk about arguments. All you ever do is repeat whatever Hastings said in his book."

Everyone stared at him, and then at me. Calling our professor just "Hastings," with no title, to his face, was a terrific faux pas. Sean was already red with anger and now he grew a bit redder, from embarrassment. But he pulled himself together and said, rather magnificently, "I apologize, Dr. Hastings."

"Never mind," he said, seemingly amused. Yes, he *was* sadistic. He had to be. Anyway, it was all very well for him—but Sean had not apologized to me.

So I sailed recklessly on.

"I understand what Dr. Hastings said in his book, and sometimes I use his arguments, yes, but I use my own as well, even with all you uptight patriarchal prigs making jabs at me every minute. I'd like to see any one of you put up with this sort of puerile persecution—" I was glad to find that my anger was making me more rather than less fluent: sometimes I got lucky that way. "Men and courage! Ha! You're only courageous if you're all huddled together in one testosterone-laden mass. And then you have the gall to act like St. Thomas is always on your side, that he was some sort of benighted woman-hater just like the rest of you."

"I think the term 'woman-hater' might be a little harsh, really," Justin interrupted me in a moment when I paused to catch my breath. "but he held traditional views, certainly, and it's anachronistic to read into his work revolutionary and, I'm afraid, schismatic sentiments that only came into being in the last century..." his voice trailed off, in a sort of vague imitation British drawl.

Before I could say anything, Nat broke in. "Talk about anachronistic! The fact that you are even trying to exonerate Aquinas—trying to make him up-to-date! Well, I'm sorry, but that is just funny to me. Of course Aquinas hated women. He was a raging misogynist—wasn't everyone? Look at Abelard. He gets a job tutoring Heloise, and what does he do? He isn't interested in her mind—even though he says she's pretty smart. All he cares about is seducing her. But Aquinas, hey, that's a different hang-up altogether. That whole business with the poker, I mean come on!

He must have been—well, let's just say 'uninterested in women,' shall we?—but either way, who cares if he thought women were inferior? Everyone did back then. Get over it, Cate."

Before I could respond, Sean said, "You've both got it wrong. He wasn't a misogynist. And he certainly wasn't a homosexual, as you seem to be implying— I'm sure his appetites were as strong as anyone's, otherwise he wouldn't have run for the poker, he would have just sat down and had a chat with her and convinced her of the error of her ways. Anyway, he was young then. But he DID see that men and women are different. The feminists have just pulled the wool over everyone's eyes, trying to make women think they should be just like men. What's wrong with saying women were made for virtues of service? What's wrong with being meek and humble and nurturing?"

"Nothing!" I snapped, "It's just that maybe men should consider being meek and humble, too!"

Hastings spoke at this point. "How about we take our break?"

I spent my break period outside, wishing for a cigarette, alone and angry on a bench in the shade. The guys were all hanging out in the lobby, enjoying the air conditioning—warm weather was upon us again—but I sat exiled in the swelter of a typical Houston spring. I was too mortified by my outbreak of rage to be comfortable going in and talking to them. And probably they were all mocking me, anyway.

Hasting approached me from the classroom. "May I have a word, Cate?" he asked. My heart sank. He was going to upbraid me for getting the class all riled up—for beating a dead horse—for resorting to *ad hominem* attacks...I could think of plenty of things he might reproach me for. But I said "Certainly," and tried to smile wisely, graciously.

"The graduate school is organizing its annual symposium," he said, "you've probably heard about it—it usually involves a set of presentations from some faculty, and some students, on a set theme or text. This year, because of the importance of this class, the symposium is going to be on the thought of St. Thomas Aquinas. All the graduate students in all departments are invited to attend—and there's usually a rather delectable wine and cheese spread afterwards...you can count on Dr. Moerio to do things right in the gastronomic department; she was a chef before she went into academics, did you know that? Anyway, each department head is usually asked to nominate one student to represent their department, but this year only the Philosophy Department is being represented."

He paused, and I asked—because I wanted to sound intelligent, "How are the other departments dealing with that?"

"Oh, Dr. Moerio ironed them out. The English Department will get a special conference later in the year—on the main stage play, I think it will be. And Politics, too, will get their chance. I don't know what, exactly. But this is the big one. There will be a number of very well-known scholars in attendance, from universities here and in Europe. Several of them will present papers, along with the four philosophy students I select to represent this department. Naturally these students are chosen for their knowledge, their ability to prosecute an argument, and the originality of their ideas. I have in mind the students I intend to nominate — and I also know the format I intend to suggest, a rather novel one."

I couldn't think of anything to say, so I just nodded, but somewhere inside me my inner child was waving its arm and shrieking "Pick me! Pick me!"

"Yes, I am thinking, instead of the philosophy students having presentations, of staging a bit of a debate. On something good and controversial, for a change. What do you think, Cate? Are you up for it?"

I had been hoping to hear this — but my mind boggled all the same and all I could say was "Yes, of course!" probably too eagerly. Then I recollected myself and asked, "What's the debate on?"

"St. Thomas' view of women," Hastings said, and grinned, genuine mischief lighting upon his green eyes behind his glasses and making him look, very briefly, young and engaging. "I'm hoping to have you, Sean, Justin and Nat debate the issue — as representatives of the department."

I was three-fourths singing jubilation as I left class — but the other fourth was bitter red rage…mostly at Sean. I had to tell the girls…tell them about the amazing thing that had happened to me, that I had been selected as the crème de la crème of the philosophy department…and that I was scared silly about it…and that Sean was a veritable rat, a betrayer. He had seemed so pleasant and friendly that day of the ill-omened creek excursion after the retreat. But though his views were less extreme and offensive than those of Justin and Nat, they hit harder, for some reason: because, I realized, ultimately he was suggesting that a woman's place was not in a classroom, but in a home. Nat was a vile atheist so it didn't matter what he thought; Justin was in a whole other class of being, who knows where he got his ideas?…but Sean was a normal man. Okay, whatever, he was an ATTRACTIVE, intelligent, normal man (and in that case maybe not so normal after all?). So what he thought actually, sadly, mattered.

I wondered whether all decent Catholic guys thought like that. If so, I suppose none of them would ever want to marry me. I would go to my grave brilliant and unloved. Well, fine, I thought. Maybe I would just be a nun…and then become an abbess, and write amazing books, and die, not at all unloved, but surrounded by admirers, and my corpse would smell of roses, and I would be instantly canonized, and eventually be declared a Doctor of the Church. Wasn't that better than marriage? As a nun, I might even keep my figure, after all the sweet lovable docile girls had lost theirs through childbearing. If I ever had a figure to keep, that is.

Portia was the first friend I found. She was sitting cross-legged under a tree near the graduate building, smoking a hand-rolled cigarette and reading Yeats. I threw myself wildly into the aura of her sympathy—

told her all about my triumph, which she was very impressed with, and finally about how I wanted to kick, kick, kick Sean. Actually, I wanted to kick all of them—but especially Sean.

I was gratified by Portia's sympathy, and glad to have made her a friend at last. "So childish," said Portia after I finished, "of him, I mean. You want to know what I think, Cate? I think Sean has a crush on you—"

"—WHAT???"

"Yes! And he's trying to express it in the classic manner of an eight-year-old boy. You know—pull her hair, put frogs down her dress, say misogynistic things, etc."

"Okay, well, that might make sense in theory but in practice it is so completely wrong. You'd have to see him in class. Then you'd know. He really thinks women are meant to be barefoot and pregnant and should never ever have the gall to actually be trying to get a philosophy degree. He's sending me that message loud and clear, every day. That's why he's nice outside of class: being a good old-timey gentleman, so long as I stay in my proper place."

"Your explanation makes him sound psychotic."

"Is it? But the question is, how far gone a psychotic is he?" she mused.

I had discovered by now that Portia was a connoisseur of character, as befits a serious actor. Unlike Danielle, who was often too practical, or Mary-Clare, who was often too charitable, Portia had no problem engaging in intriguing psychological analyses — or gossip — when it came to the men in the Suminar.

"Ideologues are psychotic," I said firmly.

She blew smoke to one size, neatly hitting the breeze blowing away from me. "Okay, sure, but Sean seems really sane to me. Like, too sane to be getting a philosophy degree. He ought to be like a carpenter or something. Can you see him as a philosophy professor? Do you think he'd keep wearing his work boots?"

"I don't ever want to see him as a philosophy professor. I hope he drops out and becomes…a…a street-sweeper, or a circus clown, or something. I am going to DESTROY him in this debate. I swear. Either that or die of terror first, I don't know."

Portia giggled appreciatively, but she raised one eyebrow. "Nevertheless…" she said.

"Look, you come and sit in on class some time. You'll see what I mean. Actually, I'd love to have your support."

She scowled a bit, pulling her long red hair back and twisting it into a knot on her neck. "I would be thrilled, thrilled I say, to sit in on that class. But I don't want Garrett to think I'm chasing him."

"Oh! Are you still? Chasing him?"

"No! I guess I was, last semester. But he's just such a wet blanket. Hanging out with him, makes me hate art and artists and want to run away with some jolly redneck with bad grammar and a big truck."

I diplomatically said nothing, but I suspected that part of his wet-blanket-ness had to do with his not having (to my knowledge) reciprocated her interest, except for as a pair of ears to listen to him talk on and on and on about whatever his latest art project was. Either way, though, Portia was well out of it.

"He's like Narcissus," I said, "only in love with his own image."

"Yes, mirrored in his art. That's a good comparison. Except Narcissus was supposed to be astonishingly beautiful, and Garrett's only so-so." She got up, and tossed the twisted remains of her cigarette into a nearby trash can. "I have class. Blech."

"I have to study. Double-blech."

"I still think I'm right about you-know-who," she called to me over her shoulder as she strode towards the class buildings.

"If he puts a frog down the back of my dress, I'll grant that you might be right," I called back, enjoying the perplexed looks from a few undergraduates who had glanced up at our exchange.

I was sure she was wrong. But still…it gave me something to think about.

26 ∼

O Fortuna, Velut Luna

Finally the Mardi Gras Fund Fair had arrived, and we were busy putting finishing touches on our prison keep, on our costumes, on the paperwork and money-tracking methods. Our juvenile delight in dressing up and play-acting, which had motivated us in the beginning nearly as much as had our hope to do a little good, now turned into grumbling about what we had been thinking, why we had opted for such a time-consuming fundraising notion, why we hadn't just had a bake sale. Despite the fact that we had collected over fifty kidnap requests, and the festival hadn't even started.

"This is taking friggin' forever," grumbled Portia, who was trying to help us paint the prison keep so it would look like it belonged on a grubby pirate ship. It looked more like a chocolate cake.

"What we need," I said, hopelessly slathering cocoa-colored paint over the particle board, "is an eighties-style montage that will make everything go by faster...with peppy music and shots of us looking cute with paint on our faces."

"My pirate pants don't fit," said Sam, one of the guards, a male FPV sympathizer we had recruited for the event. He came over and demonstrated. "They keep falling off." He dramatically unclenched his hand, and true enough, his baggy pirate pants slid to the ground. Luckily for us all, he was wearing shorts underneath.

"Well, pin them up," growled Portia, who had done a lot of the sewing, and disliked Sam. She was trying to suggest slats and boards by means of slashes of darker colored paint; the effect simply suggested darker icing on the cake. She wore tattered jeans and an old lace-trimmed tank top; both were now paint-spattered. So was one of her cheeks.

"What, you expect me to go running all over campus tackling people with my pants held up by a PIN?" Sam demanded. He was a short, stocky boy with thick sandy hair and a vain attempt at a beard. He looked less like a pirate, in his giant pants, and more like a yuppie kid wannabe-gangsta.

"Did you get a box to put the money in?" Danielle asked Felicity, who had just wandered in looking displeased with the world—as if that were new.

"Yeah, yeah, yeah."

"And a padlock?"

"We have a padlock," I said, gesturing at the door of the chocolate cake/pirate dungeon.

"No, a little one, for the box," said Danielle. She was sitting on the ground nearby, cutting sheets of paper into separate cards to be filled out by the kidnappers. She was dressed in her oldest khaki shorts, which had an unfortunate mid-nineties cut to them, and her hair straggled out from beneath a bandana, but she still looked pretty.

Felicity rolled her eyes.

"I'll get one," said Mary-Clare, "I have one for my suitcase that I never use." I had enlisted her to help, and was glad I had: she seemed to be capable of taking care of anything, and she never got angry. Even Danielle had lost her cool from time to time, and Portia and I had enjoyed several shouting matches over stupid things we promptly forgot about.

"Students Against Hunger are doing a bake sale," said Portia darkly. "Caritas is having musicians busking. All smooth and easy. Who came up with the idea of Kidnap for Life, anyway?"

That was me, and I had been proud of it, but at this moment I kept mum.

The Mardi Gras Fund Fair began the next morning. Danielle and I were on the first shift to monitor the Keep. We wore big plumed pirate hats, and fringed sashes, to suggest the idea of pirate captains. I had an eye patch, too, which I thought was rather chic.

It started slowly. I saw people swarming around the bake sale booths, nearby, and went over to buy a brownie myself. It wasn't on my diet, but I needed to keep my spirits up. After all the work we'd put into this, if it didn't come off...

Then a group of undergrad girls showed up, giggling in a typical undergrad manner. "Portia sent us," one of them said. I recognized her as a theatre major, very musical theatre-ish with dramatic eye makeup and a huge circle skirt. "She said you don't have to tell the person who kidnapped them. Is that right?"

"That's right," I said. "You can put down a code name on the form or just leave it blank."

"We have a whole list," one said. I figured it was a list of the guys they had crushes on, but as a professional kidnapper, one must maintain discretion, so I just smiled.

Sam and Colin, the guards (Portia had mended Sam's pirate costume, albeit sloppily) were dispatched.

Several of the guys were found in the library, several in the cafeteria; one of them put up a fight and had to be chased. We saw him burst out of the library, leap over a bench, dart round a lamp-post …Colin, who was long-legged, was hot on his trail, his pirate hat in his hand so it wouldn't blow off.

Sam, whose beard had fallen off, came out belatedly, blocked the guy, and they both tackled him in the soft grass; arms and legs flailed while onlookers gaped and applauded.

"Awesome!" someone shouted. "Violence inherent in the system!"

Soon our Keep was full—and there was money in our box.

The buskers—two fiddlers and a harpist—were watching us with amusement. Soon one of the fiddlers stopped playing and came over. "Can you kidnap ANYONE?"

"Within reason," Danielle said. "I mean, we can kidnap anyone on campus, but if you were looking to kidnap Kim Jong Il or some tyrant somewhere, that might be out of our league."

"Or Hugh Jackman. Much as we might like to kidnap him, I think he lives too far away," I said.

"How about profs?"

I wasn't sure about this. We hadn't even realistically considered it, in spite of the supposed bet the guys had made. There was no way they would go through with it; the idea of Hastings being kidnapped was metaphysically impossible, like a square circle. "Probably depends on the prof," I said.

"Dr. Lyons?"

"Oh, sure!" Danielle and I both said together. Dr. Lyons was a young theology professor, unmarried, popular, but not big on gravitas. He wore crazy suits and went to bars with students. I figured Lyons would enjoy being kidnapped. We were right. Our pirate kidnappers were dispatched straightaway and soon returned with a grinning Dr. Lyons in tow. The crowd in the Keep burst into cheers when they saw him and he gave them a mock salute.

At noon I had to leave the fun to get to class: Aesthetics with the aged and frail Fr. Ambrose. It should have been an interesting class, but Fr. Ambrose was a bit more effusive than he was solid. We did spend a lot of time listening to sacred music and writing about it, which was interesting, but it wasn't quite what I expected from a doctoral-level philosophy class.

"Portia's coming to look after the Keep," I said.

"Will she be okay, just by herself?" Danielle asked. "Mary-Clare has class and…" she dropped her voice, "…Felicity just texted me to say she has cramps and can't come."

"Yeah, right," I said. I knew Felicity just wasn't into it.

"Collin and I can hold down the ship," said Sam, indignantly, speaking for his fellow pirate who was out on a kidnapping quest. "We don't need to have some pirate queen watching over us all the time."

We looked at each other and shrugged. Portia was great at the creative end of things, but she wasn't exactly organized. Still, Sam and Colin ought to be fine on their own, until a new pair of pirates relieved them. "Okay, it's your party," I said. "Sail on, mateys."

On my way to the graduate building, I heard a roar and clamor from behind a shrubbery. I stopped, wondering who was resisting arrest this time. The shrubbery shook like it was caught in a gale.

"Stop him, stop him!" shouted Colin, who was stuck in the shrubbery.

Then I saw Sean, his shirt half-torn from his shoulder, with Colin clutching desperately at his legs. He was bellowing like a mad bull, twisting from side to side.

I stopped to watch, wondering who had kidnapped Sean. Then I wondered why I bothered to wonder. Some of the undergraduate girls he kept flirting with were the most likely culprits, since said girls either were not aware of or not minding his annoying sense of patriarchal supremacy. Or perhaps thinking that it made him the Perfect Catholic Man, blech.

As I watched, Sean broke free and tore down the quad. Colin was right behind him though. All the students going in and out of the library, sitting near the fountain, walking along the quad, stopped and watched in awe and delight as Colin took a flying leap, tackled Sean, and the two of them went flailing together into the fountain. Sean's shirt was definitely mostly off now, and I had a last glance of splashing water and waving arms and a pleasingly muscular chest, before I ducked away, already late for class.

Aesthetics was duller and less focused than usual, and I was happy when it was over and I could resume my pirate hat and my post. Portia had left, and Mary-Clare was on duty, looking sheepish but fetching in her hat.

"How's it going?" I asked.

"Crazy," she said. "The Keep is totally full. So's the money box. And there was a jail break, too, while Portia was on duty. Guess who?"

"Sean?" I asked.

"Mmhmm. I wonder who kidnapped him?"

"Some girl I bet," I said.

At three I left again, this time for the Suminar. I was getting tired and hungry, and was, for once, not looking forward to two hours of wrangling. I felt that I would not be quite up to par. Also, my hair was flat from having been under a pirate hat half the day.

Che and Michael were standing outside the classroom, grinning.

"Class is canceled," said Che.

"What?" this was unprecedented. Not once, this semester or the last, had Hastings canceled a single class. Apparently he was possessed of magical health, authoritarian control over his personal life, and a perfect schedule. Not surprising, really.

"Yup," said Michael.

I looked at the door, for the usual sign that was posted when lesser professors than Hastings were obliged to cancel class: no sign. Nothing on the blackboard, either.

"Evidence?" I asked sharply.

Michael giggled, almost—and Che hummed casually, staring at the ceiling. I sighed and went back to the entranceway, to see if anything was posted there.

Outside, Kidnapping for Life was still going on (I have created a monster! I thought)—the guards, their pirate costumes beginning to look a bit droopy in the heat, were solemnly passing by with yet another hapless prisoner.

"Evidence!" Michael shouted, exultantly, pointing to the prisoner. I caught a glint of glasses flashing over cropped sandy hair, a tweed-covered elbow—

"WHAT???" This time I think I squeaked in surprise and horror. "Who? Wait…no way, you guys didn't kidnap Hastings? Did you?"

Che shrugged elegantly. Michael was giggling in earnest now.

Garrett and Bart sauntered in.

"What's up?" asked Bart.

Justin, coming in behind them, glared and asked. "Is it true? That Dr. Hastings was—'kidnapped'?" It was clear that this stunt was way too undergraduate for him.

"Looks like it," said Michael.

"I sincerely hope that no one in this class was immature enough to do it," said Justin. "We pay for a full quota of classes, and so far Hastings has been the only professor to make sure we get our money's worth."

"Oh, come on, we're all here on fellowships," said Che. "And don't worry. None of us did it. It was Fr. Eliot."

Father Eliot? The university president? This I couldn't even imagine. Fr. Eliot was a robust old man with a broad face and a lot of white hair; he always seemed to be pondering something solemn and eternal. Apparently a spirit of Carnivale had infected the campus.

Che sidled over to where I was standing and muttered in my ear: "We paid him to do it! But don't tell Mr. Fancy Shirt over there."

I didn't know whether to side with Justin's gorgeous disapproval, or to join in festive aura—I managed to shake my head and squint in what I hoped looked like disapproval, while grinning a bit in what I hoped looked like understanding...but probably I just looked deranged.

Sean, wearing—I noticed—a new shirt, came in. "Class is canceled," I said to him, forgetting I was supposed to be annoyed with him. For a moment I just remembered how he had looked so very, very strong and brown and masculine, thrashing in the fountain.

He didn't look at me.

"You owe us money, dude," said Michael.

"Only," he said, very clearly and coldly, 'because some people are traitors."

"But—" I started to say.

"Save it, Cate, I saw the name on the warrant," he said. He handed a wad of cash to Michael, turned, glared at me again, and strode angrily back outside.

I was completely at sea.

Appetitus Contra Intellectum

The Wee Nook was rapidly becoming a Wee Trash Heap of Philosophy Notes. I have never been a very tidy person, which is sort of a trial, since I like BEING in tidy places. I just don't like cleaning. And with the great debate looming ahead of me, I lost even the slightest semblance of domesticity. I read and I read, took feverish notes, carried Hastings' commentary, the Summa, and many others with me everywhere in my leather bag. Toting the extra weight was good exercise, but I worried that I would start to get a crooked shoulder, like Richard III. Still, between the exercise and not having time to eat, I was finally certain that I had lost an entire dress size. Clothes I had bulged out of when I arrived at Dominican now fit me almost too loosely.

Mary-Clare begged me to take breaks from time to time, but she had to unite with Portia to get me to put away my books and notes. Danielle was never good at persuading me to take it easy, since she never took it easy herself. But the other two declared Saturday evening an Enforced Time of Rest, and convinced Danielle to take a break

"No philosophy! Keep the Sabbath holy!" Portia exclaimed as Mary-Clare opened the door for her. "That's our motto!"

She held up two bottles of Chianti, as they came in. Danielle, behind her, brandished a paper bag, out of which a baguette was sticking. I could smell the faint sharp aroma of parmesan cheese. A feast!

"You bunch of heretics," I said. "Insinuating that the works of the Angelic Doctor are anything less than holy!"

"It's you looking like a crazy woman that's unholy," said Portia. "You look like all three Weird Sisters rolled into one."

"Seriously, Cate. Have you even been sleeping?" Danielle asked.

"She sleeps with St. Thomas under her pillow," said Mary-Clare.

"For luck," I said. "Or maybe benediction would be the better word. Benediction, or benefaction? Man, I am so brain-dead, I can't even remember how to talk!"

"Brain dead...NOT good," Danielle frowned, scrutinizing me closely.

Mary-Clare was unpacking the groceries. "Oh, what lovely bread! Almost as good as my mom's!" She put her nose to the golden, crackling crust and inhaled. "Mmmm. Sourdough." She set the bread, and a platter of cheese, on the table. "This is like we imagined when we moved in...*Anne of Green Gables*, only modern," she said, curling up at the foot of the orange chair, tucking her toes under her spreading denim skirt. Earlier she had lit a row of votive lights on the table, so the room was full of dancing shadows, which hid my heaps of paper and untidy books.

"I never really got into the whole Anne thing," said Portia. She was busy uncorking a bottle, grimacing a little as she wiggled the cork. "I mean, I like a lot of stuff about her, but it was always almost too good to be true, you know? I could only identify with the characters up to a point." The cork came out with a comfortable pop.

"I have that problem with a lot of female characters," I said. "They often seem too perfect."

"Anne isn't perfect," Mary-Clare pointed out.

"Maybe not, but all her vices are lovable," Portia sighed as she poured out the wine. "I guess if I never get around to being virtuous, I could at least aim for lovable vices."

"I always find real life people more interesting than people in novels," said Danielle.

"Have you read *Till We have Faces*?" Mary-Clare asked me.

"What?"

"By C.S. Lewis. It's awesome," said Portia. "I love the main character. I think, if I were a character in a novel, that's who I'd be. I love the scene when she grabs the sword and goes for the guard."

Once again, Portia and Mary-Clare seemed to have read all the same books. "No, I've never read it. I feel like such an idiot, compared to you guys."

"Says the girl who's always got her nose buried in the *Summary Theological* or whatever it's called." Portia raised her glass to me and took a swig. We sat for a moment, sipping, appreciating the wine.

"So, other than not getting any sleep, how's the cramming going?" asked Portia, glancing at my heaps.

"I think it's about as useless as cramming always is. But I just feel like I have to be doing it, y'know?"

"I think you should just relax and let go," said Mary-Clare. "I keep telling her that!" she added to the others.

"And I agree. You don't want to be so worked up you won't be able to think clearly," said Danielle.

"No, it's not like that for me. For some reason, when I get mad, it's like…well, it's like some sort of mental high, or something. Afterwards I get depressed, but when I'm in the moment—" I gestured with my hand, an imaginary race-car taking off—"whoosh!"

"Yes, but is it worth it?" Mary-Clare reddened slightly. I knew she was asking: is it worth it, morally, to indulge wrath for so long?

"I think you're giving them too much credit," said Portia. "I mean, they're not gods, they're just a bunch of GUYS, some of them geeky, some of them kind of hot, but they're all clueless."

I thought this was mildly ironic, considering the way she had mooned over Garrett, but I opted to be charitable and refrain from mentioning it.

"Why do you say they're clueless?" Mary-Clare asked. She persisted in taking far too optimistic a view of my opponents.

"Well, because they can't even figure out how to connect their daily life with the theories they come up with in class. And that's just pathetic," Portia said.

"Yeah, it's true," I said. "It's like each of them has two identities, one in everyday life, and another for the classroom. Though I guess I shouldn't talk—I do the same thing. We all do. Except for Hastings, of course."

"I saw Hastings in the library the other day," said Portia. "Did you ever notice that he's sort of attractive?"

I had, but I said, "He's beyond being attractive. And anyway, he's married. His wife is this big-name archivist or something so she's always off in like Greece, or Russia, or Italy—weird, huh?"

"I wouldn't like that—if I liked my husband, that is." Danielle giggled. "Though I guess if I didn't like him, I might prefer to be off working someplace else. But that would be kind of sad."

"Well, she's probably uber-academic, like him, and just doesn't even notice," said Portia, kicking one leg in the air. I watched her wine glass warily. "And that's totally the problem. These ivory tower types just aren't real men. I don't mean in some dumb macho sense but—like, real, reality. They're not in touch with reality."

"Are we?" Danielle asked. "Are we women in touch with reality?"

"I think being a woman keeps you in touch with reality," I said, a little sadly. "The realities of puberty—sexuality—childbearing—they really tear down any false romanticism, I think. Men can take a distance from it all."

"I don't think it's just that they're men and we're women. I think it's that they're intellectuals. That messes people up," Portia said. "That kind of guy can get all romantic and carried away with characters in books. But if a real, interesting, strong-willed woman comes along? They run screaming away! They like their women safe inside the covers of a book."

"Some women seem to do the same thing to men, though," said Danielle. "I don't like all these generalizations. People are just people."

"That's a tautology," I said, "and not very satisfying."

"Oh, you and your philosophical dictionary! I don't even know what that MEANS," said Portia. "Cate, don't you think your life would be easier if you would just cut through all the jargon and use normal language? Really talk about things as they are? All that philosophy is just, like, a smokescreen."

"Portia, you're thinking of Garrett's babbling. Real philosophy isn't like that. It doesn't obscure, it enlightens."

Portia took a swig and slammed her empty glass down. Incredibly, it didn't shatter. "I've read philosophy, Cate. I'm not an idiot. Maybe I'm not a scintillating genius like you, but I have an informed opinion, thank you very much."

Hastily, Danielle said, "I just realized I must have been starving. Is there more cheese?"

I got up to get her some. I was preparing a come-back for Portia, but at that moment my phone bleeped.

I didn't recognize the number, but I was so frazzled I answered anyway. "Hello?"

"Cate Frank. How are you?"

Justin was calling me! Either that, or I was going mad — which was, woefully, a distinct possibility.

His voice went on, "I trust that you're having a lovely Southern evening?"

"Why yes, I am, thank you," I managed to reply. "How are you?"

My friends were all staring at me. I suppose I must have looked dumbfounded. I waved for them to ignore me. All intentions of coming back at Portia were swept clear from my head. Except for the image of Justin, my mind was a tabula rasa.

"Oh, I was just spending a little quality time with our mutual friend, the Angelic Doctor. What better way to spend a Saturday night?"

"Yes indeed," I said, immediately wishing that I could honestly say I was doing the same. Also, I had no idea how he had gotten my number. But I was too nervous to ask.

"You know, I was going over my notes this evening, and things that you said in class kept coming up," Justin's smooth voice buzzed in my ear, "so I thought I'd give you a call. I thought maybe, if you were free, we could do a little studying together?"

If I were free! Immediately, treacherously, I wished that my friends were all elsewhere and that I had been enjoying a cozy evening at home, just Aquinas and me. I glanced over at where the girls sat, nibbling their cheese and talking in low amused voices. No, I didn't really wish they were elsewhere. But still! Of all the nights for Justin to want to study with me!

"As a matter of fact, I have some friends over right now," I said—and then immediately wished I hadn't. He would take it as a cue to say good bye quickly, and I wanted to prolong this miracle. "It's a shame, really. I've been studying all day, and I'm sure having some intellectual company would have been a blessing."

"It would be! Although of course," Justin said, "we would have to study with a certain sort of solipsism. Since we are preparing to debate each other, after all."

"Oh yes, of course," I said, feeling foolish for not having thought of this. "Solipsistic study groups, my favorite sort."

"Well, maybe a study group isn't exactly the right term—solipsistic or otherwise. It sounds too formal. I was thinking more along the lines of meeting up for coffee and just discussing a few things that have come up in class. Two heads are better than one, you know—even heads that are preparing for combat against each other! " He chuckled.

"Oh! Sure! That would be great! When would be good for you?"

"Well, let's see…" we started suggesting days and times, but it turned out we were both heavily booked up all through the week. I felt almost breathless.

"It seems as though the only day we are both free is the day of the debate itself."

"Oh dear…" I said.

"Well, I don't see a problem. Do you? I mean, I'm hoping I'll be entirely prepared by then. But if you need to keep on studying, I understand. But then again, you might just want a break. A little calm before the storm?"

"I think I might be up for that, if you are," I said. As I spoke, I could just see my Intellectual Power gesticulating and shaking its head and waving its arms, trying to get me to stop talking like a simpering little nincompoop. But my Appetitive Power just kept flashing before my inner eye images of Justin's eyes, and mouth, and perfect physique.

"There's that little continental-style café over near the park—have you been there? They play classical music and have chess sets on the tables. We could meet for lunch there."

I agreed. It was within walking distance, so I had no excuse to angle for a ride. Then I hung up and immediately wanted to kick myself. My Intellectual Power, which I now envisioned as a tough no-nonsense Rosie the Riveter type feminist, was shaking its head in disgust.

"I think I have a date," I said to my friends—trying to ignore the Intellectual Power.

"What? With whom?"

"Was that Sean?" Mary-Clare asked.

"Sean? No, no, Sean hates me. There's no way he would ask me out. But it was even weirder than that. That was JUSTIN. Justin, the Perfect Guy. He wants to have lunch with me next Saturday." I sank down in a chair in disbelief. "Okay, so, not a date exactly. But the closest thing to one I've had in a few centuries or so!"

"Isn't he debating you that same day?" Danielle asked, concerned.

"Yes!" I said.

"Well, aren't you worried that he's going to try to…sabotage you, or something?"

"Are you kidding? Justin is…well, it's hard to explain. He's like, in a whole different league. He's so honorable and chivalrous it's almost implausible. I can't imagine him ever stooping to anything like that…He takes his studies really seriously." I took a big sip of wine, and shook my head. "Nor," I went on, "can I imagine him actually being interested in me. So it must be that he feels sorry for me or something. That's the only explanation. He must have realized the guys in the class were ganging up on me, and felt it was his Christian duty to make amends."

"Oh, Cate, don't sell yourself short," Mary-Clare said. "Why wouldn't he like you?"

"For a myriad of reasons. For one thing, I'm not beautiful. And for another, yes, I may come off as brilliant in class, but when has a man ever really been attracted to brains in a woman?"

"Exactly what I was saying earlier," Portia said. She gave me a long cold look.

I suddenly realized that I was acting as stupid about Justin as she had acted about Garrett. And I was supposed to be an intellectual!

28 ～

Homo Proponit

It was the day of the debate, and I woke up sweaty and sore from lack of sleep, too much huddling over books, too much coffee and not enough water. After showering and nibbling on a small uninspiring muffin, I drank my third coffee of the morning and prepared to head for the library. I planned to study all morning, study again all afternoon, and then change for the debate. I hadn't yet decided what to wear. This was yet another horrible, demanding, gut-wrenching intellectual exercise looming before me.

But also, in the middle of all this, was my lunch with Justin. What had possessed me to agree to have lunch with him on the day of the debate? Of course, Justin really was indecently gorgeous and tremendously charming—but come on! The Next Great Catholic Philosopher should be above such things.

I remembered a quotation from Kierkegaard: "purity of heart is to will one thing." Distracted and divided as I was, between focusing on preparing for the debate and anticipating my date (if it was a date) with Justin, my purity of heart was certainly compromised.

Mary-Clare, looking drowsy and absurd in a huge sack-like nightgown with pictures of garish tulips (where DID she find these things? She looked like she was wearing a hospital gown!) handed me a banana as I was walking out the door. "Don't starve yourself," she said kindly. "And relax! Everything's going to be fine! I'm going to go to the chapel and say a special rosary, just for you."

"Thanks!" I said, really meaning it. What a good friend! A far better friend than lots of girls with finer fashion sense. What was the point of fashion anyway? No matter what I picked out to wear that evening, it would not guarantee me success in the debate. Dior couldn't guarantee that. Not even Valentino. After all, from a fashion perspective, St. Thomas was just a fat Italian man in a Dominican habit.

By lunch time I was ravenous and grouchy. I also realized that I would have to change into something at least marginally attractive before walking to meet Justin — even though the walk would probably reduce whatever I was wearing to a sodden wrinkly mess. My best bet was to wear something lightweight and minimal, but I was uncomfortable about showing too much flesh in front of Justin. Especially since my flesh was so inferior to his own. However, I just didn't have the time to get worked up over it, so I just slipped into my Ralph Lauren sand-colored wide-legged trousers, a pair of comfortable espadrilles that wouldn't be too awful for walking in, and a lightweight button-down white silk blouse. I removed my hair from its messy ponytail and then re-imprisoned it in a slightly more artistically messy ponytail. I had on a pair of emerald studs and felt that to change them for anything more dramatic would be a mistake. It was a pretty conservative look for me—but I was terrified to appear to be flaunting attractions I didn't actually possess.

The walk through the park was, as I had suspected, a sweaty business—especially with my Pakistan green canvas bag carrying the *Summa* and my notes in it. Since our lunch was ostensibly a mere meeting of the minds, I couldn't very well go forth without all my study paraphernalia. I didn't want Justin to think that I was approaching this as anything other than a philial meet-up.

Houston seemed to be smelling particularly bad that day—even worse than usual, I noticed, as I stopped to re-adjust my ponytail and check under my arms for sweat-stains about a block away from the café. It seemed that I was still in good order. Not glamorous, but not horrific either.

However, as I walked on, it seemed that the smell was getting more noticeable, which was strange, since there were large plots of flowers and groundcover and a lot of flowering trees near me that should have provided some stench protection. A horrible suspicion struck. I stopped and leaned against a wall, lifting my foot with one hand to check the bottom of my shoe. Yes: I had stepped in dog poo. It was smeared all over the sole of my left espadrille.

There was no grass nearby for me to wipe my shoe on, just pavement. I found a stick beneath a tree and used it to remove most of the offending gunk, but the smell was pervasive. So I surreptitiously (I hoped) pulled up a wad of pansies and tried to scrub my sole with that…but I was terrified of compromising my hand. So finally, in a fit of desperation, I reached into my bag and pulled out my travel perfume: a few squirts should mask the odor. I hoped it would, at least. Time was running out.

Hoping I didn't smell like some weird amalgam of dog poo and a French cat-house, I marched up to the café with all the confidence I could muster. And there he was, lounging elegantly in one of the black lacquered little chairs. His hair, with just the right amount of length on top to curl, was beautiful. He was wearing a linen casual suit—Pitti Uomo?—in an ecru, and a pale blue shirt that matched his eyes. Shoes were slightly scuffed—just so—Hush Puppies. As usual, his sense of style was spot on.

"Sorry I'm late," I said.

"No more than fashionably late," he responded, rising and pulling out my chair. Though no sucker for acts of spurious chivalry, I found my heart was racing just a teensy bit faster than it should have been. I hoped Justin wouldn't notice that I smelled a little funny.

We chit-chatted. Justin asked where I was from, and when I told him that I was born in Philadelphia but had lived a while in New York City, he said,

"Amazing. I used to live in Manhattan a few years back."

"Really?" I said. "I thought so."

"What gave me away?" he asked. "Don't tell me I picked up a Bronx accent?"

"Your clothes," I said, and felt I had to explain, "I used to work in fashion…"

"Really?" He smiled. "I admit, I can't enjoy shopping anywhere else."

He asked me more questions about my old job, what I missed most about the city, and so on. Of course he was just being polite, I told myself, but what a great connection! I felt starved for East-Coast company.

The waitress approached us. Justin ordered a latte and a sandwich. Though I was famished, feeling like I could eat everything on the menu, I contented myself with a ladylike little chicken salad on a croissant: really, rather bland, but I was afraid of ordering some big goopy sandwich that would ooze mayo all over me.

"How's the studying been going?" he asked at last.

"Oh, fine," I said, "it's really just a matter of principle at this point. How about you?"

"I usually try to prepare for things like this by taking some time off, removing myself from the object of concern just a bit. A little workout in the gym…a little visit to the chapel…you know, *mens sana in corpora sano*."

"Wisdom to live by," I said.

"I find the classics give one nearly all the wisdom one needs to get by—in the area of natural philosophy, of course. Don't you agree?"

I was about ready to say "Oh yes!" After all, I was the one who lived by the "What Would Thomas Aquinas Do?" rule. But then I caught myself, and stopped to think. Did I really agree? Wouldn't that mean ruling out all the wonderful work done by recent thinkers, our own popes among them?

"I'm not entirely sure," I said. "It provides a great base, but there's a lot we can learn from more contemporary thought, too. Look at what John Paul II did for understanding the human person."

Justin folded his hands behind his head. "I don't think he really did more than draw out ideas that were already latent in the classics and the medieval tradition."

My iced mocha arrived and I took a sip. "Maybe..." I said. "But many of those ideas really do seem to be quite new, even if they were there in their seminal form. I know John Paul based the idea of the Acting Person on Thomas' work, but the notion of a person-based ethics is pretty revolutionary." I was saying this, really, just to reassert my independence.

"Possibly, possibly," Justin suddenly put his mug down and gave me a very long, direct look. "Cate," he said. Then he paused.

What was he going to say?

"I'm a little concerned about you," he went on.

"What? Why?"

"This debate tonight. I can tell that preparing for it has been exhausting for you. Not that you aren't incredibly intelligent—I've seen that in class. At first, I admit, I was a little dubious; I thought Dr. Hastings was doing some sort of ridiculous 'affirmative action' stunt, putting you in class like that. But now I can approve his actions. Up to a point."

I was getting confused, and a bit miffed. While the compliments were appreciated, I found it pretty arrogant of Justin to "approve" of Hastings. But just then our sandwiches arrived and I distracted myself for a moment, in the sudden swell of hunger. I took a few big bites, and then looked at Justin and said, "What do you mean, you can approve of Dr. Hastings only up to a point?"

Justin quickly leaned forward, concern creasing his brow. "That must have come out wrong. Please, please don't take this the wrong way. Hastings is a stellar instructor. And please don't think I think poorly of you. Quite the contrary. I admire you very much."

Little exclamation points exploded inside my head. He admired me!!!!! Very much!!!!!! I forgot to be miffed and just listened, wide-eyed.

"I think everyone else in the class just sees you as a kind of disembodied mind," Justin went on. "Hastings sees how brilliant you are. That's why he asked you to do this debate. But I see you as more than that. And that's why I worry." He fixed me intently with his blue eyes. "Your femininity makes you vulnerable, Cate."

I was flabbergasted and mesmerized. On one hand, I agreed with this: I was vulnerable. On the other hand, I resented this same vulnerability. But on the third hand, (never mind that I had no third hand) I was taking in the very fact that Justin had *noticed* that I was a woman. That he was *worried* for me. That he...*cared* about me?

Justin went on, in his soft voice, his eyes still intent. "I don't want to see you denying what is in fact part of you. Your vulnerability is in your very nature. And that is a very beautiful thing. But it also means that participating in this debate is harder on you than it is on us. I am sure you will do well, of course. But at what cost?"

"Oh, a few sleepless nights!" I tossed up my shoulders and tried to adjust my voice to a lower pitch. "I'll recover soon enough. And anyway, I have to learn to deal with the stress, if this is what I am going to do with my life, don't I?"

He leaned closer. "Do you? Do you really think that being a professional academic is going to be more rewarding for you than getting married and raising a family? Think about it, Cate. You've lived in New York. You've seen how the women there are. How unhappy they are, caught up in their careers. Do you really just want the Catholic version of that? Or wouldn't you rather be able to get married and live a woman's vocation fully?"

I was discomfited. Could I believe what I was hearing? Was this some sort of marriage proposal? If so, it was completely not what I'd ever envisioned as an ideal lead-up to romance—let alone the Eau de Dog Poo and the aspersion cast on my career choice. But—this was *Justin!* Talking to *me* about marriage! Even if it were in a remote, theoretical way...

I paused to collect my scatter-fly thoughts. "I really don't know," I said at last. "I don't know what my vocation is, in the long run. I do know my vocation right now is to be a student. I want to do that as well as I can. And doing as well as I can means that I need to take on the challenges that are offered."

"I just think," Justin lifted his mug to his lips, but kept looking at me over its rim, "that you may not be seeing the true challenge here. Did you ever stop to consider that God might be testing you? A temptation in the desert, so to speak?"

"Perhaps," I said, trying to pretend that his deep gaze wasn't making me feel tempted at all.

"Suppose God is asking you to reject this opportunity to flaunt your intelligence? That's what the world tells you to do, isn't it? Show off, get attention, get noticed. But what would the Virgin Mary do? She was meek and humble of heart."

This was not a new problem for me. I was never quite sure how to process this idea of Mary's meekness. It sometimes rubbed me the wrong way, since meekness is obviously not my forte. I am loudly opinionated, and I wear huge earrings, for heaven's sake!

I am afraid I took undue consolation in the knowledge that Mary was a Jewish mother, and that, in my experience, Jewish mothers could be maternal and loving while also laying down the law. None of the Jewish women I knew were mouse-like and trodden-on, and I secretly thought that the Blessed Mother had a good strong streak of that Jewish archetype: after all, hadn't she questioned an archangel from the Lord to make sure what was what?

I fiddled with my napkin. "Why can't I be meek and humble of heart and still debate philosophy?"

"But is that what God is asking of you?"

I was shaken. What if Justin was right? What if this whole exercise in academics was just a temptation of a more subtle sort than cinnabons and buttery muffins and White Russians and hot guys with broad shoulders?

Justin spoke softly. "I just want you to think about what I'm saying, Cate. I think I understand you better than the others. And whatever you decide, I want to let you know I care about you as a person — not just as a disembodied brain." He reached his hand out and very lightly brushed my fingers — it was the slightest touch, but it brought the quivery feeling back again. I smiled, I hoped casually, and said:

"But as a person, I love philosophy," I said. "And I can't disappoint Professor Hastings. It would be wrong for me drop out of the debate at this point."

"Of course, I can respect that. But just be sure you are thinking as God thinks. Don't worry about the world's respect."

Did this mean that if I participated in the debate I would lose his admiration? Or, worse yet, *God's* approval? Was I doing wrong?

I finished my sandwich in silence. Justin had already finished his, and he watched me as I ate. I felt very awkward.

He went on. "I think you should drop out of the debate. Hastings would understand. And I would admire you very much for your courage. So few women these days have the integrity it takes to truly be beautiful daughters of God."

The check came. "I'll take that," Justin said. He smiled at me winningly. "This is on me."

So, it *was* a date, of a sort.

"Thanks," I said.

His brow furrowed again. "I know this was probably hard to hear, but I felt I had to speak to you about it. Please pray about what I said. Call me if you need to talk. I know what it's like, trying to work out one's salvation in fear and trembling. I've been doing that a lot lately myself."

"Really?" I waited to hear more.

He stared off at the horizon. "It's been a long journey for me, but I'm pretty sure God is calling me to be a priest," he said.

Oh.

"That's great," I said weakly. "Really, really great."

I felt somewhat numb and brain-dead. This lunch had been so totally different from anything I had anticipated. Whether better, or worse, I felt too confused to say.

We rose to leave.

Justin held the door for me. After I had exited he said in a low voice, "Was it just me, or did you notice a very strange smell in there? Almost as though something was decomposing...sort of sweet, but also rotten. Did you smell it?"

Oh no! "I didn't," I said. "But maybe living in Houston has made me immune to bad smells."

"Where are you parked?"

"Oh, I walked."

"Let me offer you a ride back, then."

What terrible timing! Any other day, I would have been thrilled to get in a car with Justin. But as long as that smell was on my shoe, there was no way I was going to risk getting into a small enclosed space. "Thanks," I said brightly, "but I need the walk, to keep my energy up. And to think about things."

At least I had asserted my independence.

But maybe Justin didn't find such an assertion very attractive?

And what did it matter, if he was promised to God? As I had heard some girls at Dominican say, God takes the best, we get the rest.

As we parted, Justin took my hand and held it very briefly as he looked me in the eyes one last time. "Thanks for meeting with me, Cate. I'll be praying for you."

"Thanks. I need all the help I can get." I managed to say.

What was I going to do?

O Tempora! O Mores!

In the middle of the park, I took off my espadrilles and dumped them in a trash can. Then, barefoot, I sat down on a park bench to collect my thoughts.

Was Justin right? Was I pursuing this debate only out of intellectual pride?

Was my sinful pride all the more hideous in that it went against my innate femininity?

Did I even have an innate femininity? Or had I hopelessly compromised it ages ago, first with wild living and materialism, later with intellectualism and arrogance?

Should I drop out of the debate? If I did, would Justin think differently about his vocation? Would he want to date me? Marry me, even? What a dizzying idea. Also, a ridiculous one. I needed to drop the idea of Justin as a potential spouse...it was making me crazy.

I closed my eyes and murmured, "St. Thomas, I could use some serious illumination here!"

The reality of the situation hit me with full force: I had come to Dominican to study philosophy; I had felt a Tingling when I entered the classroom! My study of philosophy could not be at odds with my pursuit of God's will. Perhaps the Tingling had been there to tell me that my vocation was truly to be a philosopher! To give that up for a man—any man— even a man as amazing as Justin—would be to be untrue to myself.

Plus, I would be betraying Hastings if I threw off his debate in the last minute. I felt a great peace and clarity settle down on me as I walked, barefoot, back to my apartment.

Once there, I sat down and sent Justin a quick text:

"Thanks for the lunch and the wise thoughts. But right now I have to do my duty as a student."

I hoped he wouldn't be too disappointed in me.

I felt a terrible need to discuss my bizarre date with Mary-Clare, but there was no sign of her. There was a note on the fridge: "Hi, Cate! I'm off on a quest; see you this evening!"

So, Mary-Clare had left—abandoned me, really, in my hour of need. I didn't know what her quest was for. Probably groceries, I figured: there were mighty few in the fridge. The milk had gone a bit sour, but I poured some into my travel mug, added ice and coffee, and hoped my stomach wouldn't suffer from this unpalatable concoction. Then I slipped on a pair of sandals, since my discalced state would not be appreciated in the library.

Unsatisfied, hot, sweaty, and annoyed with my housemate for not being home, I set off to trudge back to the library, through the murky air.

I had already decided to spend my final few hours of cramming in the rare-books room, since I associated it with scholarship, exclusiveness, and of course my incredible good luck in first meeting and impressing Hastings there. Now I was not so sure. Luck? I wondered. If I hadn't been so "lucky" I wouldn't be in this dilemma. I could have signed up for some nice cushy little first-year philosophy classes, and wowed everyone by my brilliance; as it was I now risked wowing everyone with my utter folly...as well as with the unseemly spectacle of brillo-pad hair. And I was also risking losing a chance with the most amazing man I had ever met.

It was an unwritten rule that if profs were in the rare-books room, no student would disturb their sanctum. Plus, very few undergrads had the guts to enter at any time. A few of the brighter or rasher ones (the same ones who liked to sit in on grad classes) would come in on occasion. But there was a good chance it might be empty.

It would be just my luck to find Sean or Nat holding the fort. Or, worse yet, Justin. I just did not have it in me to face him at this point.

I was in luck: the room was empty! I picked a chair, settled myself and spread out my books, my notes, my notebooks and my pens around me, in a kind of ornamental fan-shape. I like a modicum of order when I study, at least in the beginning. The *Summa* was sort of the hub of the fan; it lay open in front of me, to the section on "The Production of Woman."

All those pages and pages and pages of words, and only a few, here, on me.

And the first article: "Whether Woman Should Have been Made in the First Production of Things": I had looked at it often enough, but I now seemed to be seeing it for the first time. "It would seem that the woman should not have been made in the first production of things. For the Philosopher says that the *female is a misbegotten male*."

I had argued, of course, that Aquinas was simply addressing the standard view of antiquity here, and in no way buying into it—but honestly! In a world where such questions could be asked, what could I really hope for? I should be happy that anyone was even defending my right to exist. As for my right to be in a philosophy class—to be a philosopher—to strive against other philosophers… I was beginning to feel as though Justin had been right. I was going against my nature. St. Thomas Aquinas would not support me in this. He was probably shaking his head over my folly right now.

I was about ready to slump over on the book in despair when I heard a very familiar voice outside the room.

"I so cannot BELIEVE I am actually going to sit here and STUDY. Like, how weird is this? You'd think I was in COLLEGE or something!"

Kimmy! Great. Just great. Now I wouldn't be able to leave the room without her seeing me, brillo-pad hair and play-dough skin and all.

"Hey, studying isn't so bad, really. Take it from me. You just have to approach it in moderation.

Never too much at a time." I recognized the voice, but couldn't quite place it.

"Like, fifteen minutes? Is that enough? Then we can go get a drink?"

"How about twenty minutes! Deal?"

Garrett! It was Garrett, with Kimmy. The world was clearly going insane. On the other hand, based on what Portia had told me about her brief unsatisfactory romance, Garrett was not really interested in intellectual women, or artistic women, or women with any ideas rattling around in their heads at all—since in his view the fundamental purpose of a woman was to listen to him. And presumably to gratify him physically—though Portia said she'd never reached the point where she'd had to try to resist that temptation.

For a moment I was afraid they were actually going to enter my sanctum, and I contemplated hiding, or running out, or something. But the door did not open, and it appeared that they had settled down somewhere outside, near the door. I heard the whine of Kimmy's noxious vowels from time to time, as I tried to concentrate on Aquinas. Aristotle's views on women suddenly seemed far more plausible. I took a sneaky swig from the travel mug I had hidden in my bag (no beverages allowed in the Rare Books Room, of course) and then spewed it out: the milk had curdled! Gobs of clumpy whitish-brown coffee went all over St. Thomas and my shirt.

I almost swore, but then remembered I did NOT want anyone to hear me in here. My shirt was a mess, covered with coffee-stains, and smelling of rancid milk; poor St. Thomas was little better. Luckily there was a bathroom in the Rare Books room. It was not a nice bathroom, not a very modern bathroom, not a bathroom I or anyone (to my knowledge) had ever used: more like a utility closet, really. But it had a sink in it as well as a toilet; I could clean up in there. I crept in, pulled a few paper towels off the roll that was lying across the back of the toilet, and then went back and tried as best I could to clean the curds of coffee and milk off the page "On the Production of Women."

The mess came off easily enough; only a few tan splotches remained. My shirt was another matter: the white silk sleeveless shirt I had worn for lunch. The splotches stood out glaringly on it. It was ruined, if I didn't rinse it out immediately.

Hoping no one would come in while I was engaged in this task, I pulled the bathroom door shut and took off my shirt. The Yale lock on the door looked rusty and unreliable, and I decided not to use it, since I didn't trust it either to turn or turn back— anyway, no one was going to come into that bathroom. Why would they want to? I ran water over my shirt, and then finally filled the sketchy-looking sink, and let the shirt soak there for a few minutes. I wished I had brought the *Summa* in with me, so I could read while my shirt soaked...but there was no way I was going to creep out there shirtless to get it! Who knows, a whole bevy of theology professors might come in and catch me. I began to think maybe the wisest course would have been for me to load up my studying paraphernalia and scoot back to my apartment post-haste, and wash my shirt there. Too late now! Now I was going to have to sit in the Rare Books room and let it dry on me—and any number of undesirable people might decide to come in, while THAT was happening. And all the while, I was losing valuable studying time, and what remained of any smidgen of composure I might have had was gone, gone, gone.

Then I heard the door to the Rare Books room open—and a horrible, unmistakable giggling. Kimmy and Garrett were coming in after all! Horror upon horror. I was now trapped: I would either have to wait until they left, or come out and embarrass myself.

Giggle, giggle, rustle, thud. I heard a sound like someone slurping on a milkshake. They were kissing! In the presence of my notes. I felt as though my notes would be scarred forever.

"Oh, man, this is so NAUGHTY! Someone's been studying in here! What if they come back?"

"Hold on," said Garrett's voice. "This is the room we need."

He was headed towards my door! I knew he was! Panicking, without thinking, I turned the rusty Yale lock—it clicked noisily.

"Someone's in there!" Kimmy's voice sounded startled.

"No way. No one's ever in there." He rattled the doorknob, and I was thankful that the lock had worked. I just prayed that they would go away, so I could get out—get back to my book and my notes, and my stress. Stressing over the debate seemed far preferable to having to listen to Kimmy and Garrett messily make out in the presence of some of the most hallowed texts of the Western canon.

"They are! I saw it! Anyway, someone's crap is lying around here. Omigawd, I know whose this is! THIS stupid book." I heard a slam, and guessed that she had smacked St. Thomas. He was definitely having a kind of martyrdom today: first the coffee curds, then the kissing, now downright violence.

"I have a real connection with that book," said Garrett's voice, dreamily. "Sometimes I think no one really GETS what he was all about. It's like, you can't go for it in a linear manner, see? That's where they all get it wrong, in my class." He was off! He wouldn't hear a word she said, and would probably forget about making out with her, now that he was on his favorite topic, himself. I hoped he would take his monologue and his partner outside in a hurry.

"I don't know why anyone wants to waste their time with crap like that. I mean ..." but Kimmy was talking to a blank wall, I well knew.

"What you have to do, is envision it as a sort of series of concentric rings. Sometimes I think Hastings gets it. But he doesn't understand me. Call me crazy, but sometimes I just wonder, if maybe he's jealous of me. I mean, I have this connection..."

Their voices trailed away. The door slammed. They had left the room, and taken what remained of their Eros with them. Good! Now I could put on my shirt, get out, dry off a bit, go back to my apartment and recover. I let the water out of the sink, and wrung out the shirt, over and over, until I couldn't get another drop of water out of it. The coffee marks were faint; they might come out with a proper washing, at least. In spite of all my wringing, the shirt felt absolutely sopping and unpleasant when I put it on again. Yes, I would go STRAIGHT back to my apartment. I unlocked the door.

Except, I didn't. I couldn't. The lock was stuck. It wouldn't budge. I tried again—it was still stuck, but I was sure I could move it. I put both thumbs under it and pushed with all my might—nothing. I suddenly became alarmed. What if it really was stuck? What if the damned thing just wouldn't work, never had worked? I took a fold of my wet shirt in my hand, wrapped it around the lock, and tried again, this time with more to grip on. Nothing. I wiggled it, slammed it with the palm of my hand, pushed the door in, with my knee, pulled the door out with my arm lifted the door, pushed down on the door, finally kicked the door. It was futile.

I was quite definitely uttering all sorts of profane imprecations under my breath at this point, but the idea of shouting for help—of banging in terror against the door until someone rescued me—was entirely out of the question. The embarrassment of having locked oneself in a bathroom...no, there was no way I could hold my head up and go to my debate. If only I had my cell phone on me! But it was out there in my leather bag. Maybe someone would come into the Rare Books room, and I could get their attention? But what if it were...Sean...or Justin...or Nat...or Hastings...or Carson...or some incredibly old, incredibly famous, incredibly saintly Dominican monk who might be visiting the school, and who might suffer from heart failure hearing a terrified voice from behind a closed door, and his death would be forever on my hands.

I realized I was losing my grip on reality.

I said a Hail Mary, and then two more, and then tried the whole rigmarole with the lock again.

I invoked St. Thomas Aquinas, Ss. Peter and Paul (they'd been miraculously rescued from prison), St. Teresa of Avila, St. Catherine of Siena, St. Catherine of Alexandria. I thought about invoking St. Antony, the patron saint of lost objects, since I was sort of a lost object...but I didn't want to be found, I just wanted to GET OUT before anyone found me.

There was a tiny window in the revolting bathroom. I wondered whether I could open it. It was dusty and grimed, and very high up. I could stand up on the radiator, though, and reach it. Looking out, I saw that a ledge of roof stuck out beneath it, not very far down. Maybe I could get onto that? And then maybe slide along until I found...what? A tree? A ladder? Superman? No, I couldn't really think of any escape that way.

I went back and began pounding on the door. I pounded lightly at first, and then with more vigor. Finally I was banging and kicking with all my might, hoping SOMEONE would hear me. Could it be possible that there was no one at all near the door? The embarrassment of being rescued from a locked bathroom was suddenly eclipsed by the embarrassment of not being rescued at all...of languishing for hours, forgotten and abandoned, and finally not showing up for the debate. It was due to begin at seven in the evening. They would look around for me...wonder where I was...when they called my name, I wouldn't be there. Or maybe they wouldn't call my name? Maybe by that time they would have figured that I'd flaked out, and decided to just carry on pretending I'd never existed? Yes, that's what they'd do—save face that way, not having to look stupid calling my name and having me not show up. I would be, as it were, deleted from existence.

I invoked St. Jude, the Patron of Desperate Causes. Mine was pretty desperate at this point. I invoked all three of the Holy Archangels, because archangels could be amazingly handy, I thought, in a case like mine. I invoked St. Joseph the Carpenter, since a carpenter would know all about doors, and locks, and be able to get me out. I wondered whether there was some patron saint of girls locked in bathrooms I didn't know about, who would only help me if she could, so I added "Unknown patron saint of girls locked in bathrooms, please get me out of here."

I felt like I was about to cry. I thought about creeping out the window, and banged one more time on the door, as loudly as I could.

"What's going ON in there?"

It was Kimmy.

30 ∽

Ora Pro Nobis

"Who's that?" I heard footsteps in the room—but it sounded like just one set. Apparently Kimmy had ditched Garrett. "I KNEW someone was in there. What the hell?"

"I'm locked in this bathroom," I shouted, probably louder than I needed to. "This damned lock is stuck. I can't get out. I need someone to get security, please."

There was a long silence. Finally: "Is that you, Cate?"

"Yes." No point in denying it.

I thought she might refuse or storm out, but instead she just started laughing—squeaky bursts of hysterical laughter. She went on and on, laughing squeakily, but she almost sounded as though she might be about to cry, too.

"That…is…just…too…hilarious," she finally sputtered.

"It is very funny. And when this door is unlocked and I come out I promise it will be even funnier. Just go get security, PLEASE. I mean, you don't have to get them, even, if you don't want to. Just go down and tell the librarian at the desk there's someone stuck in here; she'll take care of the rest."

"But," Kimmy seemed to have controlled her laughter now, though her voice still came in squeaking bursts, "what if I think it's funnier for you to stay locked up in there? "

I took a deep breath. Of course, the little brat hated me! She wasn't going to help me if she could avoid it. "What happened to Garrett?" I asked. "Did he go off to gaze in a mirror somewhere?"

"That guy? What a total douche. I got so sick of listening to him go on and on, I decided I'd rather actually go study than listen to all his bull."

"He wasn't actually interested in you, then?" I couldn't believe I was shouting this conversation through a bathroom door in a university library.

"Huh." This didn't seem to be an answer, one way or another.

"Kimmy, let me assure you: that sort of guy," I said, "is only interested in himself. Trust me. You can do better." I wasn't sure I believed this...but then, thinking of Garrett, I wasn't sure I disbelieved it, either.

"Look, girlfriend. I know guys. They are ALL interested in NOTHING but themselves. One's the same as the other."

"They're not all that bad."

"Yeah? You got a boyfriend yet? Why don't you call HIM to come rescue you, then?"

I thought about inventing a boyfriend on the spur of the moment—a rich boyfriend, far away in France, too far away for him to come galloping up on his trusty steed and release me from my prison (or for Kimmy to do any actual research into his existence)—but then suddenly I realized I didn't actually want to crow it over her. And what did I have to feel so superior about? Sure, she might be a sassy goddess, but was I much better thinking, me who acted like I was a famous philosopher, but who was actually locked up in a smelly bathroom in a damp shirt covered with coffee stains?

"I haven't got a boyfriend. Sure, I know a ton of guys, but all they care about is showing off. They don't give me the time of day. Honestly, I think I might as well just be a nun or something."

"Well, I figured that's what you were going to be," Kimmy's voice didn't sound as though she was intending to be insulting, just matter-of-fact. "But you just said they weren't all that bad."

"Not as bad as Garrett," I said, "was what I meant."

"He kisses like a dying goldfish, anyway. Ugh! "

I sort of felt like that fell into the category of TMI, but I laughed, dutifully. Actually, it was a rather amusing simile. I resolved in my heart that I would NEVER EVER kiss Garrett. Not that it was likely that this would ever be an issue. Still, dying goldfish have never been my cup of tea, in the amorous department. "Kimmy," I said to the closed door. "Look. I'm sorry I was so obnoxious when we were roommates. I was just sort of…confused when I got here. You know? And also, you were so thin and pretty that I was jealous of you."

"You have totally got to be kidding me. I'm not thin. I can't get thin to save my life."

This girl is really nuts! I thought. But I felt sorry for her. I really did! I felt sorry for myself, too. I was just filled with pity for the whole human race. I almost felt tears spring into my eyes, as I thought about the terrible weight of the world's suffering. "For real?" I asked. "You have got to be kidding ME. You have a great figure. Look, I should know, I used to work as a fashion writer. Before I started on the path to nun-hood."

"Seriously?"

"Absolutely seriously. You could be a model. But I wouldn't advise it. I've known a number of them and they are NOT happy and the guys they date almost NEVER treat them well. Men in the fashion industry are…well, like Garrett only worse."

"Really?" there was a long silence. She seemed to be digesting things. "This is a really weird conversation," Kimmy finally said. "Look, I'm going to go tell the librarian you're locked up in here. Okay? I hope you get out all right."

"Thanks," I said.

FREEDOM!!!

Yes, it had been embarrassing, stepping out the door (they had actually had to take it off the hinges—that's how stuck it was) into the presence of two security guards, one maintenance man, the campus locksmith, two librarians, and a few undergraduates who had gathered outside the door to watch the melodrama. But I didn't really care. I had a few more hours, still, before the debate, and my experience of having involuntarily incarcerated myself had left me with a strangely buoyant feeling, as though I had died and risen again. Now that I was no longer locked in the Rare Books Bathroom, I felt, I could do anything. I didn't know whether the unknown patron saint of girls locked in bathrooms had helped me, or if it had just been chance, but either way something felt as though it had worked out as it was intended. That I had sort of made my peace with Kimmy, as best we could—that was something. I didn't see us ever being best friends. But at least we didn't hate each other anymore.

I tried calling the apartment to see if Mary-Clare was home yet—no answer. I called Portia and Danielle both, to tell them my story—but no answer on their cells, either. So I arrived back at a dark and empty apartment again, not angry, but just a little worried and very, very hungry. It was four o'clock. The debate would take place in three hours. I needed to find some food, take a shower, and figure out what on earth I was going to wear. But I also needed to have my friends with me.

I found some squashed ice cream sandwiches in the freezer and began to eat one. On a rational level I knew it didn't taste very good, but in my condition it seemed wonderful, like the ultimate Platonic Ideal of ice cream. Some ice cream dribbled down my chin. I realized that I must look deranged.

The door opened—in came Mary-Clare, Danielle, and Portia. They looked excited and flushed—no wonder, with this heat! Portia was carrying a big paper sack, and Mary-Clare was carrying a smaller one.

"WHERE HAVE YOU GUYS BEEN!"

The smell of curry rose from the big paper sack. "Dinner for you!" Portia said, "actually, dinner for all of us—but for you, mostly."

"I wanted to make you a special dinner," said Mary-Clare, "and I know Indian curry is your favorite, but I have no idea how to make it! And then we got caught up on our quest, and ran out of time, so we just ordered take-out, I hope it's okay."

"It's beyond okay, it's heavenly! Look, you're not going to BELIEVE what just happened to me. Suffice it to say, I'm lucky to be here right now." I proceeded to tell them of my misadventures in the Rare Books Bathroom. "Probably," I concluded, "it was some sort of test. I had to confront Kimmy, you know? And tell her I was sorry. I've been feeling guilty for a while, for the way I treated her."

"Seriously, Cate? She was just as rotten to you," said Portia.

"I know what you mean," said Mary-Clare, "it's like how knights had to be shriven before battle."

"Shriven?" asked Danielle.

"Go to confession," Portia explained.

"You guys are the best friends ever. There was no way I was going to survive without passing out, just on a squashed old ice cream sandwich. Now, you just have to keep me from eating too much—I don't want to look bulgy for the debate. Not that I even know what I'm going to wear yet..."

"But there's one more thing," said Mary-Clare. "This is what our Quest was all about! We wanted to get it for you—it's not a big deal or anything—but we thought it would be like a special protection, an amulet...something to give you confidence."

"And we ran all over Houston," said Portia. "And nearly died of an overdose of piety, going into every little religious shop we could find."

"Including some really bizarre ones," Mary-Clare added. "I didn't know there were such things as Rastafarian Catholics, until today."

"Is that what that was?" asked Danielle.

"It was really a head shop," Portia explained. "With a lot of bongs with pictures of Our Lady of Guadalupe on them. Bizarre is right."

"And we found one of those Tridentine places. That...Society of St. Pius the Tenth, I think it is? The schismatics? And an old lady there told us that if we went to the Latin Mass every day, Jesus would pick out good husbands for us." Mary-Clare shook her head.

"Worth trying," I said.

"Anyway, we finally found your talisman," said Portia, "and then we got stuck in traffic, so WE'RE lucky to be here, too."

Mary-Clare handed me a small white object, wrapped in tissue paper. "This is for your special protection," she said, "protection from disrespectful men, especially."

I opened it: it was a beautiful, round silver medal of St. Catherine of Alexandria: my patron saint. I had actually looked for one before—always fruitlessly. She is not as popular a figure in Catholic hagiography as St. Francis of Assisi or the Little Flower. But ever since I had heard the story of her martyrdom, preceded by her defeating the top pagan philosophers of Rome in a debate on the merits of Christianity, I knew she was the patron for me.

Remembering that a great and holy woman had entered into debate with men was a comfort to me. Justin was wrong. I was right to be doing this.

"This is so beautiful," I said, "I can't believe you found it! Really. I've never been able to find even a holy card of her."

"You can wear her like a breastplate," said Portia.

"I will," I said. "Be afraid, Sean and Company! Be very, very afraid."

31 ∽

In Academicum Arena

I can, in retrospect, think of several metaphors for the way I felt, walking up to the reception room in the graduate building: the Charge of the Light Brigade...Hector confronting Achilles...Custer's Last Stand... Thermopylae. All this demonstrated was the usefulness of my over-education in providing me with many and diverse ways to express my terror. Why couldn't I think of a more triumphant image? St. Michael slaying the devil came to mind—but no, that was overkill. I'm no St. Michael. And Sean and Co, irritating though they may be, were not really bad enough to merit devilish comparisons.

I was dressed to impress: or so I hoped. It was a dress I had forgotten in the back of my closet, an asymmetrical matte silk dress, tea-length, blood-red with slimming ruching from the neckline down to the hip, a single huge black poppy on one shoulder. Somehow, I had not, hitherto, found occasion to wear it. Perhaps it was a bit much for a philosophy conference...but then, I didn't really know what sort of costume was *de rigueur* for female academics. My imagination partitioned female academics into several types:

1) matronly, blowsy women who looked like housemaids but could speak ten languages
2) intense, thin, bespectacled, androgynous women with cropped hair and grievances
3) sentimental women who affected Victorian fashions and wept over poetry
4) ambitious no-nonsense scholars in tough businesslike suits, the kind of girls who obsessively run five miles a day and eat only egg white omelets, and end up as department heads out of sheer force of will.

I didn't feel as though I fit into any of those categories.

But then, I thought, I am not SUPPOSED to fit into categories — education, like the path to sanctity, is always a strongly individual path. Whatever God wants me to be, it must be something unique as a snowflake. Not that I looked much like a snowflake.

"You look like a siren," Portia had said. "These boys are not even going to be able to open their mouths to speak! You'll win the debate the moment you walk into the room!"

"It's not too much, is it? Too dramatic, or too tight?"

Danielle, who had been brought up with a code of modesty that had never existed in my society, had looked at me, eyes narrowed. "No," she had said at last. "It's not immodest. It's a bit...daring. But in a good way."

"How are you going to do your hair?" Mary-Clare had asked.

Usually, to class, I had worn my hair up in a twist or a high ponytail. Since I was growing it out, I had been uncomfortable with its enormous, ungainly curliness, which was only exacerbated by the famed Houston humidity. I had decided to take the plunge. I wanted to appear different, somehow, from my classroom persona, and I did NOT want to hide my femininity, as though I were ashamed of it—as though I thought I had to pretend to be a man in order to win respect. If Justin thought my femininity had been compromised by my philosophizing—well, I would show everyone just how uncompromised it was.

"I'm going to wear it down," I said.

This had required a lot of gel spray, and a lot of cautious crunching, before I was content that my curls had just the right amount of restrained unruliness, or artistic wildness, or whatever. I had examined myself with a critical eye, having used nearly half a can of gel: a touch of Medusa, maybe, in my snaky black locks? Very well, then, I would petrify the males with a feminine single gaze.

I had finished my new, dramatic, philosopher-femme-fatale look with an application of beige and gold eye shadow, but I had left my lips pale and matte. Eyes symbolize wisdom—I wanted to call attention to that aspect of my being, not to my mouth (which I suppose, in my case, signified gluttony). Luckily, I had lost enough weight that the red dress sat on me sleekly, with nary a bulge in sight.

Now, flanked by Mary-Clare and Danielle (Portia had gone on ahead of us to secure seats for her and the other girls, and possibly to glare at Garrett, who knows?) I strode up to the door of the reception room where the debate would be held in my four-inch red-and-gold peep-toe heels, not wobbling, head held high, a neat sheaf of notes in a black leather folder under my arm. No one looking at me (I hoped) would have dreamt of the turmoil I had been through that day, the mess I had left at my apartment, the churning in my stomach.

The reception room was carpeted and wallpapered and lit with candles and a buffet on one side — but a narrow podium, row of four black seats, and spotlit microphone reminded me of the purpose of this academic party. I swallowed.

Dr. Hastings, urbane in his usual suit with a nicer tie, greeted me with a rare sincere smile, and nodded politely to my friends — also a rare gesture, as he tended to ignore both faculty and students who were outside his sacred purlieus.

"Very elegant, Cate. Smashing, to tell the truth."

I could feel myself start to blush, but luckily for me Hastings turned away to greet a colleague, before he could see my red cheeks. I was surprised that he would give such a personal compliment. Clearly he was in a good mood — looking forward to the match. As for me, I had a sudden wish that someone would offer me a flask of brandy — like they do in Edwardian novels. Smelling salts would do, also, and a cigarette. Oh, how the temptations of the world intrude, even when one's heart is set on higher things!

A number of professors and students were already sitting expectantly. I recognized a few of them from my other classes. They were not just from the philosophy department—I saw Portia's favorite Theatre professor, and a few boys from Theology—probably ready to snare me in their subtle traps: each was armed with a pocket-sized abridged *Summa*. I feared them not.

In one of the four chairs near the podium, Justin sat, wearing an Italian suit (Giorgio?) with a dark ivory silk shirt, and pin-striped tie that accentuated his masculine perfection. Now that I knew he was meant for God, I could admire him in a manner of remote aesthetic appreciation. I had no chance with him. And if I did, my participation in this debate was destroying it. He, too, had a black leather folder, which was unzipped, and he was looking intently at his well-organized notes. Of course he was early. Of course Sean and Nat were late.

As I slipped into place, Justin gave me a perfunctory nod. I understood his position. I just didn't agree with it.

I noticed, in the audience, Portia talking animatedly to Danielle and pointedly ignoring Garrett, who seemed lost in his own thoughts. Bart was there, off in a corner by himself—he is something of a mystery, I thought—with his big battered *Summa* in one big red hand. Che was arguing with Fr. Eliot, the university president, about something—Che seemed comfortable arguing with anyone about anything, and almost never let himself get riled. He glanced up at me and gave me a wink as I passed—then puckered his lips, miming a whistle. Well, that was Che—nothing embarrassing there. I winked back. Michael was not there yet. I assumed he was attending to Sean, perhaps in the manner of a squire arraying a knight for battle.

Really, I had to stop thinking of it as battle.

The room filled up quickly, and although I tried to keep my attention on my notes, my mind was getting blurry—the way things blur when they go by you too fast. I wished time would just stop, slow down, so I could take a deep breath and recollect my thoughts. The famous Dr. Carson came in. I was always surprised to find how boyish and cheery Dr. Carson looked—not gaunt with pondering the Eternal. Certainly, the guru of the Theology department was far more approachable and human-seeming than our remote Hastings. As soon as he sat down, several of the theology students flocked to him, and he seemed to draw them all into the discussion with ease.

Nat came in, wearing a seedy black button-down shirt and, inevitably, blue jeans. At least they weren't dusty and torn. But still, blue jeans! Justin gave him a look, under one arched unsurprised eyebrow, which ought to have withered him, if he'd had any sense. His shaved head shone beneath the golden lights, and his scruffy beard looked more like fungus than ever. He sat down next to Justin, who ignored him, and continued to peruse his papers.

Hastings stepped up to the podium, with a single sheet of paper and an expensive-looking pen (I knew by now that he was a devotee of technology, but liked to give an impression of being old fashioned—the pen mightier than the software, and all that). He glanced impatiently at the empty chair between me and the podium, and then turned and asked Justin something. I was suddenly aware of how casual Hastings was, how relaxed: this was nothing to him, but to me, it was everything...my first conference! And even if it was in-school, it was in front of famous academics, not just a bunch of MA students and unknown untenured professors. What, oh what, in the name of God, had I been thinking, imagining I could impress Hastings? The man knows the *Summa* like I know my shoe closet! Probably I should have just stuck with the shoe closet. I am *so* in over my head.

Sean came in. The door banged a little too loudly, and I looked up and saw him, his tall frame twisting a bit as he made his way past knots of people, up to the front of the room. He looked...the only word for it was hot. Not just handsome, not just attractive, but genuinely hot. His clothes fit him right, for a change...maybe his mother had come for a special visit to help him dress? His trousers, flat-front and gray in some thick-woven fabric, were faultless. His shirt, white with a touch of Western flair in the pearl buttons, was also textbook well-dressed Texan. Never before had I noticed that his jaw was so square or his hair so made-for-running-fingers-through.

Great. Just great. I belong in the shoe closet for sure. Here I am, supposed to keep my mind on the eternal, the transcendent, the absolute, and I am thinking about...Sean's hair? I don't even *like* him. He doesn't like me. What if he totally wipes the floor with me in this debate?

...St. Catherine of Alexandria, PLEASE help me, even if I don't win, please don't let me be transmogrified into a floor-mop for these ravening misogynists. Please don't let Hastings be embarrassed by me. Please help me remember whatever it was I thought I was writing about when I read it. Thank you.

I glanced up surreptitiously at Sean. Again, we had one of those horrible awkward moments: just as I looked at him, he had taken the same moment to look at me with, I thought, little friendliness. Yet his eyes were so...intense...

St. Catherine, please, also, help me to STOP THINKING ABOUT SEAN. At least until this ordeal is over...

"Faculty and students of Dominican University — and of course our esteemed guests — it is my great pleasure to welcome you all to the Fourteenth Annual Graduate Symposium." Hastings was speaking: the debate was about to begin. For one terrible minute my brain started to go blank. Then I took a deep breath and the world came back into focus.

Hastings was introducing us. There was some awkwardness, since we had sat down, not in the order of presentation, but according to each person's desire NOT to sit beside certain people: I had avoided sitting next to Justin, and then Nat had avoided sitting next to me, and Sean had just taken the only seat left: right next to me. Deep breath now, Cate.

"…Justin Hale, whose theological background has considerably enriched the class' understanding of Thomistic terminology. He will be presenting on 'The Only Acceptable Gender Theory: The Order of Nature and the Order of the Divine.'"

The only acceptable gender theory, according to Justin, was certain to be one in which I was relegated to the status of submissive nobody. I almost sighed—it might possibly be tolerable, being submissive to a man as gorgeous as Justin. Oh, and, of course, if he weren't already promised to God.

Hastings went on: "And to my right, Sean Fowler, a careful and dutiful scholar who can be counted on to read a text with diligence and a sense of tradition—his paper is entitled 'Beyond Biology: Aquinas' View of Marriage.'"

I had to admit that Hastings made Sean sound a little less than exciting. Perhaps he had been placed in the group as a sort of stabilizing influence? His proposed paper didn't sound as though it were likely to make me break out into a rash, at any rate. But, I thought: we shall see, we shall see.

"And the intrepid Catelyn Frank, who has held her own with extraordinary finesse, as the sole female in our seminar class on Aquinas. Miss Frank will present on 'Misbegotten or Misread? Thomas' View of Woman in the *Summa*.'"

I, intrepid. Well, if intrepid means foolish…

I caught Portia's eye—she was smirking a bit—as though she could see I was about to suffer from horrible stage-fright, and was reminding me that in the grand scheme of things this was, after all, just a conference. Not actually a battle to the death. Danielle gave me a tiny, surreptitious thumbs-up sign behind her notebook. Mary-Clare just smiled. I felt encouraged.

"And finally, Nat Santorini, a first-year doctoral student who has often impressed and spurred on the class by playing devil's advocate. Mr. Santorini's paper is entitled 'Power Play: Women in Aquinas' Classical Anthropology.'"

I could only imagine what sort of travesties awaited us there. Probably Aquinas re-cast as a fat monkish Nietzsche, if such a thing could even be imagined. If it could, surely Nat would be the one imagining it.

Dr. Hastings asked Fr. Eliot to lead us in an opening prayer. As the tall, hefty Dominican approached the podium with jovial gravity and began to pray, I was reminded of my patron saint, and felt more cheerful myself. Then the prayer was over. The debate began.

Quaestiones Disputate de Gender

The order for the debate, Hastings had told us in advance, had been arranged so as to best showcase the different perspectives: first Justin, as propounding the most conservative view; then Sean, as offering a more moderate alternative; then me, with my neo-feminist reading, and finally…whatever on earth Nat was planning on throwing at us. Presumably Hastings was saving the two more controversial presentations for the latter half of the debate.

The typical conference paper is about twelve pages in length, and requires some fifteen to twenty minutes for presentation. Hastings had encouraged us all to be as brief as possible, without sacrificing the subtlety of our argument, so as to leave more time for the question and answer session between each paper. After the entire debate was finished, the audience would also be invited to pose questions. I hoped I would be prepared to field them.

Justin came to the podium, shoulders straight, notes in hand. He glanced around, as though assessing his audience, and immediately began to read. His voice was even and pleasantly modulated, and his charm was apparent even through the large words he used.

"Discussions of philosophy and theology are often plagued by the problem of ambiguity in vocabulary," he read, "and perhaps this phenomenon is nowhere more problematic than in the case of the word 'nature.' Let us explore, today, the way in which this ambiguity leads to a problem of interpretation in St. Thomas' view of man and woman—or as some would put it—inaccurately—St. Thomas' gender theory."

If it's inaccurate, why mention it, I wondered?

Then, as I had suspected, Justin went on to analyze various possible translations of key passages. I could see the classically-minded scholars in the audience nodding their heads, eyes bright. Some of the students, I suspected, were nodding in order to convey an impression of total comprehension. My own Latin being less than stellar, I sympathized with them. I also began to wonder what business I had putting myself forth as an Aquinas scholar—even an amateur one—without Justin's classicist and medievalist background.

I glanced at my friends. Mary-Clare and Danielle were gazing at Justin. I think they were happy to have an excuse to look at someone so handsome. But Portia was rolling her eyes.

...Yes, even if Justin was fascinating to watch, what he was saying was kind of boring.

Justin went on to explain how the order of nature as outlined in the *Summa*, in accordance with Aristotelian natural philosophy, presents us with a prototype of the divine order intended in heaven. I wondered how he was going to prove that one: personal insight into the Beatific Vision a la Dante, maybe?

"It would be a mistake to regard St. Thomas' reliance on Aristotle's biology or physics," he said, "as reducible to the sort of natural scientific theory comparable to the modern variety. The supposed 'inaccuracies' in these ancient sciences are irrelevant, because the structure of the universe, as outlined by Aristotle and utilized by St. Thomas, is intended not to reveal to us anything so banal as mere material composition; it is intended to reveal the divine order of being itself, as the Creator intended."

Dr. Nero, a tall white-haired physics professor, could be seen wriggling uneasily at this point. No doubt he was dying for the end, when he could lambast Justin for dubbing the natural sciences "banal."

The presentation went a little over twenty minutes, concluding with the statement that "therefore we may see that when Aquinas uses Aristotelian biology to designate the differences between men and women, what he is indicating here is not an actual natural difference in the strict modern sense, but a difference in the order of being." He turned the page, fixed his eyes on his audience one last time, and read, "Thus the natural subservience of the female to the male thus is not extrapolated out of some outmoded biological theory." He seemed to glance in my vague direction. "Rather, it is an expression of the divine order, the order intended by the Creator, according to which all beings are subjected to him, and ordained to live out their vocations in fear and trembling."

Yep. I had been relegated, all right. If Justin was right, I would be stuck as a sort of cosmic scullery maid even in heaven (if I ever got there).

Prof. McCaffery, Portia's wild-haired drama professor, started to rise from her seat with one thin fist clenched like an avenging deity...but then the man sitting next to her tugged her on the elbow and whispered something in her ear that made her grin, in a sinister sort of way. Clearly she was lining up to lambast Justin, too. It almost made me feel sorry for him. But still, I had my question ready.

I raised my hand quickly, and Hastings nodded at me. "If Aristotelian physics is irrelevant and inaccurate," I asked, "how, then can it be said that we accurately deduce a divine order from an erroneous system?" I leaned forward. "Shouldn't the actual order of being be manifested in a system that conforms to the natural world?"

Justin turned to face me. "I'm not sure your question makes sense," he said, a bit coldly.

I took a deep breath. "If in the order of the divine, the female is subjugated to the male," I said, "how do we know this through a biological system you've just admitted is outmoded and false? This makes no sense." I appealed to the audience. "Divine truth should come to us through the true order of nature. But if you're not getting it from nature, then where did this idea come from? Because from what you're saying, it sounds like it came not from God but from Aristotle. But you don't really mean to say that, do you?"

Prof. McCaffery actually clapped her hands at this point. Everyone turned to look at her, some glaring, some smiling — then they looked back at me.

"The order is evident in the actions of nature," Justin said. "The flaw is in the explanation of this action...Aristotle's explanation. But there's no confusion in what we see, even if Aristotle was wrong about why it...is that way. The order is very clear."

Not to me it isn't, I thought. But before I could say anything Nat muttered, sort of generally to the room: "Talk about disregard for the material world!"

"Nat, do you have something to say?" Hastings asked.

"Yeah, sure. He claims the science is unimportant. Sounds like Gnosticism to me. Would you say that understanding nature is itself irrelevant or unimportant?" He cocked his head at Justin, grinning.

Justin seemed particularly irritated by Nat. I could understand why. "Not at all. I would say it is subjugated in importance to the understanding of divine things. There is an order in everything."

"But how are you so sure? What's the source of your certainty? What's the source of Aquinas' certainty?"

"Illumination," said Justin. I saw Sean roll his eyes. Clearly Justin had talked himself into a theological conundrum at this point. Remembering Hastings' view that Aquinas' debt to Aristotle was overrated, I figured that our professor was mentally rolling his eyes, too.

"So you're falling back on theology after all, then, Justin?" Nat asked.

"There is such a thing as natural illumination. But some people just aren't capable of it." Justin spoke pointedly.

Hastings rose and cleared his throat: the conference was getting controversial already. He suggested that further questions be saved for later, and invited Sean to come forward.

Sean's paper was less ambitious than Justin's, and more palatable. Rather than using an admittedly inadequate biological system as proof for a divine order, Sean clearly stated his intention to look at Aquinas' understanding of man as a being not reducible to biological explanations. "In the case of marriage, in particular," he read, "we find that any approach to man as a mere animal fails to do justice to the dignity of the institution. Sacramental marriage particularly cannot be fully explained by means of recourse to biology."

He cleared his throat. Was he nervous? If he was, he was cute being nervous. " — And while within the context of mere generation, which can be understood to be a wholly animal action, men and women are acknowledged to be unequal (see Q. 96, Article 3), it does not follow that this inequality is present in the sacramental union of man and woman. So while it may be said that 'woman is naturally subject to man,' (Q. 92, Art 1) we must enquire whether marriage can be understood entirely in light of this natural subjugation."

Natural subjugation may not be to my taste, but at least Sean was willing to recognize that Aquinas' view of marriage allowed for a kind of equality. After Justin's austere views, Sean seemed almost…refreshingly revolutionary. I smiled at him as he read—and then suddenly remembered that for some reason he hated me. Quickly I looked down at my own papers again.

Sean went on to address a number of quotations in which it seemed as though Aquinas was stressing the inequality between the sexes (thus reminding me what a difficult task I had taken on)—and in each case argued that we need to distinguish between the natural relation and the marriage relation. Not that he went so far as to assert a natural equality…still, after Justin, Sean seemed courteous and moderate. I had to admit that I liked, with a few reservations, the idea of marriage as transcending inequality.

When Sean had finished, Justin immediately raised his hand and said, "You're reading contemporary personalism into Aquinas!" in a tone of mild accusation. I was a little surprised. Just earlier that day, hadn't he said those personalistic ideas were already in Aquinas? Perhaps I made a greater impression on him than I had thought!

"I don't think so," said Sean. "It's based upon the efficacy of the sacrament, the equality of the marital union—not on the…the person."

I detected his slight fumbling over that word, and couldn't help myself—I had to attack where the enemy was weakest. "What would you say," I asked, interrupting Justin who had just opened his mouth to keep arguing, 'is the distinction between person and nature, in Aquinas' thought?"

I felt wickedly triumphant (mea culpa, mea culpa) because I knew Sean had been absent with strep throat the day we had discussed Question 29, in which the issue of divine personhood is addressed. It was unfair of me, maybe, but for heaven's sake, I had been beleaguered by these guys, all semester long!

Sean took a deep breath and ran one big hand through his curly hair, disheveling it somewhat. "Person and nature," he said. He gave me an evil look. I almost regretted my question. Now he actually had a reason to hate me! But he went on: "Person derives from the Latin 'persona,' which means, a mask. So while nature is the essence of a thing, person is…the way it manifests itself."

"That sounds to me like just a scholastic version of Kantianism," I said. "I believe actually Aquinas follows Boethius' definition of a person as an individual substance of a rational nature—in fact, he rejects the idea of person as 'mask' because it could really only work on a metaphorical level. For Aquinas, each of the divine Persons is a perfection of one of the three relations of paternity, filiation and procession. For Aquinas, it could almost be said, person is relation."

"Yes, of course," he murmured. "And...?"

"And so, if person is relation, wouldn't it be possible for the relation between man and wife to be equal on the level of person, not just assured by sacrament?" I tried not to sound smug.

"I suppose it would be possible," Sean said, scowling. "But the divine relations are perfect, and the human imperfect."

"Yes, but in that case, wouldn't men and women just be equally imperfect?"

Prof. McCaffery clapped her hands again. I looked over and saw Portia give me a thumbs up. To my surprise, the ethereal and saintly Fr. Elliot was smiling and nodding. Clearly I had touched upon some important point of theology, without knowing it. Thank God I had touched on it correctly.

"Thank you, Sean," said Hastings quickly. I wasn't sure whether he was just trying to keep us on schedule, or whether he was worried about chaos erupting too soon. "We will now hear from Catelyn Frank."

33 ❧

In Defensionem Feminam

The intrepid Catelyn Frank, whose knees were about to turn into jellied consommé and melt down into the bottoms of her gleaming red patent leather Louboutin heels, had just been called to present her paper at her first conference. I rose to my feet, willing my knees to stop shaking, and went to the podium.

"Misbegotten or Misread? Thomas' View of Woman in the *Summa*." I said. My voice quavered only a little. I gave a slight cough and went on, trying not to think about how many eyes were on me.

Suddenly I thought about how vulnerable I was up there, my body shielded from all those peering curious eyes by nothing more than a shred of red silk—why hadn't I rented a suit of medieval armor for the occasion?—and a fit of absurdity struck me. For one split second all I could think about was a single ridiculous thought: that I was naked under my clothes. And from there to the horrible realization that everyone else in the room was also stark naked underneath their clothes—in fact, everyone in the world. For a moment the mingled horror and

silliness of this thought almost dumbfounded me—
then with a stern wrench of my mind I fixed my
meditation upon the image of St. Catherine of
Alexandria, and then on St. Thomas Aquinas, as he
appeared in the chapel. My knees stopped shaking,
and my mind became very clear.

"One of the most famous, or perhaps infamous
quotations on the nature of women, from the
tradition of Western Catholic thought," I read, "is
Aquinas' reference, in Question 92, Article 1, to
Aristotle's assertion that 'the female is a misbegotten
male.' This quotation has been used both by
misogynists trying to argue for a theological or
philosophical basis for the oppression of women, and
by feminists asserting that the tradition of the
Catholic Church has long been one of patriarchy and
oppression. The usual response to an excerpt so
widely quoted is to suggest that (mis)readers take a
closer look at the context. In this case, however,
anyone arguing for the equality of woman in the
thought of Aquinas may find herself at a
disadvantage—since the context of the quotation is
the question of whether woman should have been
made at all—'in the first production of things.'"

A few giggles from the audience, and a snort from
Portia. I was off!

I went on to explain further the wording of the
context, the fact that Aquinas was not actually asking
whether women should have been made at all, but
rather whether they should have been made
alongside man, since from woman, according to
scripture, sin entered the world. I then argued that

woman should not on account of this be viewed as evil, since the common good of her creation is clearly stated by Aquinas to be greater than the individual evil of temptation.

The gist of my argument, though, depended on what Aquinas meant by "misbegotten."

"It is not an appealing word. It is not a word one wishes to have applied to one. However, let us take a closer look at the meaning of this word, in the context of the *Summa*. It does not mean, as one might suppose, that woman was made by mistake, as the Manicheans posited that the material world was made according to an error on the part of an over-exuberant Demi-urge. Nor does it mean that woman is nothing more than a deformed male — as though nature, had it proceeded rightly, would have produced nothing but men. This, however, makes no sense, in the context of right reason or the thought of Aquinas.

"The term 'misbegotten' refers, rather, to a theoretical stage in reproduction according to the Aristotelian biology to which Aquinas alludes, 'for the active power in the male seed tends to the production of a perfect likeness according to the masculine sex; while the production of woman comes from a defect of the active power, or even from some external influence, such as a South wind, which is moist (Q. 92, Art. 1). I am inclined to skip over the biology altogether, archaic and amusing as it is, but I will pause long enough to say that there is nothing so very wrong, in my view, with having been brought into being by a south wind."

I really hoped Hastings wouldn't loathe this little jest—I glanced at him and saw him smirk a bit, and sighed with relief. A few chuckles ran through the room.

"So we see, then, that the charge of 'misbegotten' may be taken as wholly irrelevant, directed as it is towards an event in a biological system which does not in fact exist. As the *Summa* is not Sacred Scripture, we need not look for the theological meaning of this assertion. However, the assertion could still be taken as evidence, by some, that Aquinas truly believed women to be inferior. I answer that: in light of Aquinas' views about the overall intention of nature, he would not see a single defective causal event as yielding in any sense a defect of nature or substance in the product. For 'as regards universal human nature, woman is not misbegotten, but is included in nature's intention as directed towards the work of generation' (Q. 92, Art. 1)."

I cleared my throat again. I could see I was doing well with the audience, but I didn't want to lose them.

"Moreover, Aquinas asserts that woman was made not only to fulfill this intention of nature, but also 'for the purpose of domestic life' (Q. 92, Art 2). Here, I would suggest, we find the true relation of man and woman—not only as ordained for generation, but ordained for the domestic church, the family. It might be objected at this point that Aquinas asserts that "woman is naturally subject to the man." Indeed, he does assert this, but in the same section he explains that the "subjection" here referred to is "economic or civil." We are able to recognize a certain order in civil affairs in which a ruler is head of his subjects—but we do not from this conclude that the ruler is in any way truly superior to his subjects. Aquinas thus asserts here, then, not that the male is naturally superior to the female, but that there is a necessity for order in the household, even as in the state."

"Furthermore, in the third article, he goes on to present an argument that is no doubt familiar to you all. Some may be surprised that the argument comes not from a contemporary feminist theologian, but from the Angelic Doctor himself: 'It was right for woman to be made from a rib of man. First, to signify the social union of man and woman, for the woman should neither use authority over man, and so she was not made from his head; nor was it right for her to be subject to man's contempt as his slave, and so she was not made from his feet' (Q. 92, Art. 3).

"It might be a little more to my taste, had Aquinas phrased more strongly the reason why woman was not made from man's feet—but I think we can excuse him the very few prejudices of his time which we find here, and focus instead on the remarkable theology of marriage and family here presented, in which woman is seen indeed as not only partner in generation, but true partner, true equal, and true companion. Far from defending an outmoded patriarchal ideology founded on domestic oppression and the sophistical notion that 'Might makes Right,' St. Thomas Aquinas here appears to be arguing for the dignity and equality of women—as, indeed, the true Church has always done."

I was finished.

I almost moved to sit down, but then remembered that it was time to be bombarded with questions.

And the first hand was (of course!) Nat's.

Nat: "So are you saying that Aquinas is the true church? Are you arguing that the Summa is infallible?"

Me: "Of course not, I am simply asserting that Aquinas, unlike others—such as, say Tertullian, who is NOT, of course, a saint or a doctor of the church—here remains in line with true Catholic tradition."

Justin: "What about Aquinas' assertion that in men the discernment of reason predominates?"

Me: "In order to address that, we need to take a look at what is meant by discernment of reason, and whether it is the only perfection of reason identified as proper to human nature."

I was on a roll! I felt as though I had just downed a glass of potent Chianti. Philosophy was coursing through my veins. I was doing well! Almost all those prestigious academics in the audience were smiling at me with approval!

A few more questions—none, I noticed, from Sean. I now knew he really would hate me forever. In the midst of my triumph I felt a small ache of disappointment. My feet were aching, too, in my high heels. I was relieved when Hastings called on Nat, and I could finally sit down.

I admit I didn't really pay much attention to what Nat said. I knew it was going to be insane, and I wanted to listen and relish the insanity, but I was too busy in my mind going over my own presentation—anxiously I went over every bit of it, and although I naturally thought of a few elements I might have improved, overall I was pleased—and the one question I had dreaded, the one Justin had asked, I had found an answer to!

And then I heard Nat's voice:

"The desire for violence against women," he said, clearly but with little expression, "often transmuted or translated or transliterated into an imputation that women desire such violence, has always been present in the Western intellectual tradition. The general trend in contemporary thought is to negate or deny this desire—to distance oneself from its expression in certain works of the hallowed canon. In certain cases when this desire (and imputation of desire) has been boldly stated—such as in Nietzsche's *Zarathustra*, for instance—it has been necessary for many to clearly establish this politically necessary distance. But in cases where it is hidden, or perhaps sublimated, it has not failed to find its devotees. I suggest that latent in Aquinas' view of man and woman is just such an expression of desire."

This was worse than I had even imagined. If I had not been appalled, I would have had to congratulate Nat, mentally, for coming up with something more egregiously horrid than even my athletic imagination could conjure.

"The story of Aquinas chasing a woman out of his room, with a red-hot poker," Nat went on drily, "is relevant in this case, if biographical details may be permitted to assist in the work of hermeneutic. One might almost say that the shadow of this poker is to be found throughout the Summa, wherever woman is spoken of. Freudian interpretations of such symbols come to mind here. But let us not forget that a poker is a domestic implement. And thus Aquinas' expression of desire must be seen within a domestic context, unlike Nietzsche's, which is very clear, very open, and very warlike. This is a hidden, a repressed desire: one that is kept, so to speak, behind closed doors."

I was furiously jotting notes—for one thing, I had never heard that the poker was red-hot. It was just a poker, for heaven's sakes, and probably the poor young man was surprised—indeed, alarmed—to suddenly find a strange woman in his room.

Also, Nat had not yet presented a single shred of textual evidence. I wondered whether he would. I couldn't wait for him to finish, so I could DESTROY him.

"Interesting to note," he went on, "is the fact that when Aquinas speaks of sins of concupiscence, he speaks always of a man sinning against himself—or, in the case of adultery, against his neighbor (see Q. 72, Art 2, and Q. 73, Art 5)—never against the woman with whom he sins, or the wife to whom he is untrue. One can derive from this that according to Aquinas, the injustice or violence done against the woman is negligible or irrelevant. Or perhaps even desirable? The woman as a victim appears to have been excluded from his ethical economy, even as she is demoted in his ontological hierarchy (as she is constantly spoken of as being lower in reason—see Q. 74 Art 6, and Q. 92, Art. 1)."

"What does this exclusion connote? To borrow a felicitous phrasing from Aquinas himself: perhaps a 'lingering delectation'…"

"This is obscene!"

Every head turned to look at Justin, who had risen, glowering. "This isn't scholarship!" he said. "It's obscenity!"

Nat turned to look, too, and in his surprise dropped his papers. They spilled over the edge of the podium and fanned out on the floor in front. For a moment he stood as though too shocked to move.

Hastings half-rose: "Justin! Sit down please. Wait until the paper…"

"I'll get them!" Justin shouted. With a sudden leap, he went for the papers on the floor, even as Nat was trying to squeeze around the podium, arms outstretched, glasses awry, snatching desperately. Justin began to snatch up sheets of paper, crumpling them as he went. Nat, seeing what he was doing, started grabbing papers to protect them. Sheets of paper crumpled, fluttering around them. I felt my mouth hanging open in disbelief.

To my shock, even Hastings was discomfited. He hovered irresolutely, as Justin grabbed at the papers in Nat's hand, and Nat clawed back at him, trying to grab them back. "Justin! Nat! Stop this! This is…" Hastings shrugged suddenly and stepped back, helpless.

Still, no one in the audience had moved. It was one of those moments you imagine, sometimes: when suddenly, in the middle of a decorous and dignified gathering, the sort of place where everyone is eager to make things move smoothly and gracefully, where an unwritten etiquette prevails, someone breaks loose from the restraints of conventionality. And no one knows what to do. It is too unforeseen. Too…just too WEIRD. For a moment everyone tries to pretend it isn't happening. It's like when a crazy person gets on the subway and starts causing trouble: no one wants to be the one to have to do something about it.

"This presentation is disgusting!" Justin said, brandishing his handful in the air. Then with fierce movements of his hands he began to crumple and mash the papers. Nat leapt and tried to grab his pages, and Justin swung away, crumpling as he moved. "No one should be forced to listen to this vileness!"

Suddenly Nat didn't seem to mind having lost his paper. Grinning, shoving his glasses back onto his pointed nose with one bony hand, he leaned back against the podium. "Freedom of speech, sucker!" he said. "You're exposing the real nature of your ideas, the way you're acting — can't bear to hear anything you disagree with!"

Justin faced him, breathing hard, crumpled papers still in his hands. For a moment, they really looked like they were about to start fighting.

Out of the silence Fr. Eliot rose from his seat, a tall white-haired figure, stately in his white Dominican robes, like a portly angel. "ENOUGH!" he boomed. I had never guessed that his voice could boom quite so loudly.

He took two big steps towards Nat, grabbed him by the shoulder, and walked him back to his chair, robes swishing seraphically.

"Buffoonery," he said enigmatically, as he pushed Nat down into the chair, "is only proper to those who have earned the right to be fools for God. If you wish it, earn it!"

Then over he marched to Justin, and plucked the papers from his limp hands. "Is this zeal for your father's house, or is this pride, my son?" he asked. "Is the Almighty not equipped to defend himself? Thousands post over land and sea to do his bidding!" I recognized the paraphrase of Milton, and almost smiled.

To my surprise, Fr. Eliot smoothed what was left of the pages and handed them back to Nat, who for the first time now looked truly shaken, like a small boy caught in a guilty act.

'Thanks," he muttered down into his own lap.

Hastings stepped forward. Fr. Eliot patted him on the shoulder—for once, our austere and terrible professor looked like someone who needed a pat on the shoulder—and whispered something in his ear. To my surprise, the old priest was grinning.

Hastings looked over at me and Sean, and then at Nat and Justin. Then he ran his fingers through his hair, and asked:

"Does anyone have any questions?"

34 ∽

Da Mi Basia Mille

Portia, Mary-Clare, Danielle and I were gathered around the canapés; Portia had managed to get a hold of a whole napkin-full of baked *brie en croute*, and was actually licking her fingers while I tried to answer five different people at once—all faculty members—as they pushed up to me, admiring, complimenting. Neither Nat nor Justin was anywhere to be seen. Sean was off on the edge of the room, talking to Michael and looking a little glum. Well, he hadn't done too badly—at least he hadn't started rioting and tearing papers—at least he hadn't openly defended using archaic science as a pathway to illumination, or suggested that a holy saint of the church harbored illicit desires. I wanted to feel warmly towards Sean, in this my moment of triumph.

"That was poetry!" Prof. McCaffery said. "I have to admit, I never really cared for St. Thomas before this—shhh, don't tell…oh, never mind, there are people all around, okay, I confess, I NEVER CARED FOR HIM." She lifted her pointed nose, and declaimed theatrically. "But you really made me see him in a new light. It's so hard to get around that language, it's true…"

Then Dr. Brown, one of the politics professors, clinked his plastic glass of cabernet against mine and said, "Cheers, Catelyn. That was magnificent. You have a rare gift for seeing distinctions where they need to be seen." He was a dapper swarthy man whom, I had heard, his students feared as much as we feared Hastings.

I almost didn't know what to say; I managed a dignified, "Thank you." At least, I must have looked dignified, compared to Portia licking brie off of her fingers, beside me.

"Fellow conspirator!" Che approached us, but to my surprise I found that he was addressing, not me, but Portia.

"Don't be asinine," she said, but smiled greasily.

As no professors were congregating to gaze in awe at me at that moment, I turned to Portia. "What have you been conspiring with Che about? Revolution in Central America? Liberation Theology in the classrooms?"

"Nothing at all so devious," said Che. "But devious, all the same. Remember that Kidnap for Life thing?"

"I'm not likely to forget it any time soon," I said, "Dear Lord, that thing probably took ten years off my life!"

"Well, listen to this, and tell me if I don't have the makings of a spy," Che said. "I had a bet on with Sean—I bet that you would pay to have him kidnapped! I was going to ask you to do it. Bribes may have been in order. But the night before the event, I saw how busy you were, and I was like, no way is she going to take time on such frivolity, not the serious Cate we all know! So I accosted Portia here — since I know she's an actress, and a damned good one, too — and I bought her a drink and I asked her to do me a favor. I told her SHE had to kidnap Sean."

I looked at Portia, aghast. "What? You did? You never told me? Why in the world would you do that? — Oh no!"

"I didn't think it was important," she said, surprised at my reaction.

"Oh no!" said Mary-Clare. "Oh no, I see where this is going!"

"What? What?" asked Danielle.

"But wait a second," I said, my mind racing. "Sean said he saw the warrant for his kidnapping, and he swore my name was on it!"

"Oh, no! I didn't do that!" Portia said. "I wrote — well, it was his idea…"

"Hey, I was asking a great Shakespearean actress to help me out," Che said. "So I told her to write 'the dark lady,' in place of a name, on the form she filled out. Wasn't that clever? SO…when Sean asked who had him kidnapped, the guard would just say 'the dark lady.'"

I closed my eyes. It was all making sense now.

"So I didn't have to lie, but he figured it WAS you, and he paid up, with no sweat at all. Tell me," he popped a mini cheesecake into his mouth. "Am I sinister and brilliant, or am I sinister and brilliant?"

"Oh bloody hell, Che," I wailed. "You have no idea!" Heads turned to look at me: what did the star of the conference have to wail about? "You don't understand! He thinks I broke my promise, even though he kept my secret. He must think I'm a two-faced snit."

"Ha. Not you. You're the crowned queen of philosophy," Portia said, "And Cate, oh dear, I am SO sorry. No, that's not good enough. What a mess. I am sorry though, I am. If I had known—you never told me you promised him anything! Why didn't you? There's no way I would have done that, otherwise." She turned a baleful look towards Che. "Jesuit!" she said. But she said it with some humor. Che was hard to be angry at.

"I've got to explain to him…" I said, looking around in every direction.

But Sean had vanished from the party.

Danielle said, "Cate, you were amazing. I was so proud to listen to you, and know you were my friend. But you know, for a moment I was worried those two guys were going to start physically fighting, actually with fists. You were right in the line of fire!"

"I thought they might, too," said Mary-Clare. "And you know what's odd? I wasn't sure whether I was scared they would fight, or sort of hoping they would fight. Isn't human nature a peculiar thing?"

"Peculiar, indeed," I said.

"Come on," said Portia, "make your rounds, let your adoring subjects kiss your ring or lick your shoes, and then come and meet us all back at my house. You deserve a Dionysian revel, at the very least!"

Post-debate party at Portia's house.

Portia must have pre-arranged it, because there were far more people there than had been at the debate. She was in her element, shaking a cocktail in a shaker. By the time we got there, there were at least a dozen people in the house and she had changed into a glamorous thrift-store fringy dress, very Roaring Twenties, with a feathery headdress in her hair. "Come hither, come hither," she called, shaking madly, as we walked in. Then the fire alarm went off. "Crap," said Portia. "Hold that thought. And this." She handed me the shaker. I shrugged and poured its contents into a glass from a nearby table. I took a sip: a nice stiff mojito. Excellent.

A number of people, other grad students, plus the students from the cast of Portia's play were in the room. When I came in, there was a spattering of clapping, which embarrassed me but also pleased me, of course. I'm not above academic flattery.

I noticed Che sitting on a sofa between two girls (typical) and I thought I heard Garrett's voice droning on about something around a corner. I was a little surprised that he would be there—I thought Portia had gotten over that unfortunate crush. I saw Nat sulking in the corner with a cigarette, and Michael was in the opposite corner, nursing a beer and arguing with Bart over the debate.

Justin, of course, was not there: part of me was sorry. Sean was also not there. Most of me was glad.

To tell the truth, I was nervous about seeing him: I could understand why he hated me. Plus now that I had trashed him in the debate, he surely hated me even more

"I've actually never been to a party before," said Mary-Clare shyly. "I mean, a party with…cocktails. …I wish I could spout witticisms like Oscar Wilde. But instead I feel sort of ridiculously intimidated. I don't know why."

"You shouldn't," said Danielle. "People are just people, you know. And anyway it's mostly just people from the U."

"Very frightening people indeed," I said.

Danielle got herself a Sprite from the fridge, while Mary-Clare eyed a bottle of red wine. I saw that she was nervous about pouring for herself, so I got her a glass. "Cheers," I said. "Maybe I'll be lucky and Sean was so abashed by his defeat that he's run off to join a monastery."

We mingled a bit, and then went out onto the back porch where Portia was arguing about Art with a tall thin curly-haired young man while smoking a hand-rolled cigarette. I was tempted to ask for a drag, but remembered how the last time I had bummed one of her hand-rolled cigs the tobacco shreds had stuck to my lipstick.

"Hey! Philosopher chick genius! This is Dennis. He says beauty is all relative," said Portia, jabbing a long blood-red nail at the young man. "Cate, will you tell him what's what? I can't. I know he's just as wrong as can be, but I don't know how to convince him."

"If he won't grant my first premise, it's no good," I said, leaning back against the porch railing. "All I would be able to do is bludgeon him about the head for a while, until he sees sense. But I didn't bring my *Summa*. It's the best for bludgeoning."

Dennis didn't seem to know what to say, so Danielle rescued me. "Hi, Dennis," said Danielle. "Don't mind her, she's not actually violent." She sat down demurely in a faux Adirondack chair, next to a flickering citronella candle that was filling the velvety air with its pungent odor.

"Why do you think beauty is relative?" Mary-Clare asked Dennis, doing her best, I could see, to pretend not to be shy.

"Well, you know, it just, like—think about different cultures, you know?" Dennis shrugged, and batted at a mosquito.

"What do you mean?" Mary-Clare asked, sipping her wine.

"Well, like, back a long time ago men used to like fat chicks, and in Africa they like chicks with long necks or something, or those things they put in their lips, and some people like really fancy houses with a lot of junk in them, and other people like stuff all square and white, so it's really all just in the eye of the beholder, right?"

"Couldn't it be that there are different kinds of beauty? Think about music. What sounds good in a jazz club might not sound good for a classical concert, but there's still a difference between good jazz and bad jazz, right?"

Dennis said slowly, "You mean like, there's a difference between hot chicks and ugly chicks?"

"Oh, well, it's different with people. You can't just treat them like objects, can you? A person isn't just a painting or a sculpture."

I looked over at Danielle and grinned. Mary-Clare was doing fine. Then I looked past Dennis at Portia to give her a grin, too—and saw to my horror that Sean was standing right behind her. He had a beer in one hand and was looking straight at me, an appraising expression on his face.

"Oh!" I exclaimed, idiotically.

"Can we talk?" he asked.

I didn't know what to do, so I did probably the stupidest thing I could have imagined doing: I turned around to run, and fell off the porch. That is, I half-fell, half-jumped down the three steps, landed on the sidewalk, twisting my ankle slightly (stupid high heels), and sort of tottered towards the shrubbery.

And Sean was there, leaping towards me, grabbing my arm and helping me regain my balance. His arm was strong, powerful, but he set me back on my feet so easily that it was almost graceful.

"Th—thank you," I sputtered.

Everyone seemed to be looking at me. I managed a smile and said, "Sure, we can talk." I think I was still a little wobbly.

We walked down the sidewalk around the corner of the house, and then I turned to him and blurted out, "Look, I know you're mad at me about that stupid kidnapping thing, and of course you DO have a right to be, except that it wasn't me that did it, actually, so in fact you DON'T have a right to be mad at me—I mean, your will was functioning under the aspect of the *bonum* but your intellect was unenlightened. So now that I've enlightened your intellect—not the way God does, but just as a sort of participation in the Divine Illumination—I hope you won't be mad at me anymore. I mean, I can't say I'm sorry, can I, since I didn't do anything? But if I had done something, I would say I was sorry, so on behalf of my theoretical self in a totally nonexistent parallel universe I apologize, really I do. And I think my ankle is sprained. Yes, I am an idiot."

For lack of anything else to do I leaned against the wall of the house—but then quickly stood upright again, having felt the sticky stringiness of cobwebs. I knew I was now such a mess that going back to the party—or even emerging into the light—would take a supreme effort.

"You're not an idiot," Sean said. I guess he had been in class long enough with me to be used to my tirades of non-sequiturs. "Actually, you are one incredibly brilliant woman."

"I am?" I said, rather stupidly.

"Cate, you were amazing in that debate tonight. You beat me. Hands down. And I'm cool with that—" he held up his hand, "—not just because you're a woman and therefore you don't count, but because your arguments really were superior. You kicked butt. Well, at least my butt. And I respect you for doing it."

I was trying to follow this—having been distracted by the scatological reference—down, down, presumptuous human flesh!—and I swallowed. He had paid me a compliment. A real, solid compliment. Amazing. I had won his respect.

He put his hands in his pockets. "And I'm not mad at you. Che told me what happened—he gave me my money back, too actually, though I really don't care about that. It was just a stupid bet. I guess I—" Here he hesitated. "Well, I guess I'd started thinking of you in a certain way and then when I thought you had broken your promise...I thought I had made a mistake about you—and that was hard, not just because I felt like a total schmuck but...I'm not making much sense, am I?"

"I think I follow you," I said. I felt a little breathless all of a sudden. In the darkness around us crickets stridulated, and the voices from the back porch seemed suddenly very remote.

"I should just shut up. But—well, I wanted to say, you were amazing. Not just your paper—that was brilliant, though, of course—but you. You were amazing. The essence of Cate was—is—amazing. And now I really should shut up and walk away..."

But he didn't walk away. My eyes had adjusted to the half-light now, and I could see his face, his splendid, rugged face, clearly against the honeysuckle bushes in the background. The honeysuckles, mixed with the aroma of the citronella, were having a hypnotizing effect on me.

Maybe on Sean, too. "I forget what I was saying," he said with a little laugh.

"You were just saying I was amazing," I tried to sound light-hearted. "Why would I want you to stop saying that? Please, feel free to continue developing that most interesting line of thought!"

"I don't know if I should."

Yes, I was definitely feeling breathless. "Why not?" The honeysuckles' scent was exceptionally sweet. Was that why?

He took a small step closer. "Because I don't mean amazing in a purely...I guess people would say Platonic sense, even if that's an inaccurate use of the word..."

"It IS inaccurate!" I insisted. I suspected I was babbling, but I breathlessly went on. "Plato is all about beauty, and love, and passion...if you get past the Republic...I mean, in the Symposium, remember, desire is absolutely essential to his philosophy! I wonder, where did people get such an inaccurate idea about Plato—?"

And then Sean was kissing me. And I? I was kissing Sean...

"Uh—Cate? Oh!"

Portia had suddenly appeared, followed by Mary-Clare—they swooped around the corner and then stopped short, having almost bumped right into Sean. I think he and I both sort of jumped away from each other—but not quite soon enough, since as Portia came up to me she gave me a round-eyed look, her mouth forming an astonished "O."

Mary-Clare, clearly trying to pretend she had seen nothing out of the ordinary, said, "We were just looking for you—thought you had gotten lost—Danielle's looking for you around the other side of the house. We...wanted to give Dennis some further proof of the existence of beauty."

Sean said, "Oh, that's funny. Cate and I were just discussing beauty and Plato. While admiring the shrubbery. That has a very Monty Python sound to it. Shrubbery!"

"Shrubbery!" I agreed. "And Plato!" We both laughed, and everything was normal. We all traipsed back onto the porch, but since I was still a little wobbly (for a different reason) Sean gave me a hand up the steps. And he kept on holding onto my hand. When he finally let it go as we rejoined the party, it was only with a very meaningful squeeze that told me our conversation would pick up at a more opportune time.

35 ∾

A Posteriori

Post-post-debate party.

"He was kissing you! Holy Moses! He was! I saw it!" Portia exclaimed.

The party was over. The four of us were in Portia's room eating kettle-cooked potato chips and drinking fruit-flavored seltzer: Danielle was adamant about making sure the single beer she had drunk was out of her system, before she would drive us home, and we were joining her in solidarity.

"Nice timing, ladies," I said. "Everything was going beautifully until you guys had to come crashing around the house...honestly, what did you think was happening?"

"We thought you had been abducted, of course! By ninjas!" Portia said.

"Actually, I really just thought you'd gotten lost in the undergrowth," Mary-Clare said.

"In the middle of Houston?"

"Well, you have to admit," she said, a little apologetically, "odd things DO happen to you, Cate. Remember our retreat?"

"True," I admitted.

"Honestly, I wanted to make sure he wasn't annoying you and if he was, I was going to give you an opportunity to escape," said Danielle. "You mean you've actually *liked* him all this time? Why didn't you say anything about it?"

"It grew on me slowly," I said, stuffing a chip into my mouth with unladylike fervor. Suddenly I had discovered that I was ravenous.

"He grew on you slowly...like a species of fungus," said Portia. "Just kidding! I like Sean. I really do, even if he has a patriarchical complex." She lay stretched out on her side, languidly, head on hand, her feathery headdress awry, her hair strewn over the floor. She looked very much like a fin-de-siècle vixen who had partied too hard and too late.

"He's great," said Mary-Clare. She was sitting next to me, cross-legged, staring down at the pile of chips in her lap. "I think—well, I think if you and Sean really do end up dating, or whatever, that would be just splendid."

"I have to admit," I said, "I think so too. Dear, beautiful women—I don't usually gush like this, but I am feeling a little gushy this evening—I would have told you, but I was trying to not even think about Sean myself. I didn't think he could possibly feel that way about me, too, even if it weren't for that stupid Kidnap for Life mix-up. I thought—well, I have so much to be thankful for, you know, and I wanted to focus on that, instead of pining for something I couldn't have? And anyway...who knows what will come of it? He said he'd call me tomorrow. But maybe he won't. He probably has lots of other options. I don't want to get my hopes up."

"What? Why would you think that? He *kissed* you!" Mary-Clare said. "Oh, Cate, I'm sorry for our awful timing." She looked up and gave me a quick smile.

"For some guys kissing doesn't mean crap," said Portia, a little darkly. I assumed she was thinking of the fickle Garrett.

"Sean's kind of old-fashioned, though, I think," Danielle mused over her seltzer. "I think with him, it would mean something. But you're right to be sensible, Cate. Still…I think he'll call you. And then you have to call *me* and tell me immediately! If you don't mind…"

"Of course! *If* he calls. We'll see."

I tried to feel as sensible as I sounded.

36 ❧

Post Scriptum

First year down — six to go.

I had handed in my last paper that morning. The campus was still blanketed under that tense hush that always accompanies finals, but here and there you could see a few others who had come through the dark woods of despair and out into the light of hope. Two undergrad boys went yelping down the scuffed stairs past me, and earned a scowl from a thin, nervous looking girl two steps ahead. A mustached professor went by in khaki shorts, looking harried, clutching a stack of blue books.

At the top of the stairs I nearly bumped into a kissing couple, and was inclined to scowl myself — especially when I realized the male part of the equation was Garrett. The girl, I did not recognize: the parts of her I could see were tanned, curvy, and scantily clad. I wondered how long his dalliance with Kimmy had lasted. Then I wondered how Kimmy was doing. Not too awfully I hoped, but the hope was slim.

"Cate," said a voice as I was opening the door to the departmental office—it was Hasting, looking a little harried himself. "Last paper for the semester?"

"Yes. Ethics. And now that it's finished I hardly know what to do with myself! Any reading suggestions?" (Why did I ask that? I didn't actually want to read ANYTHING. For at least a week. I wanted to lounge and luxuriate. So basically I just said it to show off an academic diligence that was totally fabricated. Will I never learn?)

Hastings appraised me, head tilted back. "You're taking Phenomenology in the second summer session, right? Maybe you should brush up on your Husserl."

"Excellent idea." Brush up. Was this a reference to my need to brush my teeth? (Exams had taken their toll on my appearance.) Oh dear. "Thank you. And also, thank you for an excellent course. I am happy to find that my expectations in coming here have been far exceeded." Oh dear Lord. I knew I sounded stuffy and pretentious, but that was unavoidable as long as I was afraid to open my mouth all the way.

Hastings smiled, spectacles glinting. "Well, I hope they will continue to be. But I have a feeling it might take a lot to challenge you. Keep up the excellent work, Cate. And maybe take a break from the studies for a day or so—you don't want to burn yourself out, you know."

I smiled back, keeping my mouth tightly closed, like a grinning Etruscan statue.

So now, teeth brushed, showered, and restored to my usual on-the-verge-of-achieving-happy-weight self, I lay on my bed, reading Husserl, while listening to Vivaldi and eating ripe cherries (a lot less fattening than baklava, and just as good, really), and contemplating the bliss of summer vacation.

A little mound of cherry pits was beginning to grow on a crumpled napkin beside me, but I was engrossed in Husserl. Actually, that's not quite accurate: I was reading Husserl, trying to get engrossed, and pretending that I understood what I was reading. Perhaps it had been a mistake to get so complacent, just because I was (apparently) good at deciphering Aquinas? A whole world of philosophical challenges was spreading out before me.

Okay, let's be honest. I was not actually doing a good job of even pretending to understand Husserl. I was thinking about Sean. That frustrating and exquisitely handsome Catholic man named Sean.

He *had* called me, after all. In my old life, guys never called back: you hung out, you drank a bit, you made out, and then maybe after that something more would happen, and then MAYBE after that they would consent to remember you existed. What a misery that had all been.

But now I was different. And Sean was a different type of guy. He had called back, and we had had a delightful conversation, including some choice Thomistic banter. Danielle was right—he was old-fashioned enough to be, apparently, serious about this…serious enough to ask me out on a date.

I did not want to think of the Tingling, or analyze what the future might portend. No, I just was content and happy, and looking forward to my first real live date with a Catholic man.

Granted, for the date, we were going to a rodeo—a RODEO???—after dinner at a steakhouse, which meant I would probably end up with gravy dripping down my front, *so* appealing—unless I ordered a salmon or something boring like that. Even if I did order salmon—or a salad, ugh—the idea of a hot date at a rodeo, with screaming cowboys and bellowing bulls and a lot of pungent smells, and leather, and worryingly tight jeans, and peroxide Barbie-doll cowgirls, and who knows what else, was a new one in my romantic book.

But then, my romantic book probably needed some serious revisions. I was prepared to try anything, even if it did involve the smell of cow poo. And perhaps that would add a realistic touch that would keep my romantic impulses from running away with me.

So much to be thankful for: friends, honeysuckle, ripe cherries, philosophy, men with broad shoulders, Vivaldi, good wine, forgiveness, humid summer nights, enlightenment, the quest for holiness…Life is never dull!

∽ *In Finem* ∽

The Authors

Rebecca Bratten Weiss grew up in the middle of nowhere in North Carolina and Ohio. After completing her homeschool studies, she pursued her B.A. and M.A. in philosophy at Franciscan University of Steubenville, and is still trying to finish her Ph.D. in Literature from University of Dallas. She has worked as a landscaper, horse trainer, bartender, cook, theatre costumier, and professor. She comes from a long line of Jewish grandmothers, though she has not (yet) experienced "The Tingling." Currently she resides in Hopedale, Ohio, with her husband Brendan and three children Dominic, Avila and Gideon. She works part-time teaching English at Franciscan University, part-time as an organic gardener, and full-time as a domestic diva. In her spare time she rides horses and writes poems. She considers herself a renaissance woman, which is just a fancy way of saying she lives in a condition of perpetual chaos.

Regina Doman grew up in Philadelphia, worked in New York City as an assistant editor, but alas, has never achieved truly elegant sartorial style, despite occasionally perusing glossy magazines in an attempt to Learn Something About Fashion. She however, did meet and marry the Perfect Guy, at least for her, and he is very handsome and devout, plus he kindly edits her manuscripts. Regina has written a bestselling book for children and several well-received books teens: this is her first attempt at writing a story for adults. When not writing or editing books and manga comics, Regina helps her husband attempt to civilize their abundance of children on a homestead in Virginia's Shenandoah Valley while seeking to achieve her ideal Happy Weight.

~ *Cum Gratiam* ~

The authors would like to thank their friends who encouraged them, overtly or inadvertently, on this mad escapade, including Katie Doman, Kate Slattery Stapleton, Jaime Gorman, Susie Lloyd, Daria Sockey, Mary Stanford, Connie Marshner, our mothers and sisters, and other women who shared laughter and experiences along the way. In particular they want to thank the members of the writers' group where they first met and gained mutual respect for each other's writing talents: chief among those intelligent, talented and supportive women were Ronda Chervin, Judy Bratten, Molly McGovern, and Helen Valois.

~ *Vide* ~
www.catholicphilosopherchick.com

CHESTERTON PRESS

is the publisher of quality fiction that evangelizes the imagination through telling a good story. Find us on the web at www.chestertonpress.com.

www.chestertonpress.com

CPSIA information can be obtained at www.ICGtesting.com
Printed in the USA
BVOW06s1448060815

411953BV00011B/94/P